HOUR GLASS

MICHELLE RENE
Amberjack Publishing
New York | Idaho

AMBERJACK
PUBLISHING

Amberjack Publishing
1472 E. Iron Eagle Dr.
Eagle, ID 83616
http://amberjackpublishing.com

Publisher's Cataloging-in-Publication data
Names: Rene, Michelle, author.
Title: Hour glass / by Michelle Rene.
Description: New York, NY; Eagle, ID: Amberjack Publishing, 2018.
Identifiers: ISBN 978-1-944995-49-2 (pbk.) | 978-1-944995-50-8 (ebook)
| LCCN 2017946539
Subjects: LCSH Calamity Jane, 1856-1903--Fiction. | United States--
History--1865-1921--Fiction. | Deadwood (S.D.)--Fiction. | Autism-
-Fiction. | Brothers and sisters--Fiction. | Western stories. | Historical
fiction. | BISAC Fiction / Historical
Classification: LCC PS3618.E57485 H68 2018 | DDC 813.6--dc23

Cover Design: Faceout Studio
Chapter images used under license from shutterstock.com

Dedicated in loving memory to my grandmother Marieta.
This is also for my grandfather, my Pa.

Sorry about all the cussing. Jane said it, not me.

"I figure, if a girl wants to be a legend, she should go ahead and be one."

-Calamity Jane

1894

1

IN THE CORNER OF the bar, a gaggle of fellows crowded around an unseen victim. Some poor bastard, no doubt. Tension radiated in a way that signaled someone was very near to death. People grouped together, afraid to say a word. Every person in the place held their breaths with the gravity of the moment. A single laughing voice cut the air. It was a laugh I recognized.

"Yer mighty big for yer britches, if you don't mind my sayin' so! What are you planning to do with that shotgun?"

As soon as I laid eyes on her, things went sideways.

There was no mistaking that voice and the person

behind it. I pushed through the folks crowding around the men. Most clung to the fringes of the fray, but a few of the braver ones had closed in, hoping for a better view. There she was, as always, in men's buckskins, swaying back and forth a little, using the bar to keep upright.

"Call me a coward again, Jane. Do it so all the folks here can hear it fer themselves."

Jane snapped her head up and looked at the red-faced man holding a shotgun to her chest. She smiled. Nothing had changed. I nearly laughed like an idiot.

"I'm sorry, Randall Foster, did I offend you? I mean—and forgive me fer speakin' plainly here now—I was just callin' a spade a spade. If you beat on a lady, that automatically dubs you a fuckin' coward."

"Whores ain't no ladies," Randall sputtered.

"Well, there you go now. I reckon half-wits like you aren't known for havin' the mind to tell man from woman. I mean, let's face the fact that it don't matter much when yer favorite partner is of the livestock persuasion."

Enraged, Randall Foster lifted the shotgun and cocked it. The action cracked the air of the room but didn't seem to affect Jane. She slurred and wavered on her feet, then laughed into the barrels of her possible demise.

"See there's the problem now," Jane taunted. "Yer always pointing that there piece at women, or did you not notice that part?"

He faltered, sweat running down his face in little

beads. I moved closer to him, so close I could smell the salty sweat collecting in the hair behind his ears. Killing a person in a flash was one thing, but staring someone down long enough to talk? That was another thing entirely. Especially when that person was Calamity Jane herself.

Everything was still. Jane looked relaxed, courting death at a ball only she seemed to be invited to. Some damn things never did change.

"Yep, that's what I thought. Coward."

Rage rippled through Randall's torso and into his shoulders. One squeeze of the trigger and the deed would be done. Jane, my friend, would be gone forever.

I pulled my pistol out, cocked it, and pointed at his temple.

"Drop it," I said.

Jane laughed and slapped her knee. "Ha! I tell you Randall, this ain't yer fuckin' day!"

"I said drop it," I repeated, pressing the pistol harder to his temple.

Randall slowly lowered the shotgun and placed it on the floor. Behind me, the rest of the room relaxed just a touch.

"You the law?" he asked, turning to look at me.

"I ain't. But the sheriff is on the way."

"Why do you care about an old drunk like her?"

He nodded his head toward wobbly Jane, bent over laughing. The whole affair was nothing more than entertainment to her.

"That ain't none of yer concern," I said with all the menace I could muster.

"She ain't worth yer life," replied Randall making a move toward his gun again.

"I think she is."

Before he could reach the gun, I turned mine and cold-cocked him with the butt on the back of his head. The fight went out of him instantly. Just as he hit the floor, the sheriff came racing into the saloon, mistaking me for the problem.

"Don't move! Put the gun down!"

I did as I was told, holding my hands up for the law to see. Jane slapped the bar, laughing for all she was worth.

"What happened here?" asked the sheriff.

"Well you see here, Sheriff, this cowboy you're yellin' at saved my life. All these good folks can testify to it."

The sheriff eyed Jane, recognizing her. She was, after all, very memorable, if not by sight then by reputation. He scanned the room of bystanders. Several nodded in agreement to her statement. He took this for truth, moving his revolver back to its holster.

"Who have we got here?" asked the sheriff, motioning toward the unconscious Randall.

"That hunk of cow shit is Randall Foster," said Jane, leaning against the bar. "Works as a hand at the Buffalo Bill Show I'm currently travelin' with. Beat on a girl. Now, he's wantin' to shoot me fer callin' him yella. That's the whole story. Anyone'll tell you the same."

The sheriff looked as though he smelled something funny and gestured to the bar behind Jane. "Fred? Fred Whittacker, you back there?"

A timid, balding man slowly rose from behind

the bar. He wore a striped shirt and the ugliest set of suspenders I'd ever seen outside a theater. "I'm here, sheriff. Right here."

"It all happened like she said?" the sheriff inquired.

"More or less." Fred said, his eyes glued to the bar.

"Good enough fer me. Get him to his feet."

The sheriff and his deputies lifted and dragged Randall out of the saloon. He moaned and protested, but there was nothing to be done. It was off to the holding cell with him.

Jane slapped the bar like a thunderclap. Fred jumped straight up at the sound, and then flinched when he saw Calamity Jane had turned her scowl on him.

"All righty, Fred, you lilly-livered rat. A bottle of yer finest Reverent. Hand it over."

"Jane, you ain't paid fer the last bottle o' whiskey you drank . . ."

"Don't you sass me, Fred. You didn't come to my aid once. You hid back there like a skunk. Hand it over, else I tell everyone in town 'bout it."

Defeated, Fred retrieved a bottle of Reverent Whiskey from underneath the bar and pushed it toward Jane. She grabbed the whiskey and walked toward me, slapping on the back.

"Come on, stranger. Let's have us a drink on ole Fred here."

Stranger. She called me stranger.

Like a duckling, I followed her out into the light, past the crowd outside the saloon, and into the thoroughfare. She didn't say much of anything, and I didn't either. There was no sign at all she recognized me. It had been eighteen years since we had last seen one another, more or less. I had the face of a twelve-year-old the last time she looked at me.

Jane led me just outside of town where a makeshift camp of painted wagons and crude stages constituted the Buffalo Bill Show. People milled about, aimless, in various stages of dress. Some in costumes and others painted to look like the clowns that taunted bulls for sport. I couldn't tell if they were setting up shop or tearing down.

We stopped at a wagon parked under a tree. The wagon was painted purple, and along the side a home-made sign advertised *Calamity Jane, Famous Pioneer Woman*. She plopped down in the shade, pulled the plug on the bottle of whiskey, and drank a hearty share.

I stood and watched her.

She tipped her hat enough to look up at me with one bloodshot eye. Little red spider legs infected the edges of her nose the way they do with habitual drinkers. There was a haze about her, but, apparently, not enough of one to soften the dubious glare she cut at my formality.

"What are *you* looking at?"

"The infamous Miss Calamity Jane, I reckon," I said, motioning toward the sign.

"Miss Calamity Jane sounds too official. Only salesmen and snake oil vendors sound like that. I already got my whiskey fer tha night. I have a reverence for Reverent you might say. Don't need much else, and you're welcomed to fuckin' partake with me."

I sat down near her, suddenly nothing more than a boy again. A kind of hope filled me after seeing her in that bar, but pinholes were being poked through it, and the light of truth was shining through them. She slurred a little as she spoke, keeping one eye on me but not entirely registering my face. Jane hadn't recognized me, and the idea pained me more than I could have guessed possible.

Still, I went ahead and asked like a fool. "I was wondering if you remembered me."

The legendary woman sat up and pushed her hat back enough to fully take me in. Even though she swam in a fog of Reverent, I thought I saw a glimmer of recognition in her eyes. A flash of color. Regardless of glimmers and their nature, she shook her head at me.

"Sorry, cowboy. I'm thankful fer yer help just now, but I don't know yer face."

My heart sank. What had I expected after all? Calamity Jane might have changed *my* life, but I hadn't registered in hers. To mean something to a person like that? Who was I kidding? With a heavy soul I lowered my eyes and nodded to the woman. I replaced my hat and stood up, meaning to leave with all the silent dignity I could muster.

"Thank you for yer time, ma'am."

"Tell me, cowboy, what did I do to make such an impression that you'd stand up for me like that? Did I know you in another fuckin' lifetime? Or did you just like the stories?"

I smiled but not enough to seem mocking. "Stories?"

"That's what I do these days. Tell fuckin' stories.

Thought you might've seen the show."

I shook my head. "Just got in today. I haven't seen yer show. I woulda figured you'd be ridin' or sharp shootin' like you did back in Deadwood."

The name "Deadwood" seemed to stir something in the woman, and she looked at me a little harder. Her eyes were sharp despite the heavy drunk weighing down her head. I could tell she was trying to cut a clear path through the whiskey haze to the truth standing between us.

"They weren't too happy about me doin' them things drunk, so now I only do 'em on the days I'm sober. Pert near blew a fella's hat off once."

Jane pulled the cork on the bottle next to her and took a long swig. I had witnessed grown men cough and spit up on a lesser swallow. The buckskin-clad woman in front of me swallowed it down like cold water from a creek. Mother's milk took all sorts of forms, I reckoned.

"What days are the days you're sober?"

"What's today?"

"Thursday."

"Well then, not fuckin' Thursdays."

I laughed without meaning to as she took another long pull from the bottle. Jane wiped her mouth with a lick and cracked a smile.

"Tell me, son. You know me from Deadwood?"

"Yes, ma'am."

"And I should know you?"

Hurt had filled my guts with poison all over again, and now anger cramped my innards as well. After it all, after everything we had seen and done together, Jane really didn't remember me? I was just another person in a sea of faces to her, another man in a saloon. A bit of grit caught in my eye, and I pretended it was the reason for water building under my lids. I thought . . . I don't rightly know what I thought or expected, but it wasn't this indifference.

"I reckon you shouldn't," I said with a little scorn in my voice.

I turned on my heel and was about to hightail it away to go drown my troubles at the nearest saloon, when I decided to say some parting words. Even if this drunk of a woman didn't know me, I knew her, and she would hear about it.

"I remember you, Jane, but not the person in front of me. I remember the woman who saved my life. You see, I figured a thing like that would have registered with you, but I reckon it didn't. I reckon none of it did."

"By all means, cowpoke, pop your corn. Say exactly what you mean," she said with a little grin around the edges of her mouth.

There was something knowing in that grin of Jane's, but my dog was too wound up at that point to quit its hunt. Had I remembered in full the nature of Calamity Jane, I would have pulled the reins. Had I taken a blasted second to cool down, I would have stopped myself before it was too late and that trap of hers was sprung. Damn fool that I was didn't see the punch line underneath it all until it was too late. All I saw was hurt from a drunkard.

"After all that happened, it seems I left less impact than a bit of shit on yer heel."

Her smile didn't falter. "You know, this is a family show we run here. No cussin'. You owe me a copper penny," she said, holding out her hand.

Something familiar rang in my head, but the insult of her apathy flustered me too much to recall it with any certainty. For all my years in manhood, I was twelve years old again, angry and rattled at the feet of this woman. The nerve of her was worse than I had recalled. No wonder so many had had it out with her. My eyes were red hot and threatened to flame.

"*You* cuss more than anyone I ever knew," I said.

"How this life is fraught with ironies. Now hand over that penny."

I wanted this to be over. The bottle of whiskey she held reminded me what was waiting for me only two whoops and a holler away. With a sour glare I fiddled a copper out of my pocket and thumbed it to her. The penny hit the ground with a muffled thud just inches from Jane's boot. It turned up tails, and I began my retreat.

"I know you, Jimmy Glass," she shouted after me.

Her words were a little slurred, but they rang true. She neither stood nor followed me. Instead, she waited for me to come to the proper conclusion on my own. There was nothing for it, so I turned back to the drunken woman leaning against the wagon. Her manner was a patient one, waiting for me to catch up to her. Heaven help the man who made the mistake of discounting her as a dull-witted drunk. Calamity Jane was smiling that sideways smile of hers, the kind that could change a person's life . . . or end it.

I stared down at the penny in the dirt, the one she wasn't going to pick up, and remembered that part too. "You know me?"

"Yeh, I know you. Don't go pulling a kite at me like that. I knew yer face the instant you showed it in the saloon. Before you even pulled the gun. But yer a might bit uglier than I last saw you."

We laughed a little as my back went down. She patted a bit of earth next to her, and I sat as instructed. Everything shone purple now that the sun had begun its retreat for the day. Up close, Jane's face looked more worn than earlier, like she had lived a few lifetimes since we'd spoken last. Tanned, leathery skin parted around the lines of her eyes like cracked earth around a dying river. Eighteen years wears different on different people. Those steely blues, though, they still rang true when she held me in them.

"You're a cowboy now?"

"Yep. I just brought in a herd. The work's good; I get to travel my fill."

She nodded. "Plagued with a case of the goddamned wanderings like me, I take it?"

I smiled and nodded in turn.

"Worse things out there to be plagued with, kid."

As if adding to her statement in some iconic way, Jane took a long swig of whiskey.

We watched the last remnants of the daylight pass beyond the horizon under the cool westerly wind. Somewhere, men laughed and jested at one another. Glasses clinked, and women sang rowdy songs while dancing across the wooden floors of dance halls and brothels. We only got bits of the sounds carried on the air with grit and the scent of cow manure. Off to the east was the Chinatown. We might have smelled the odd incense and opium of the celestials, but where we were sitting was upwind from their camp. Silence was an easy thing for me, but not for Jane, not for long.

"I saw it in yer eyes, you know. The fear I wouldn't recall you."

"You are the legendary Calamity Jane. I reckoned you might forget."

"I ain't no legend."

"You got a card in poker named after you. The Queen of Spades is called a Calamity Jane."

"So I hear tell. I 'spect that has more to do with my unwaverin' ability to dig a fuckin' grave than anything of real value. Gamblin's for dumb shits anyways. It's what got Wild Bill killed in the first place."

"I thought it was in reference to the idea that to ignore a Queen of Spades was to court calamity. At least, that's what I heard. Not much of a gambler, myself."

"That's a goddamned blessing."

A pause passed between us as Jane stared off into the spot of sky the sun had recently occupied. There was a longing there plain as day. It reminded me of old poems I read in school of fishermen's widows standing vigil and waiting for their loves to return from the ocean. Unlike the dead fishermen, the sun would return again, and so would the crowds and the laughter of children as Calamity Jane told and retold her amazing tall tales of the Old West. Tales that were dying a little slower than she was, but dying all the same.

It was a funny thing how the west was already old. When I was a kid, it was all new, but with the trains and the law came a different era. The dawn of a new kind of people. The legends like Calamity Jane and Wild Bill were fading into the sunset. They were spectacles—legends on display—because there were no real places for legends anymore. As if reading my mind, Jane broke our silence with an answer.

"I ain't so legendary to forget people. Not people like you and . . . your sister. How is Hour anyhow? What I did back then . . ." Jane tripped on her words and gnawed at her nail to cover the blunder. It was an odd thing for her not to know what to say or how to say it. "Did it work out? I always wondered . . . Is she all right?"

Jane was hesitant, and I wanted to hug her for it. We had been on her mind all these years. We weren't just a footnote in her tales. Maybe nobody else knew of us, or what happened eighteen years ago, but she did. My face had not been lost in a sea of faces. Jane knew me. She would always know me. I sat beside not a legend, but my old friend, the woman who saved my life.

2

IN AUGUST OF 1876, home was a shanty in the Black Hills outside of Deadwood, South Dakota. At the time, the entirety of the land of Deadwood Gulch and the gold-filled Black Hills was legally the property of the Lakota Sioux people as part of the Laramie Treaty. Two years prior, General Custer had reported the discovery of gold. Pioneers flooded the land to pan for the yellow. It wasn't long before the land was annexed into the South Dakota territory by the United States, but before all that came to pass, it was where our father had planted his claim and our home.

The air was getting cooler, which was the nature of autumn in the Black Hills. I don't reckon I'll ever forget how the air smelled that morning: full of wet leaves, whiskey, and cinnamon. Sunlight filtered in patches and bits through the tall trees around us like bright stamps on our persons. A decent rain had fallen over night, so the piece of land we occupied was ripe for planting a garden if we were the type to be so inclined to do such things.

My sister and I made our way out to the water's edge, finding our favorite set of flat stones to make our base for the morning's toilet. She went away behind some trees to do her business, always cautious about me seeing her unmentionables. A silly thing since I'd changed her messes only years earlier, but at six years old, my sister had discovered modesty, and I allowed her the privacy it required.

When she was finished, we washed our hands in the rushing water. I took it upon myself to wash her face with a bit of a rag that had been soaked. Once a week we cleaned our faces and nether parts. The job would become more and more unpleasant the colder the air around us became, but both of our mothers would have insisted if they were alive.

"Pa is sick," she said.

I was gently wiping bits of dirt from her cheek as she stared off the way she was wont to do. My sister rarely looked into a person's face the way that was common. Conversation, too, was strained and nearly impossible with folks other than me and our pa. It was the staring, though, that clued people in to her other-ness. Instead of meeting eyes, she'd gazed off blankly over my shoulder to something that was visible only to her.

"Yeh, I heard him moaning. He'll be all right."

"I don't think so."

"Why do you reckon so?"

"He got blisters. The bumps like Mr. McCreeny."

I shook my head. I had seen the bumps too, but unlike her, I didn't come out with what I already figured was truth. Mr. McCreeny was a nice enough fellow to us and our pa. We helped each other out quite often, but news traveled fast among miners, and we all knew Mr. McCreeny had been taken to see the doc in Deadwood. That was about a week ago, and the stories trickled in like rainwater through leaves. Miners from all over were coming down with a sickness that covered you in bumps and left you feverish and weak.

After we were clean, we made our way back to our shanty. The moaning could be heard from outside, and my back tensed at the thought of Pa and his misery. I was plagued with the need to somehow get him all the way to Deadwood to see the doc. Being a boy of only twelve, I was not nearly strong enough to help him to town on my own.

I asked my sister to wait for me while I went inside to check on Pa. He looked worse than before we left that morning. Pa groaned when I entered, rolling here and there trying to escape the pain of his fever. The sickness followed him this way and that, unrelenting in its torment. With trembling fingers, I approached his cot.

"Pa? You sick?"

Only moans escaped his lips. When he managed to open his eyes, I could see they were red where the whites ought to be. He blinked hard, trying to bring my face in focus, but it seemed little use as his gaze couldn't rest on my eyes. Red, swollen bumps plagued his face, arms, and legs. They looked painful. I feared touching the things lest they sprout legs and infest me as well.

"Pa, we need to get you to the doc in town."

He nodded but made no motion to stand. His body shivered violently, and I flung an extra blanket on top of him. When I left him, thick spittle was leaking from his mouth. It foamed and gathered in between his cheek and pillow. There weren't nothing for it. Somehow, I had to get him some care.

I found my sister sitting outside on a stump drawing swirls in the dirt. Beside her was the old wagon Pa used for hauling. The idea struck me like a rock upside the head. We could load Pa onto the wagon and make our way with him all the way to Deadwood proper. There, someone could help us get him to the doc. It was the only way with him unable to move under his own power.

A second thought flashed in my mind. Hauling a grown man out of the gulch to town would take quite the doing. Could we even make it, just the two of us? The alternative would be to leave and set off to Deadwood on foot to seek help, leaving my little sister alone to care for Pa until I got back. That was not a prospect that I cared to entertain, either. Not all of our neighbors were as kindly as Mr. McCreeny, and the woods were ripe with all manner of scoundrels. She was still a child and probably wouldn't call out for help given the way she was. No, I wouldn't leave her alone to care for a sick man and fend off whatever lay hidden in the gulch. Dragging the wagon up to Deadwood together was our only option.

I gave her soft tack to chew on as I loaded the hand wagon with every bit of comfort and provision I could find. We had two packs meant for children our size that I filled with clothes and food in case the journey found us in a tight spot. Things being as they were, we might need to stay at the doc's with our pa for a spell, and it wouldn't do to have to travel all the way back down here.

My sister said nothing as I explained the plan to her. She rarely said much, and the words she did use were often straight to the point with no nonsense in between. I didn't even mind that she spoke staring at my boots instead of my face. Such was the way of things. She could keep her own company if she wanted. There were enough thoughts rattling around in my head that I didn't need any additions.

Finally, I was able to wheel the wagon into the shanty by way of moving our makeshift table. It took some doing, but we managed to coax Pa off of the cot and onto the wagon. It was a tight fit, and my sister had to help him bend his legs up so they wouldn't drag on the ground, slowing our progress like two hefty anchors. When the deed was done, I inspected our work. Pa looked like a crumpled doll in a baby buggy, but it would have to do.

I had her take point at the front of the wagon while I pushed from the back. Since most of the journey would be uphill, I decided that her pulling and guiding us was the best plan of action. Pushing the wagon would take the most strength, and if the wagon were to slip, I'd rather it roll over me than her. At first, she was dubious of her position, thinking that I gave her the easy task because she was a girl and smaller. But she soon realized that neither task was an easy one.

It took us most of the day to make our way to town. I allowed us respite once every hour or so, as to not kill our legs maneuvering up the wet earth and through the trees. The journey was a hard one, and not a lick of luck joined in it. The thought that some good citizen might discover us and give aid was met with quiet disappointment. At one point, a large bit of earth gave way under my feet, and I had to grab ahold of some exposed rocks to not fall down the hill. The wagon was spared when the wheels got caught up in some roots that had been unearthed in the small landslide.

By the time we reached the bustling boomtown of Deadwood, we were tired, muddy, and hungry. The only blessing of the trip had been that Pa had fallen unconscious about an hour in, so the ever present groans of pain no longer sounded in our ears. I switched places with my sister since the bulk of the effort would go to pulling the old wagon instead of pushing. She accepted the reprieve without so much as a glance as we entered the town, so alive and vibrating with people.

Pa had allowed us to come to town with him before, when it was time for a run to gather supplies and food. It was difficult not to gawk at all the marvels of such a place. In mining camps, things were quiet until they weren't. The noisy parts were rarely happy, so the onslaught of noise in the town always set my teeth on edge, like I was in the middle of something large and terrible. It was exciting too, in its own way. Everything you could ever dream of was in town. Silk dresses and fur blankets. And the girls. Oh, the girls! They were painted and dressed up like cakes in all sorts of colors. The use of such women was known to me, but at the time, they were still beautiful mysteries in my young eyes.

But that day, none of the excitement felt exhilarating. The rain had made the main thoroughfare a muddy mess of well-worn wagon tracks and hoofprints. My sister and I were covered in thick mud up to our knobby knees as we tried to maneuver our hand wagon through the streets. We were tiny mud urchins in the larger-than-life crowd that swarmed around us. One man nearly ran us over in his haste as a buxom woman shouted at him like a scolding schoolmarm.

"Tom Gibson, you dumb-ass bastard! Ain't you got the lick of sense not to run over children?"

The man rode off, embarrassment flooding his cheeks, but said nothing by way of apology. The woman gave us a hard look. We must have seemed quite the sight to a woman like her. She had a pretty face for an aging lady. Of course, at the time, any woman over eighteen seemed like an aging woman to me. Nevertheless, she was a looker with a round bottom and an ample bosom tucked neatly into a red and black corset. Her dark hair was piled high into an elaborate hat, and she had several lengths of fur scarves wound around her neck, trailing down to her waist. The furs were so clean,

I reckoned somewhere in them the animal still lingered, liable to jump out at me at any moment. The rest of her costume was just as clean. Her whole dress would have cost a month's worth of our food, I reckoned.

"You. Kid," she said, calling to me.

Her voice was loud and sultry. There was the slightest hint of an accent I couldn't yet place. Most folks around the mining camps spoke with funny accents. Norwegians, Germans, Irish, and of course, the Celestials in town, but hers was of a different lilt. I stopped my wagon to answer.

"Yes, ma'am?"

"That feller on your wagon dead?"

"No, ma'am."

"Then what ails him?" The question came out as curiosity edged with kindness.

"It's our pa. He's real sick. My sis and I, we're trying to take him to the doc."

She pursed her lips and stared down at us over her finery. Pa twitched a little but did not wake, even with all the hubbub around him. My sister focused her gaze at Pa's feet.

"He looks to have smallpox like the rest of them," she said after her brief evaluation.

"Yes, ma'am. I 'spect that sounds about right."

The woman cocked her head and shouted into the building she was standing in front of. She didn't take her eyes off us for a second.

"Joseph! Go fetch Jane."

A rustling came from inside, and somewhere in the background, we heard a door open and shut. Within ten minutes, a short, squatty man appeared followed by a rather tall fellow dressed in an apron over buckskins with a bandana over his mouth. They both took one look at our cargo with somber eyes. The portly man moved at once to relieve us of our burden as the taller man beckoned us to join him and the woman on the slatted porch. We did as we were told, too tired to argue or question. A few others were hailed to help as they worked together to move our pa in his wagon. The struggle to get the thing moving again took a few minutes and a lot of cursing, but they managed to shove it through the mud.

"You brung him here by yourselves?" asked the one in buckskins.

"Yes, sir," I replied.

The woman next to him smiled a little as if there were some joke I was not privy to. She stifled a giggle with a gloved hand. He gave her a frustrated look before he turned back to me.

"That yer pa?"

"Yes, sir."

"I ain't no sir, boy. Where are y'all from?"

"Pa works a claim in the gulch near the creek. We brung him up from there." I looked over my shoulder following the wagon. "Where are those men taking him? To the doc?"

"No. There's been an infestation of the smallpox, so we had to make a pest tent down yonder to quarantine those infected."

I shuddered a little at the thought of having to go to a pest tent. I hadn't seen such a thing in life before, but my imagination wasn't doing my spine any favors. The man in buckskins eyed me up and down. It was then I noticed his apron was stained with splotches of blood and all other manner of fluids.

"You dragged your daddy all the way here in that wagon? That's quite a thing to do."

"I had to. No other way to get him here and look out fer my sister."

"You two have a place to stay here?"

"No, sir. We'll just make our way back home once Pa is settled, I reckon."

"Goddamn it, kid," said the man in buckskins as he yanked down the bandana from his mouth. "Do I have to show you my complete lack of pecker before you get it in your head that I ain't a man? And I definitely ain't no sir."

With the mask pulled aside, it was obvious that the man with whom I was speaking was actually a woman. Her skin was tanned and leathery, and she wore the uniform of a pioneer. If she had any bit of femininity about her shape, it was hidden beneath the layers of buckskin. Her hat was a man's hat, worn from use, ornamented with Indian feathers. Everything about her had read "man" until she pulled away that bandana to show the more delicate features of a woman's mouth. Her crystal-blue eyes glared down at me as I froze in place. The buxom woman next to her looked like she was about to burst with laughter.

My lips trembled, struggling to find words to say. Never had I heard a woman talk like that, much less to me. It left a fellow dumb.

A bark of laughter finally erupted from the woman in finery, and she slapped the strange woman on her back with good humor. "Oh, you poor kid. You ain't the first to make that mistake. I'll tell you that!"

"And thank you ever so fuckin' much, Miss Dora DuFran, for yer lovely candor," the other woman spat back sarcastically.

"Oh Jane, you ain't no delicate flower. And you, young man, just had the pleasure of meeting the infamous Calamity Jane."

She gestured with a gloved hand like an auctioneer displaying his next item for sale. I stared dumbstruck at the two completely opposite women. Dora DuFran continued to chuckle as Jane softened at my confusion. Stories abounded about Calamity Jane. Rumor had it she was a sharpshooter and a better horsewoman than most Sioux. The latest tales were about her and Wild Bill Hickok. They had only been in Deadwood a short time before he was killed during a poker game.

Now the infamous Calamity Jane was kneeling in front of me, a soft smile on her face. The voice that came from her lips was calm and pleasant. I breathed out the embarrassed gasp I had been holding.

"Yer pa, how long has he been sick?"

My shoulders relaxed, suddenly realizing how tense they had been. I looked around, but Pa was no longer in sight. In all my confusion, the men had already moved him to the pest tent at the other end of the thoroughfare. A quick glance told me my sister was all right. She sat nearby, drawing in the mud with a stick. I made to answer Jane as best as I could.

"A few days, I suppose. He weren't feeling too good all week. But it was yesterday the bumps started showing real bad."

"I see. You got a mama or somebody nearby to care for you?"

I shook my head. "We can just go on home."

"No, you ain't gonna do that. Two youngins out in the gulch alone? Not as long as I'm breathin', kid."

"Then where . . .?"

"You can stay right here with me," said Jane, standing up tall above me like a statue.

Dora DuFran ceased her laughing, suddenly looking very serious. She scowled at Jane. Her look told me more than words could.

"Jane, you ain't got a place to stay."

Calamity Jane returned her level look. She had the air of someone about to gear up for an argument they planned on winning by sheer will alone. By the way Dora DuFran was settling into her own stance, I figured this might be just another battle in an ongoing war between them. They both had the appearance of seasoned veterans of such arguments.

"Did you or did you not just this morning offer me a room in your establishment? I believe yer words were regarding my service to Deadwood in the pest tent."

"Yes, I said that, but . . ."

"And did you not say that a servant of the city such as myself ought not be sleepin' on the streets and in the alleys?"

"I did, but . . ."

"Was I mistaken in hearing from your own lips

something to the effect of: as a citizen and business owner in a community such as this, you wouldn't be worth yer fuckin' salt if you didn't allow a civil servant such as myself shelter in this hour of fuckin' need?"

"Now Jane, you know I did . . ."

"Well then, it sounds to me like I got a fuckin' place to stay, doesn't it?"

Dora DuFran, in all her extravagance, smirked at Jane. She seemed bemused by the whole thing, but Jane looked overly annoyed. The mood was thick and made the air between them pert near soupy with tension. I didn't know what to say to relieve the pressure, but without something to relieve it, the very space between them was liable to explode. Then, in the midst of the silence of that particular bit of thoroughfare, I heard a sound I hadn't heard in years. It was the music of a little girl giggling. That sound could cure just about any illness in the world as far as I was concerned. The sound wasn't coming from just any girl either. As I turned around, I saw the laughter was coming from my own sister. She was staring at the two women, giggling for all she was worth.

I hadn't heard her laugh at anything in years. No one had.

The battle was over, and my sister, of all people, had ended it.

3

THE ROOM IN QUESTION was a barely-used storeroom in the back of Madame Dora DuFran's brothel. Calamity Jane herself helped us with our packs as Dora led us through the saloon, past the kitchen, and into the storeroom beyond. As we made our way, I saw so many women in various stages of dress, that it made my head swim. A candy store of girls painted all sorts of colors. The bits behind my eyes strained from trying to take it all in. My sister, on the other hand, barely looked up from the floor to notice.

The place was called Diddlin' Dora's, and Dora herself escorted us, in all our filth and mud-caked clothes, through her establishment; she smiled and charmed with every step. Men from the bar called out to her as though she were a dear friend, offering to buy her a drink. She merely smiled and replied that all her drinks were on the house. Raucous laughter ensued— the kind that only came from the desperately drunk and the deliriously happy.

With every smile, every nod, and every wink, Dora DuFran further exuded the virtues of her Diddlin' Dora's motto: "Come here to have fun with the three D's: dining, drinking, and dancing." Apparently, Deadwood was not her only location. The ambitious Madame had begun opening Diddlin' Dora's locations in Sturgis, Rapid City, and Belle Fourche.

We entered the backroom set aside for Jane and were ambushed by the scent of sawdust. It was roomy, at the very least, inside that wooden storeroom. A few pine boxes filled with whatnots were stacked up here and there. The windows were a blessing if I'd ever seen one because the light it let in kept the place from feeling completely like a coffin. Dust floated in the beams of light pouring in through the panes of glass. There were walls though, real ones—a fact that elevated the room higher than our drafty shanty made of canvas any day.

A single cot sat lonely off to one side.

"We'll just get two more cots and fit 'em down here, won't we, Joseph?"

Madam DuFran directed the question at the squat man who had recently returned from aiding in Pa's journey to the pest tent. By way of deduction, he must have been Joseph, and by the way she smiled at him, I guessed him to be her husband. The pair had the matching rings of married people, all right.

"Yes'm. I reckon I know where I can grab a few things here and there to make a nice bed for the youngins."

He tried to smile at me. I nodded the way a man might to another. The idea of being dealt the card of a youngin didn't sit right with my blossoming male sensibilities. With a puff of my chest, I tried to make myself seem taller. Air and bluster were weapons when need be. I caught Jane sizing me up with a gaze that could cut crystal. Joseph hurried off after supplies for our stay without seeming to notice my manly display.

"Think you're big for yer britches, kid?" asked Jane.

"No, ma'am."

"Well, I think you fuckin' proved a bit of your grit, pullin' yer pa all the way here by yourself. That must've been quite a ways."

"Jane, you probably shouldn't cuss in front of the kids," scolded Dora.

"I don't reckon this one is much of a kid, as far as kids go. Still got the face of one, though. You best keep your girls on a tight leash in case they mistake him fer a new pet."

"My girls'll smell the lack of money on his person and leave him be."

Dora DuFran crossed her arms over her bosom with effort. Any commotion over such a mountain would definitely have required extra effort. I tried not to stare, as it would not befit a gentleman to do so. Not to mention the bosom in question belonged to the woman who was kind enough to put us up while our pa recovered in the pest tent. Admittedly, the idea of working

Pa's claim and keeping an eye on my sister was not something that I looked upon with interest. Thankful didn't begin to properly describe the feeling I had for our little place in the sawdust storeroom.

Jane knelt down and looked me in the eye. Her tanned face twisted in a manner that read she was taking my measure once again. Those crystal-blue eyes stared into mine like a sky that both comforted and frightened me. For a second, I thought of my sister and the way her eyes looked when she actually focused them on a person. Such intimacy in this stare, but I could smell the liquor on her breath, and the whites of her eyes were not as bright as they could have been.

"Please, ma'am. Is Pa gonna be all right?"

She put a calloused hand on my shoulder. It was rough and warm.

"I don't rightly know, son. With a thing like smallpox, there ain't much to be done but to nurse 'em and provide 'em comfort while they ride out the symptoms. I promise, I'll do my damnedest to help your pa."

"Jane's been nursing all the folks who are infected, kid. She's a regular angel," added Dora with a sideways grin.

Jane stood back up, spurred on by Dora's verbal invitation.

"And don't you go listenin' to a word this woman says neither. Ain't a bit of truth comes out of her gullet, just like the rest of her limey ancestors."

I smiled and wanted to laugh at the mock angry face Dora put on for us all. These women were so odd in their banter. Trying to remain serious was a chore.

"Better than some piss-poor prairie trash, Miss Calamity Jane!"

Jane laughed and sidled up to me. She threw a rough arm around my shoulder and hugged me like a friend. Her whisper was loud and comedic.

"Never trust a fuckin' Englishwoman, especially those that hail from Liverpool. Ain't nothin' but bastards and bedrails up that a-way."

I had no idea what most of it meant, but I laughed on cue as I gathered I was meant to. Dora fussed at us both and called us each a bastard in turn. It was all in good fun until the women noticed that my sister wasn't looking at any of us. There was no laughter from her. She hadn't even managed to lift her head from the floor. Everything here was new, and my poor girl was not good with new.

Jane and Dora focused on the girl staring at the boards. To me, her manner was habit, one I knew so well. It wasn't until we made the effort to be around people that I saw how others reacted to her peculiar ways. They'd hover around her a little, staring like she was hiding the part of her that was human from them. It was probably how I should have acted around her, but I just couldn't. She was my sister, and I understood her.

"Ah see, Jane. I told you. We shouldn't be cussing around the little one. We embarrassed her something awful, I bet. She's blushing."

"She don't really talk much. It ain't you," I struggled to explain.

Jane pointed that focus of hers on my sister, and I tensed all over. Everything that was hard in me was fragile in her and for her. My hair was all burnt blond, meant to blend into the trees, and my eyes were dark and solid to the sun. Her hair was jet black and slick, and her clear blue eyes gave away her mixed heritage, if you could get her to look at you. As Jane moved closer to her, I wanted to stop her, but she walked so delicately, as if approaching a scared horse.

"I heard you laughin' earlier, little one, so I know you can talk."

"She talks to me but normally don't with other people. She don't much like lookin' at people either, not even me and Pa most of the time."

"What's your names?" asked Jane as she settled into a squat in front of my sister.

"I'm James Glass, but folks call me Jimmy."

"Glass, huh? What sorta name is that?"

"German, I think. Pa says we're German somewheres back. His pappy or somethin'."

Jane tried to make eye contact with my sister, but she just stood quiet, staring at the floor. Her little shoulders were stiff. She was curling in on herself slowly. Everything in me wanted to rush to her and protect her, but doing so let on too much. These women weren't stupid.

"And you, little poppet, who are you?"

"She's my sister."

"Yeh, I figured as much, but she looks a little different."

I swallowed a big breath and let it out. They'd know sooner or later. Time to bet on them being the kind type. So far they hadn't shown me otherwise.

"Her mama ain't mine. My mama died when I was born, and her mama was Lakota. She died, too, a few years back."

Jane nodded slowly.

There rarely was a way of knowing what people would do when confronted with a half-breed like my sister. Folks around the hills rarely took an Indian's presence kindly. But Jane smiled at the helpless girl in front of her, and it eased the hairs on my neck.

"I can see that with all the purdy black hair," she said sweetly as she rustled my sister's hair.

Tension stiffened my back and hers at the same time. I could not recollect any time anyone had done such a thing to her, not even me or Pa. Touching was normally on her terms. A routine. How she would react to this, I did not know. In a second, her face was looking up into Jane's with an expression I hadn't seen before. It was a kind of reverence, a wonder. Two sets of crystal-blue eyes searching for answers in one another. My mouth fell agape watching the spectacle, but Dora and Jane just smiled.

"Don't worry, poppet. I don't mind Injuns none."

With all the new things happening, I almost expected her to say something to Jane, but nothing came from her but air, as was her usual when talking to strangers. She still stared at Jane though. It was wordless but more than she normally gave up.

"What is your name then, Miss Glass?"

She opened her mouth to answer, and the tiniest hint of a whisper came out. More of a breath of a word than a proper one.

"Ower."

"Hour? Yer name is Hour Glass?"

"That ain't her name," I tried to interject.

"You're meanin' to tell me yer name is Hour Glass?"

"No, it ain't."

"Well, if that don't beat all. You know, with a face as purdy as yours, I bet you will fill out into an hourglass. None of *this* face and figure for *you*, little darlin'," said Jane, gesturing to her own face. "If'n I were a bettin' woman, I'd bet you'll grow up to have an hourglass figure, better than Madame Dora DuFran right over there. Wouldn't that be somethin'?"

Jane smiled so grandly at her that it was infectious. Even my sister's face seemed to light up. Her little mouth closed, and the tiniest of grins pulled at the ends of her lips. I didn't want to spoil the whole thing, but someone had to set them straight.

"Her name ain't Hour, it's Flower. Her mama was Lakota, like I said, and . . ."

"Oh, pish posh," scolded Dora. "You think half the people walking around Deadwood use the names they were given at birth? Not a chance! Jimmy Glass, you might be the only one using the name that your parents gave you. Just ask good ole Calamity Jane, here. Hour is a fine name."

"Littlelin', if you'd like us to call you by your proper name, just say so."

She stared up at Jane with nary a sound. Jane smiled greatly at her.

"And if you want us to call you Hour from now on, I ain't gonna make you talk. I just want you to nod that purdy head of hair you got."

Without a pause, Flower, now Hour, nodded her head. Never in her life had I seen her react like that to a stranger. She barely conversed with me that much. Something in the air, maybe, made her take to someone like Jane the way she did. It had been since we lost her mama that she responded to any woman, let alone a complete stranger.

Calamity Jane jumped up and made a spectacle with her theatrical bow.

"Well, hot damn, Hour Glass. It is a pleasure and a privilege to meet you at long last."

4

THE SOUND OF HEAVY boots ended our impromptu revelry. Joseph DuFran rounded the corner and pushed his way into the room without a word of polite conversation. He tossed an armload of blankets and buffalo skins into the room, his forehead sweating from exertion. The plump man was a little out of breath. Excitement followed in his wake.

"What's the fuss, Joseph?"

"Charlie Utter is back, Dora. He brung what you asked for. Told me I ought to hustle to get you since he's good and ready to be rid of the cargo."

"Why's he in such a goddamned hurry?" asked Jane.

"'Cause I think he's having him a . . . well . . . some kinda reaction," replied Joseph.

"To the cargo? What's that mean?" Jane said, twisting up a scowl. "Dora, what the blue blazes did you order Charlie to bring you?"

"Cats."

The room grew suddenly silent as several pairs of incredulous eyes made their way to Madame Dora DuFran's spot in the room. She shrugged and smiled.

"You hired Charlie Utter to haul that ugly wagon of his all the way to Cheyenne for a bunch of cats?" Jane asked with a crooked face.

"Don't be foolish, Jane. I had him bring 'em from Rapid City."

A laugh escaped my mouth, followed by a snort. I couldn't help it. This whole affair was the funniest thing I ever heard of. Someone had to be playing a joke.

"Don't encourage her, Jimmy Glass. She ain't half as clever as a mule."

"And you're twice as stubborn, Jane. Come on with me, if'n you're so disbelieving."

Dora stormed out of the small room with Joseph and Jane on her heels. Not wanting to miss a beat, I grabbed Hour's hand and followed behind them. Through the saloon we sped, leaving a trail of confused girls in our wake. We made our way out of Diddlin' Dora's and into the crowded thoroughfare. There was already a number of people surrounding a wagon with a red-faced man atop it. A distinct mewing sound trilled in the air, drawing a small crowd.

Jane wasn't kidding about the ugliness of the wagon. Never had I seen a wagon painted so garish, with a hodgepodge of colors that didn't match one bit. Even the letters on the side were in different colors, like someone trying to make a thing colorful but only achieving the look of someone who had a lot of different paint buckets to empty. Charlie Utter was dismounting from the driver's seat as Dora strode up to him as prim as a peacock.

"Charlie Utter, as I live and breathe."

"At least you is breathing," said the red-faced man. "I tell you what, Dora. There ain't no way I'm gonna make a trip like that again for you. I don't care how much you pay me."

He wore a rounder hat, like a Jacobson but with a shorter brim. It covered a sweat-stained head with flattened hair that curled at the ends. Charlie was a shorter fellow but capable. A person could tell by the way of his eyes. Not to mention he was wound tight and strong. His face was reddened and not by the sun. His nose had the look of someone who had been sneezing often, raw and rubbed away.

"Oh Charlie, ain't but a crate of cats," cooed Dora.

With a flick of his hand, Charlie removed the blanket that was covering the cargo in the back of his wagon. Several sacks of mail surrounded a large wooden crate filled with meowing masses of fur. The din of meows turned into yowls as he made the great reveal. The slates of the crate were wide enough to ventilate the creatures' piteous moans for freedom, but not so large as to allow them an escape route. Several heaps of fur within bustled about and began hissing at one another as well as the humans outside.

"Oh Charlie, they're perfect."

"I don't know how perfect they are, but I will tell you they're ornery. Bunch of hissing, spitting devils, the lot of them. Why did you want all females anyhow? Girl cats don't get along with each other too well."

"I didn't want any Toms yowlin' and sprayin' all over the place. We get enough of that as it is with the clientele."

"Well, you just be glad I picked up some mail while there, or else the trip wouldn't a'been worth the dollar for extra handkerchiefs I'm gonna charge you. I swear it were the most unruly and aggravated cargo I ever did haul. Cornered Injuns put up less of a fuss. That's the truth of it."

Charlie Utter sneezed a few times to emphasize the point. Dora waved him away.

"Yes yes, Charlie. I'll pay the fee. Whatever you say. Joseph, get the girls to come and grab them a cat."

"That's the oddest damn thing I heard you say today, Dora," said Joseph.

He disappeared into the brothel, and shortly after, a line of women and girls in various costumes came filing out of Diddlin' Dora's. Some were fully painted and wide-eyed like the candy I'd seen earlier, while others looked bleary-eyed and tired. I could only conclude the difference being the night shift versus the day. A particularly pretty young one with bouncy blonde hair moved to take the spot closest to me. She wore a maroon dress with black lacy bits, and the outfit fit well in all the places men found fascinating. The smell of cinnamon wafted over me, and I tried mightily to keep my head on my shoulders.

"What's this all about, kid?" she asked with a cock of the head.

"Uh . . . Jimmy. The name's Jimmy."

"Pleasure, Jimmy. I'm Missy, but everyone calls me Lil' Missy. Now, what's all this about?"

"Dora . . . she uh . . . bought some cats."

"Cats?"

"That's enough, Missy," interrupted Jane. "He ain't got no money."

Missy made a piggy face at Jane and stuck out her tongue as all eyes turned to Dora DuFran. The grand lady took to grandstanding like a hog to slop. No doubting that. With the aid of Charlie Utter's hand, Dora mounted the wagon. With a wave of her arms, she made her announcement loudly to the crowd.

"All right girls, come and pick you out a new friend. There's plenty, so don't rush. Every one of my girls here at Diddlin' Dora's gets her a cat."

Charlie unlatched the crate as Dora gingerly plucked a growling black cat out of the lot by the scruff of its neck. The cat, though still plenty pissed off, sullenly curled her tail up and tucked her legs, as was the instinct when carried by a mother. A skinny brunette stepped forward and cradled the cat in her arms, a happy smile across her face. With a crooked finger, she scratched behind the cat's ears, and the feline forgot her previous anger.

The rest of the girls lined up, all suddenly excited for their new prize.

"I'll bite, Dora. What's with the cats? A pussy for the pussies?" Jane called up with a cackle.

Dora handed another cat to another waiting set of arms and then scowled down at Jane. The look that woman gave could have cut a mountain in two, it was so sharp. I was right glad it weren't directed at me.

"You really shouldn't cuss in front of the little one."

The lot of us looked over to Hour, who was enraptured by the cat handling procedure and not caring a lick about what anyone was saying. She didn't watch Dora so much as Dora's hands as she handed out one furry bundle after another. Charlie Utter smiled from his wagon at Hour. She seemed to inspire that in kinder people. I didn't know the man from anything but reputation, and that in particular spoke very highly of him from the start. Everyone liked Charlie Utter for his fair dealing and sturdy spine.

"I tell you what," he said, rummaging around in the depths of his garish wagon. "Here you go, little darlin'. Take this."

He handed what looked to be an empty milk jug to Hour. She took it and gazed inside at its lack of contents but said nothing. I reckoned the milk had been used to feed the fussy cats on the terrible trip to Deadwood. Not a lick was left now, but my sister focused on the play of sunlight against the curving glass.

"This is a swear jug. Any time anyone swears in front of you, especially Jane, they have to put a penny in it for you. What you say to that?"

Hour briefly looked at Charlie Utter's face and then back down to the jug as though it had magic hidden somewhere inside. Maybe it did. Her mouth formed a little oval with astonishment as she tried to unlock the secret in its glass innards.

"Charlie Utter, you sorry son-of-a-bitch—" began Jane, but she was cut short.

"Jane swore," said Hour just as plain as day.

Everyone looked to her then, amazed that she said something so succinctly and precisely, except Charlie Utter, who didn't know about my sister's lack of verbal abilities among strangers. It was as if she and I were talking alone, the words came so easily from her mouth. Moments ago she couldn't even recite her name fully and now a whole sentence. Well, most of a sentence anyway.

Then she held out the jar to Jane, ready to collect her penny. Her face was resolute, as if there were no other recourse than this. Mr. Utter had gifted her the magic jug, and Jane did swear. Everyone began to laugh loudly. Even some of the girls collecting cats laughed without knowing exactly what was going on. Charlie slapped his knee with hysterical glee at the sight.

Jane acted temporarily insulted but nonetheless fished out a copper penny from her pocket and plopped it into Hour's new swear jug with a wink and a smile at the little girl. Her sour face turned back toward Charlie Utter as did her tongue.

"Oh so very clever, Mr. Utter. Tell me, is you're good-fer-nothin' brother around here with you?"

"No, Jane. Steve ain't going to come around Deadwood for a while after you pistol-whipped him like you did."

"He deserved it, and he knows it."

"Yes he did, but that don't mean he wants to come

back to court calamity with Calamity Jane."

"Oh, piss out your ass, Charlie fuckin' Utter," shot Jane.

She spat at the ground and immediately pulled out a penny and dropped it into Hour's outstretched jar before Hour could ask her to. I laughed silently to myself thinking about how lucrative Mr. Utter's new jug would be the longer we stayed with Calamity Jane.

Lil' Missy was the last one to step forward and receive a cat. Hers was a rather wiry Siamese cat with blue eyes, which she named Puddin' on the spot. When asked why call the creature Puddin', she only answered with a shrug of her pretty shoulders and hugged the cat to her chest. All the girls milled about with their new pets, stroking and cooing at them in turn. Most of the cats desperately wanted down and away from the clamor of the crowd.

"Now, take them to yer rooms before they get loose. They are yers to keep and care for. Don't say I never brung you nothin'. Hurry on now, the dinner rush will be in two hours. Go on," shouted Dora over the raucous flirting.

All the girls filed back into Diddlin' Dora's one after another, holding their new friends. Dora smiled, pleased with herself. She made to descend from Charlie Utter's garish wagon, but a rustle inside the crate stopped her. We all peeked inside when we heard the meowing. Beneath the hay and a bit of fabric, appeared a calico kitten, smaller than the rest. Its little green eyes searched around for what had become of her traveling companions. Dora gently lifted the kitten as she had done the others and examined her above us all.

"Joseph, did every girl get a cat?"

"Yes'm. Looked to be that way."

"Then it looks to be we got a spare."

"I procured an extra cat in Rapid City in the event one got loose or somethin' likewise happened to them. They were a rowdy bit of company, I tell you what. Not this one though. She weren't too bad, as far as cats go."

"Looks like she's the runt of the litter," observed Dora.

The kitten mewed as a new set of hands reached for her. It all happened so fast, the whole thing was like in a dream. Hour handed me the swear jug as she moved forward and reached for the kitten. Her finger twitched with the intensity of her want. Her eyes were transfixed on the furry creature like it was made of gold. Jane followed her progress with her eyes but didn't speak up until it was clear Hour couldn't reach the kitten under her own power.

"Dora, I think you got yourself a taker for that one," said Jane, nodding down at Hour's outstretched hands.

Dora smiled down at my sister and handed her the kitten with more care than she had shown any of the other cats. Hour took the small thing and held it to her cheek, seeking to feel the warmth of fur on her face. I had never seen her show such affection to anyone or anything before, not even me or Pa. Then again, we never bothered having pets out by the creek. No point with wolves and wild dogs and the like.

The kitten tucked herself neatly against Hour's jaw. Soon, we could all hear the steady rumbling of her purring. My sister shut her eyes to better feel her purr, rocking her body ever so slightly left and right.

"Ain't that sweet," said Dora.

"It sure is, but I don't buy it for a minute that you bought them cats and sent Charlie Utter all the way to Rapid City fer them out of the good of that ample chest of yours, Dora DuFran. That dog just don't hunt. What's this all about?"

Dora smiled and sauntered her way to the edge of the wagon with a little swagger in her step. Charlie Utter and Joseph helped her down, and she strode up to Jane in a grandiose way.

"You've heard, I'm sure, of the word *cathouse*?"

"I heard some such ridiculous thing."

"Yeh, you heard it, because it's my word. I came up with it. Gonna make it famous long after I'm dead and buried. Ya'll will see."

"You came up with a word for a house with a bunch of whores, and then you propagate it by filling said house with cats?"

"I'll explain for those among us who may be slow," Dora said while nodding to Jane. "Them cats cost me nothin' in the grand scheme of things. You know what costs a fortune? Food. You know what else costs a fortune? Dead girls. The cats offer me a two-part battle against them both. They kill and eat the rodents who would eat my food and leave their nasty little leavins in the grain, and they give much needed companionship to the girls. Girls with something to care for and about don't go runnin' off or dyin' on me. It's a win-win. It's a cathouse."

Jane smiled at her friend.

"You are a clever woman, I'll hand it to you, Madame DuFran."

"Thank you, Jane. Now, little Hour, what sort of name you think you gonna give to that sweet, little girl kitten of yours?"

"Fred."

Hour answered her, much to my disbelief, but she did. The name was as clear as a bell, and we all laughed at the notion of a girl cat named Fred. Charlie Utter slapped his knee again, wiping tears from his face with the handkerchief.

"I'll be damned. A girl kitten named fuckin' Fred," he said with a chuckle.

Hour's head shot up and looked at Mr. Utter with that intense stare she had given Jane only minutes earlier. She pointed at the jug I was still holding for her with one hand while she held the kitten with the other.

"Swear," she said clearly.

Jane and Dora nearly busted with laughter. It was infectious. Despite the reason we were in Deadwood enjoying the kindness of these people, I couldn't help but laugh. My sides ached in a pleasant way, and for the first time in a long while, I felt like everything might be all right. We would stay here with these people, Hour and me, and Pa would get better. For a minute, I wished that Hour could laugh the way we did, but I didn't worry about it much. She had gained a fine new name, a kitten named Fred, and a swear jug all in one day.

"What's good for the goose is good for the gander, Charlie Utter!" shouted Jane.

With a sour smile, he pulled forth from his pocket a shiny copper and dropped it into the swear jug I held out for him.

5

THE FIRST NIGHT IN that tiny room of Dora's, voices I thought were long gone from the world drifted in. Perhaps it was the creaking stiffness of the place or the cot I was unaccustomed to. Either way, I floated in between the here and there like a ghost hearing voices on the wind. One moment awake and the next stepping toward a woman I once knew. An impossible woman. A woman long since dead.

Hour's mother came to take me to a place I hadn't gone to in years. I didn't see the woman in her entirety, yet I knew it was her because it was that silent, insistent way of hers. She whispered words long forgotten; words meant to take me places.

With a flash, I was a young boy walking through

the tall, wet grass next to my pa, who led our mule loaded down with furs to trade. His pistol was in the holster on his hip and his rifle sat strapped to the mule's saddle.

Before us was a Lakota camp. The smell of meat and smoke wafted toward me. That's when it stopped feeling like a dream. Teepees covered in skins were arranged near each other. I tried to catch a glimpse of the symbols painted on the hides but didn't stare long so as not to appear rude. The Lakota customs were odd to me, and I didn't want to offend. Women and children eyed us from inside their homes. One woman grabbed her little one from running too close to us and yanked her away.

"*Wasichu*," she whispered to the girl before tucking her back inside one of the teepees.

"Pa?"

"Yeh, Jimmy?"

"What's 'wasichu' mean?"

"I reckon it's white man or white devil. Somethin' along those lines."

"We in trouble here?"

I reckon not. Injun Joseph is yonder, up there with the men. He's a half-breed and vouched for our good nature. See there? That's him tellin' them our bonafides. We're here under invitation for trade."

I followed his pointing to see a man I knew well enough. Pa and Joseph knew one another, and he smiled at us as we approached. The other men did not seem terribly pleased with our presence though. The scowls on their faces, darkened by the sun, were hard. The men wore their hair straight and long like the women and tied bits of leather and feathers throughout their black strands. I wondered at the limit of our so-called invitation.

Next to Pa and Joseph was a woman. She was younger than her companions but held the same incredulous expression, arms folded over her chest. Her two long braids were carefully tied and adorned with round charms of carved wood. She wore a dress made of hide so fair it looked almost white in the morning sunlight. I wanted to ask her if it was buffalo hide, and if the triangular bits sewn in a pattern throughout it were bone, but the severity of the air around her made me keep my young mouth shut.

Pa must have seen my amazement and whispered down to me before he went to meet them.

"Joseph said she and some other Lakota were kidnapped as kids and held as slaves at a white camp for a while. She's a legend 'round here 'cause she escaped and led the warriors back to the youngins. While she was there, she learned a piece of English, so she helps translate since I can't talk Sioux."

My mouth hung open as I stared in awe at my pa. He handed me the reins of our mule as he patted my head. I was left there as he approached the congregation of people before us alone. The only kind face he found was Joseph's, but my pa grinned and nodded politely at the introduction of each person. He was quite a charmer, my pa.

Then the gathering removed their respective weapons and laid them on the grass at their feet, a sign of peaceful disarmament and negotiation. Pa removed his pistol, Joseph his rifle, and the three other Lakota men laid down their various weapons and blades. All complied except the Lakota woman. I couldn't help but notice she had a small knife tied to a belt around her waist, but she made not one motion to remove it, and no one asked her to.

Pa smiled at her wider then, as if her unwillingness to comply won a bit of admiration. He flashed the grin that often won the favor of people he dealt with, but the lady didn't budge one inch with that scowl of hers, and her arms remained fixed in their place across her chest. She was having none of his usual charms.

Trading talks began, and I soon began peering around at other things to interest my young mind. Women scraped at the hide of a carcass just out of sight of my father. They eyed the meeting with curiosity but kept themselves hidden with their work. Some younger men stalked the edge of the treeline near the tall grass. I reckoned maybe they were trying to flush out hares.

A gaggle of kids about my age played at a game nearby that I didn't understand. There were pronged sticks and a ball of sorts, but the mechanics of it eluded me. What didn't elude me was the sight of a smaller boy, much smaller than the others, trying to join in. Every time he did though, one or more of the kids yelled at him in words I also did not understand. The scene was the same in any culture, and I knew a little kid being bullied by bigger kids when I saw it.

Again and again, the small boy tried to grab at a stick and join the game. Each time he was rebuked, and the rejections were getting more and more severe with the other boys' irritation. I watched the spectacle, but with each shove to the side, my feathers ruffled more and more.

The final straw was when three of the larger boys teamed up against the smaller one and shoved him into a mud heap just a ways from where the game was being played. They had taken the effort to pick up a few handfuls of the black stuff and throw it on the boy as further humiliation. I guessed it was to embarrass him so much that he'd give up. A few others laughed at the little one, and it was about all I could take.

I led Betty, our mule, to a nearby tree. She huffed at me a bit but went willingly when she spotted a patch of clover in the direction I was taking her. After tying her reins to the tree, I stalked over to the fray in progress. The boys didn't hear me approaching, so I yelled good and loud as I came up behind them.

"Hey! Leave him be!"

I never figured my words would have such an effect. The Lakota boys practically leapt out of their skins at the sound of my voice. I weren't a small boy for my age, but most of the boys were far bigger than me. They turned on me with wide eyes and trembling mouths. It didn't dawn on me that my white words and white skin had been the real reason for their fear. Nevertheless, those boys high-tailed it away, leaving me with the smaller boy stuck in the mud.

He tried to scramble loose and run too, but the poor kid slipped in the slick of it all and fell back down again right where he was before.

"Don't worry none. I'll help you."

It took a bit of doing, but I managed to lift the child out of the mud by grabbing him under his armpits and dragging him back to the grass. His body was stone stiff, and we would have been done a lot sooner had he tried to help matters. I wiped as much of the muck off of his legs and rear as I could with my hand, but he would surely need a bath. There didn't seem to be any bruises when I checked him over. When I got around to looking over his face, two eyes the size of plates stared at me in terror. I turned behind me to see if there was something horrible coming our way, but there was only my old mule, Betty, in the background.

"You okay, kid?"

He didn't respond, just stood like a statue staring at me with those wide eyes. *He couldn't be afraid of me, could he?*

It was then that I noticed how quiet the camp was. When I took a second to look around, all the Lakota people, even the party with my pa, were watching me. The boys I'd scared off were hiding by the tree line now. The women with the carcass stood in a frightening stance holding knives covered in animal blood. A quiet awe settled over everyone, rattling my bones. The most disconcerting part of it all was the Lakota woman from the meeting with the knife; she was standing not five feet from me and looking down at the two of us. Her face was painted with an appraising look, but at least her knife was still sheathed.

"He afraid of you," she said.

"I didn't do nothin', ma'am. Them boys pushed him."

"I saw."

She turned to the kid and said something in Sioux. His eyes softened a bit, and he relaxed by a degree. She said something else, and he held out his tiny hands to me as if he was expecting to get something. They were trembling a little, but he didn't seem as afraid.

"I told him you had gift for him," she said to me.

"Gift?"

"A gift from white boy has white man's power. If he has it, the boys let him play."

I thought about everything on my person that might make a proper gift. Taking inventory, I realized I had a knife that I didn't want to part with, one belt—the only belt I owned—a few arrowheads I'd been collecting, and a dozen extra bullets for Pa's pistol. I reckoned a Lakota boy wouldn't care too much about a few arrowheads I found, so I reached into my pocket and produced one of the bullets. The boy's eyes sparkled as soon as he sighted it. Very slowly, I laid the bullet in his tiny hands, and he closed his fists around it. With a flash, he ran away from us, a trail of mud and grass behind him.

"Was that a good gift?"

"Yes. He liked it. He can play game now."

When I gazed back up at her, I noticed she was pretty. I hadn't ever thought of Indians as pretty or not before, but I hadn't thought of much of anyone as pretty or not before. When trapping in the wild, pretty weren't a thing that gets discussed. What made her seem pretty then was that the scowl was gone from her face, and her arms were relaxed by her side. That tense nature of hers was calm while she looked at me, and that made her pretty.

"I'm Jimmy Glass," I said, holding my hand out to her as my pa had taught me.

She looked at my hand curiously but took it in her own with a small shake.

"You are watcher, Jimmy Glass. You watch people."

"I reckon. What's yer name?"

"It's a hard name for white words. 'Without' is one, but the last is not word I know."

"Do you know any words like it?"

The woman thought a moment, seemingly searching her memory for a way to communicate it with me. She made a square symbol with her hands.

"Like box, but slave. Slave goes inside box. Kept in box."

I loved word games. Pa had bought me a book of riddles at a trading post we had come across, but this one was difficult since my own vocabulary weren't impressive just yet either. For a minute, I thought about asking Pa or Joseph over to help, but I wanted this game all to myself. Besides, they had gone back to discussing adult things with the men.

A little light flashed in my eyes with an idea.

"Maybe a jail?"

"No. I don't know that word."

"Or a cage?"

"Cage. Yes, that is word. 'Without Cage' is my name."

I marveled up at her with a smile. What a thing to be named. A woman without a cage. Thinking back on the story Pa had told me about her, I could see how she came by it.

"It's nice to meet you, Without Cage."

"It's nice to meet you, Jimmy Who Watches."

We both turned to look back at the gathering of men she had recently abandoned. One of the Lakota men motioned her to return to them, and she nodded.

"That white man, he father to you?"

"Yes'm. That's my pa."

"He smiles too much."

I laughed without being able to help myself.

"It ain't a bad thing, I don't reckon."

When she watched Pa, her brows furrowed as though she were trying to understand something foreign to her. Perhaps he seemed like a very odd duck, like the Lakota seemed to us. However, when she looked back down to me, those brows lifted and softened, and she was pretty once again.

"You are kind. Your mother is where?"

I looked down at my feet.

"She's passed, ma'am."

"Passed?"

"She's dead. Gone when I was born."

Her eyes softened more, and she nodded gently to me. Somehow, I knew that was her way of apology. Nothing needed explaining there. It was a thing to be sorry for in any language.

"This one, he raise you alone?" she asked pointing at Pa.

"Yes'm. He's a nice fella if'n you can get past all the smilin'."

I grinned at her, and she didn't smile back, but a part of her looked like she wanted to. She nodded to me again and went off to rejoin the trading party. For my part, I made my way back to our mule and watched from a distance. The tension that existed between a white man and a group of Indians seemed to lift by a few degrees. It might never lift completely, but it was enough to where Without Cage unsheathed her knife and laid it bare on the grass before her. Her scowl did not change into a smile, but her face softened enough to show my father how pretty she was.

6

WHEN I WOKE, MY memories of the past faded into the morning air, as dreams often do, and I found myself continuing with the everyday rigors of normal life.

Two days flew by quicker than a crow could fly in summer time. Our little home in the sawdust storeroom was cozier than either of us had known for some time. The shanty back in the gulch was nothing if not drafty, and it was colder than snow spit all times of the year but summer. The sawdust home, as I began to refer to it, was of better construction and solid against the weather outside. Hour and I both slept longer than we were accustomed in the room with the soft blankets and bedding Joseph had rustled up for us. After that first day of hauling Pa up from the creek, my body ached in a way I couldn't fully explain. The makeshift beds were a powerful comfort.

Hour and Fred snuggled deep in a buffalo pelt on the floor next to me. Jane slept in her cot with us the first day. It was admittedly strange for me to sleep in a room with a strange woman. Though we had all become fast friends, Jane was still a near stranger to us. She was a kind stranger, but a stranger all the same. I wondered if sleeping with us was a strange thing to her too, since she drank quite a bit before finally settling into her cot. She also tossed and turned a great deal the first night and cussed up a storm in between.

By the second night, Jane didn't come sleep with us at all, and I worried that we had made things uncomfortable for her. Ever the dedicated nurse, Jane worked all during the day, and sometimes into the evening, at the pest tent for the quarantined sick. *Surely*, I thought, *she must have been exhausted from all that*. I waited up for her, hoping to ask after our pa and maybe to offer some rolls I had hidden away from dinner, but she never came to bed.

The raucous crowd at Diddlin' Dora's went all night long, it seemed. However, there was a witching hour sometime around four in the morning, where the patronage was sparse at best. I decided to choose that hour to go check up on Jane. I weren't happy thinking of us as a burden, and I aimed to find out if that was the case.

I woke myself, as I was always able to, at just the correct time. Hour was sleeping hard with Fred curled in the crook of her legs, so I moved with all the stealth I could manage around our room. My coat was ready at hand, and I successfully snuck out of the sawdust home without Hour or anyone else being any the wiser. As I crept through the brothel, not a person crossed my path. All the girls had turned in for the night, and there were no patrons to speak of.

No sign of Jane presented itself in the saloon, and the dining hall was silent as a tomb. My wanderings took me outside to a quiet thoroughfare. Blue-cast shadows fell over the sleepy town of Deadwood in the early hour. It was cold enough for me to see my breath a bit in the night's air. Somewhere in the distance, a horse neighed against the silence of the morning. I crept along, still quiet as could be, until I finally found Jane slumped against the brothel's outhouse in the alleyway. She was unconscious with a half-empty bottle of alcohol in her hand. My first thought was full of fear she might be dead.

With a catch in my breath, I ran to her and shook her shoulders. Jane moved a bit under my grip, and I could see her breath coming out in foggy whiffs like mine. Each cloud blew out into the morning air and rose into a disappearing fog overhead. She wasn't dead, but she still didn't open her eyes or respond to me. The slight smell of urine wafted over me as I tried to move her again.

"Jane? Jane, you okay?"

I shook her some more, and one squinty eye opened enough to look my direction. It was quickly shut, and she grunted a little before moving her body away from me so that she might go back to sleep. Looking at her present position, I dubbed it entirely too uncomfortable for any mortal person to stand, no matter how drunk they were. Not to mention, she didn't have a blanket or anything of the like to keep her warm.

"Jane. Miss Jane. You ain't s'posed to sleep out here. Miss Jane, wake up. I'll help you inside."

She moaned a bit before opening both eyes and looking at me incredulously.

"Who's there waking my person at this hour?" she asked through slurred speech.

I could smell the cheap whiskey on her breath as she spoke.

"It's me, Miss Jane."

"Who the fuck is 'me'? It's goddamned dark out here."

I sat still and quiet, worried about a pistol-whipping the likes of what she must have given poor Charlie Utter's brother. Jane raised the brim of her hat to better look at me.

"I know you. You're Jimmy Glass."

"Yes'm."

"Why are you rousing me, Jimmy Glass?"

"Miss Jane . . ."

"Stop yer callin' me 'Miss' and the like."

"I'm sorry. I was just worried about you."

"What fer?"

"You never came back to the sawdust room, and I thought you might be in trouble."

"I ain't in trouble. Just sleepin' is all. Now leave me be."

I hesitated for a second, not knowing what to say or do. How does a gentleman leave a woman unconscious by an outhouse? My feet itched with cold and indecision.

"Say your piece, kid."

"Is it . . . is it us?"

"Is what you? Speak up, kid. You want a mind reader, you can mosey on down to the Celestials down the way. I ain't the type."

"Do you not wanna sleep in there next to us? Is we keepin' you awake? We can leave, if that's the case."

She laughed, but it came out in a snuffled sort of snort.

"It ain't you. I don't sleep well anymore under a roof. Prefer the sky. Feels less—I don't know—fuckin' pinned in or something. It's been this way a while really, and it's been especially bad since Bill . . ."

Jane trailed off, but I knew where that train was heading. Everyone knew about how close Calamity Jane and Wild Bill were. His murder had been quite the hubbub. The news had even made its way down to our claim by the creek. She lolled a bit and resettled herself against the wall of the outhouse. It seemed she had made up her mind, but still I worried.

"Jane?"

"What the hell, Jimmy Glass?"

"You gonna be safe out here?"

"I'm goin' heeled kid, and I tell you what. I reckon I'm a better shot drunk than most of these cowpokes are sober. Go on now and leave me."

"Okay."

Walking away, I watched her curl up as a dog might in the unforgiving early morning air. She crossed her arms and settled back again. Her hat was tipped down over her face, and she was snoring before I managed to make it back to the main bit of the thoroughfare. I crept back to the sawdust home and fell asleep with a heavy conscience.

Sometime around late morning the next day, we woke to a hollering so loud it caused all the hair to stand up on Fred's raised hackles. The kitten was dancing about the room sideways, her fur spiked along the top, with all the clamor and noise leaking through the boards of the storeroom. Hour seemed not terribly upset by the yelling down the hall. For once, she seemed more preoccupied with the kitten than anything else. I left her to calm Fred as I ran out into the dining hall to see what the commotion was all about. Others joined me as I hurried out to find Dora and Joseph squaring off against a sopping wet and angry Jane. Joseph was holding an emptied mop bucket and looking frightened. Dora stood between the two, a stone wall between warring opponents.

"Get back here, you bastard!"

Jane was yelling and panting hard. She had a revolver pulled from its holster and was staring down Joseph like a crazed Indian. Dora raised one determined hand to stop her.

"Calm down now, Jane. I told him to do it."

"Then my beef be with you, Dora. What the fuck is the idea splashin' water on a sleeping person in the fuckin' cold of the mornin'?"

"'Cause it ain't the cold of the mornin', Jane. Shucks, it's almost noon, truth be told. It's time for you to wake up and walk off that drunk of yers."

Jane spat on the floor, eyeing Dora as though she had the devil beside her.

"And what particular business is it of yers as to the nature of my drunk, Diddlin' Dora DuFran?"

A flash of annoyance crossed Dora's brow, and she fixed her hands on each of her formidable hips. The two women squared off at one another as everyone around spread to allow the quarrel ample room. It was as if all parties involved were readying for a gunfight.

"They go at it like this once a month at least," whispered a voice near my ear.

When I turned, I saw the sweet face of Lil' Missy. The girl was sidled up next to me and chewing on a lock of her hair. The powder on her face made her look like an angel. It took quite a bit of work not to stutter as most reason and sense left my brain.

"It . . . it don't rightly look like a fair fight. Jane's got a gun. Madame Dora don't," I managed to say through slightly numb lips.

"Ah see, that's where you're wrong. Madame Dora got her a derringer fashioned special for her garter holster there on her right leg."

I took a second to look at Dora's right leg and noticed the split in her skirts on that side.

"She ain't much of a shot. I seen her try to hit a snake we found in the pantry once. Mostly, she just flashes it at customers who are startin' a bit of trouble."

"Surely they ain't gonna fight. I mean, not real fight?

Jane and Madame Dora's friends, ain't they?"

Missy laughed just loud enough for the two of us to hear. That cinnamon smell was still on her, and the intimacy between us reverberated in the boards I stood on. I knew what she was, and I knew it was her job to make dumb men feel the way I was feeling right that minute, but I didn't care. No girl had ever paid so much attention to me ever, and my knees quivered from it.

"They're the quarellin' kind of friends, best I can figure," she whispered to me.

"Quarellin' kind of friends?"

"You know, the type that is around forever, always going 'round and 'round, but never really backin' down or going away."

"I don't reckon I had a friend like that."

"Humph. Just wait a piece. You will."

The women were shouting again, and the argument was getting loud. It was getting so loud that Hour had emerged from our room and was heading straight toward me with little Fred in her arms. Arguments and shouting often made Hour fall back into herself, and the moment I saw her, I worried what seeing this big fight would do.

She was doing so well here. Hour was talking a little, even to strangers. She had a pet now to care for, and my normally picky sister was starting to eat real meals again. Mostly all I could get in her at home was soft tack and the occasional bit of broth. The last thing we needed with Pa in the pest tent was for Hour to slip backwards. As soon as she approached, I took her shoulders and turned her to face away from the fray.

"It's loud," Hour said so small I barely heard her.

"I know. I know. It's okay. Just hold Fred. Missy, can you walk my sister back to the storeroom, please?"

Missy looked at me thoughtfully as she gently laid her hand on Hour's back. My sister flinched a little at the touch of a stranger and started shaking her head back and forth. Something made Hour catch herself, and she petted the kitten to calm them both down. Hour was getting upset, but Missy didn't shy away. After a long pause, she allowed Missy to lead her into the hallway.

"Sure thing, kid. What're you gonna do?"

"Break this up."

"Good luck with that one."

I watched them begin a slow journey back toward the storeroom. Missy was trying very hard to coax Hour without touching her too much. The gentle cooing words she whispered to her made me fall even more in love with her.

By the time I stepped out into the fray in the dining hall, Jane was pointing her gun all around as though emphasizing her points. When I stepped in between the two warring women, she instinctively pointed the revolver at me. I put my hands up in surrender, and she immediately dropped the thing back in its holster.

"This don't concern you, kid."

"But it does . . . sort of."

Both women stared at me as I lowered my hands and plastered the correct amount of chagrin on my face. Mock guilt can still read as guilt all the same, and I had me a deep well of it to draw from.

"I asked Madame Dora to wake you. It's my fault."

Jane squinted at me, and Dora drew her hands up across her chest without saying a word to confirm or deny my claim. I couldn't see it, but I reckoned she was pulling quite a face in my direction.

"You told them to splash me with water?"

"No, ma'am. I just asked if they might wake you so we could go down to the pest tent to see my pa. Hour's been askin' after him. I'm awful sorry to cause such a fight."

If I owned a hat, I would've been holding it over my heart at that point to better sell my contrition. Dora smiled a bit and nodded when I ventured a look her way. I reckoned she saw my lie for what it was—a peacemaker. Jane's hackles visibly lowered, and that rough face of hers softened.

"All right, kid. We'll go. Just let me clean up and get a biscuit, all right?"

"All right."

"Meet you out front."

"Yes'm."

Jane disappeared into the kitchen, and Dora winked at me.

"Quick thinking, kid."

We shared a look and a nod. I made a quick stop to check that Hour was all right and saw Lil' Missy playing with her and Fred in a happy fashion. Satisfied with leaving my sister alone there, I went out to wait for Jane on the front porch of Diddlin' Dora's, facing the thoroughfare. Deadwood was laid out before me, at least the main bit of business in Deadwood was. Saloons, brothels, and gambling casinos as far down the street in each direction as I could chuck a rock. It was noontime to be sure, but the sun wasn't out to illuminate the place. An overcast sky full of sad-eyed clouds choked what little light the sky afforded us that day.

Still, Deadwood was booming with activity. For a place that sort of sprung up overnight, the main thoroughfare of Deadwood hummed like an ant bed that had been kicked over morning after morning. Everyone, whether waking up from a hangover or going off to work, was bustling hither and yonder. In the quiet of the creek, I forgot what it looked like to have so many folks moving about each other. The sight was comforting in a way, like life was still moving even though ours had been put on hold. Hour and I were not alone in this world, no matter how much our isolation made us feel on occasion.

Jane joined me, noticeably drier and calmer. She was tying a stained apron around her waist as she walked up to me, and she threw a handkerchief at my chest. I caught it with a question in my eyes. Without hesitating, Jane tied hers over her mouth and nose.

"The pest tent ain't no walk in the fuckin' park, Jimmy Glass. Put this on and do what I say, or I ain't gonna bother with you."

I tied the handkerchief as instructed and followed her across the thoroughfare. The pest tent was aptly named, as it was merely a series of makeshift tents held together by wooden poles and canvas outside the doc's place of business. The structure was rickety at best and stained with the odors and fluids of the infirmed.

I shuddered a bit at the thought of Pa being in such a place, and, briefly, I wondered why Jane spent so much time there.

Jane held back the flap so I could walk inside with her. I wasn't tall for my age, so I didn't have to stoop, but Jane and the doc did. The tent's ceiling didn't go high enough to accommodate a reasonably tall person's head. We passed the doc as Jane weaved me through the labyrinth of cots. I recognized him from a few months back when he treated Hour's summer cold. He eyed us from behind fogged spectacles and his handkerchief. His apron was stained with blood as the man he tended to coughed more sick and blood into his rag.

As we went, we helped. Men and a few women reached for us and pleaded for various things. Mostly, they wanted water or blankets. Feverish people begged for blankets the most, even though I couldn't reckon why. They were already so hot to the touch, I could feel them through the sheets. We obliged them all the same.

Jane instructed me to fetch this or retrieve that as we moved along. She was so patient in her demeanor with the sick people all around her. The woman who had, less than an hour ago, been railing against the world with gun in hand, was now carefully moving from man to man, dabbing sweat and blood from their foreheads and offering cool water to their lips. I wondered where my pa was in all this but didn't dare rush her. These people needed her desperately. It was a plain thing for most anyone to see.

When we finally made the rounds and found Pa at the end of the second tent, I barely recognized him. In two days' time, he had become a different man entirely. His face, a face I knew better than my own, now belonged to a stranger. He and I shared the burnt blond hair of his family, but now his beard was stained dark with blood and sweat. The bumps that had begun to spring up on his face and hands were greater in number and bigger than before. Some looked painful and hard, like marbles under his skin. Others had burst and bled. Jane carefully dabbed his face with a wet rag, and he shivered beneath her touch.

"Pa?"

I whispered to him and placed my hand on his shoulder. I could feel the heat of his skin through his tattered shirt like the feverish people we helped before, so I pulled the blanket he had up to his neck. Pa's eyes were shut tight, and he didn't react to my calling his name.

"Pa? It's Jimmy. Can you hear me?"

He moaned a little and turned his head to me. With a labored effort, he opened his eyes to look at me. They were sticky with thick tears. The whites of them were gray and cloudy. He didn't seem to be able to focus. I wondered if he could see me. Blinking his eyelids seemed to hurt.

"Mr. Glass. Yer boy is here," said Jane.

"Jimmy?"

"Yeah, Pa. It's me."

"Jimmy?"

He tried again to seek me out but shut his eyes instead. Fidgeting this way and that, he moaned in pain. His head lolled to one side, and he was again unconscious.

"Pa?"

"It's all right, kid. He's just in a bad part of the sickness. He needs to sleep is all. Come on now, I'll walk you out."

I didn't want to leave him, but there was nothing for it. He was gone to the world now, and only a terrible person would try to keep a sick man from sleeping. Jane walked me back out of the pest tent with her hand on my shoulder. When we made it outside, she turned to go back in.

"You stayin'?"

"Got to, kid. Doc can't do it all himself."

"I can stay and help."

"No, kid. That's kind but no. You got a sister to look after. I ain't no doc, and I don't know nothin' about her particular ailment, but I'm bettin' she don't do well on her own fer long."

I looked down at my boots, sobered greatly by what I'd seen. All the bluster, all the laughing, all the joking around Jane did with the others—and all the while she was working in that pest tent with those horrifying faces. While folks frolicked and laughed and ate mere feet away, she was here tending to the needy. Among the piss and blood and sweat, there were rows after rows of terrified people. The look of death was in each one of them. It was even in . . .

"Jane, is my pa gonna die?"

She looked at me solid. I could tell the idea to lie to me was bouncing around in her mind. Most adults thought about lying as a first choice when dealing with kids, but I was just enough beyond a child's age for her to reconsider it. Jane pulled the handkerchief down around her neck so her words could better be heard.

"Did I ever tell you about my time I was with a pioneerin' group headed for Virginia City?"

"No, ma'am."

"Well, I was with my family and a few others. I was a young thing, not much older than you, and considered quite the shot and rider. The route they chose weren't the safest. We were constantly plagued with the fear of Injuns or rustlers or the like, but the most exciting times were with the streams. Those streams were hell to cross as a group if you didn't know what was ahead, so me and the men had to go scout them suckers before the wagons got there. Fording streams, that was exciting times, 'cause there was boggy places and quicksand that could swallow up a rider whole, pony and all."

Jane shifted her weight underneath the gravity of the story. I didn't even wonder for a second if this was a true story or not. At the time, I didn't know her well enough to wonder.

"I had many a narrow escape fer me and my pony, seein' as most of the fellers lacked the courage of a young Calamity Jane. There was this one particular stream that roared up some ragin' waters because of the rains that had come down the day before. The others left to go tell the group that we'd have to double back, but I wasn't satisfied with that. Among the calls and hollers against it, I rode my pony out into that stream, damned fool that I was, to find us a workable route."

"What happened? Did you find it?"

Jane spat a bit in the dirt and laughed.

"Hell no. That current swept my pony's feet quicker than anythin' could've. She took me and herself underwater and down the stream we went. She thrashed and I cussed so much, the dear Lord ain't forgiven me yet to this day. But you see, I figured I was goin' to die that minute."

"But you didn't."

"I'm standin' here before you to show that I didn't wash away with the flood that day. No, I was plenty scared and sure that I would, but then I thought of my Mama and my pa. The water rushed over us, and I thought about how it would be fer them to lose their eldest to such a damn fool thing. Then, I thought of all my brothers and sisters. I thought of them cryin' over my would-be broken body, and I decided that day weren't gonna be my final day. I grabbed my rope and flung it over a passing tree limb that had broken in the storm. With a little help from my pony and those pioneerin' boys I was with, I was saved and lived on to tell the tale. My pony too."

"But I don't understand."

"Go back to yer sister, Jimmy Glass."

"But what about my pa?"

"Things can look bad, kid. They can look real bad. All you need is one broke down limb to give you a fightin' fuckin' chance. Go back to Dora's and do yer part. You take care of Hour."

"Where will you be?"

"Me? I'm gonna be here danglin' some branches."

7

THE NEXT AFTERNOON BROUGHT Jane back to us in a state. Word came through the telegraph office that the Overland Mail stagecoach was headed from Cheyenne that very day with a new doctor to help out at the pest tent, along with a gang of actors bound for Deadwood to take over the new theater. Messengers said the doc was an ex-army sawbones, but he had heard of the town's need and decided to come help. All of this sounded like good news to me, but Jane's unease became clear when the stage was late to the show.

I watched Jane pace to and fro along the boards of the brothel's front porch. Indians had been spotted near Whitewood Creek, and they weren't the friendly type. Stagecoaches were robbed on occasion, and passengers were sometimes murdered due to the back-lash of the government's backing out of the Laramie Treaty. With every bit of yellow mined from the hills, the illegal settlement of Deadwood became more and more a part of the United States. The Lakota were not a people to be trifled with, and the prospect of losing the doctor when we needed him most was a worry. The last thing the sick people needed was for him to end up yet another dead trophy.

"I'm goin'. Dora, I need me a horse."

Dora followed behind Jane, trying to calm her pacing.

"Jane, you don't even know if anything's the matter. What's the point runnin' out there after a stagecoach that's probably just fine?"

"I got a hunch they ain't fine. I learned long ago to trust my hunches. Give me a goddamned horse, Dora DuFran."

The two women stared one another down for a few minutes, neither willing to blink first. I watched them from the doorway and figured the argument from the day before may have ended, but those two were still holding grudges for the war.

"I ain't lettin' you go alone, Jane."

"Who's goin' with me? You, in all your finery, or Joseph?"

"Joseph has business in town. Can't spare him. How about Charlie Utter?"

Jane shook her head.

"Na, not Charlie. I 'spect he's halfway to Sturgis by now with the mail."

Both women grew silent and thought together. Watching them, I wondered what sort of mountains could be moved if those two ever stopped quarrelling and worked together. What sort of things might get sorted in Deadwood if one sobered and the other lowered her guard? I hadn't known many women other than Hour's mother, and I certainly hadn't ever met a woman like Dora DuFran. That was about the time both of those eyes turned on me. Something lightened her face all over, and she smiled at me the way she did in the saloon when she was flirting up a customer.

"Take Jimmy," she said to Jane.

"Yes'm. I'll go," I was eager to prove my metal. There weren't no point hiding my excitement.

"Hell no, you won't," said Jane.

Dora strode over to me, her boots knocking hard on the wood floor with every step she took. *Knock knock knock.* With a flick of her hand, she flipped up the right hem of her skirt to expose a perfect derringer pistol tucked in a specially-made garter holster around her leg. Spit sort of stuck in my mouth as I tried hard to swallow it down. She removed the tiny gun and placed it in my hand. The thing was heavier than I expected.

"See, perfect size for him. Don't worry, kid. It'll shoot straight as long as you don't have to shoot too far or at anything that's movin'."

"Thank you, ma'am," I took the gun from her and turned it over in my hand, examining it.

But Jane interrupted my fascination, reaching for the pistol. "You ain't shootin' nothin', kid. And you ain't goin'. Who's gonna tend to Hour?"

"Oh Jane, you worry 'bout that girl too much. Lil' Missy just loves her. I'll have her watch over Hour. Besides, it'll be a cold day in Hell if'n you could get that child to look up from her kitten. She'll be fine, and you need someone to watch your back."

Jane scowled at us both before she beckoned me to follow her out into the thoroughfare and to the livery. I nodded to Dora with a grateful bow. The great Madame shushed me along with a wave of her hands. I'd felt so helpless for so long, and now, she'd given me an honest to goodness adventure. It might not be curing Pa, but it was helping a man to town who might. That was about as good as I would get.

"I 'spect to get my gun back now, and tell Jane I want them horses back in one piece too. Go on. Follow Jane."

I caught up with the annoyed woman a few feet from Dora's. She was flustered and agitated. Ornery as a mule and puffing air out of her nostrils like one too. I tried to figure out why Jane seemed so out of sorts. It wasn't until we made it to the livery that I understood. Jane was sober, and it wasn't a state of mind she preferred. There was an edginess to her that didn't suit, and her normal state of humor was masked by a dark cloud of anxiety. It seemed there were bugs underneath her skin. The type only she could feel.

We saddled two of Dora's horses and rode out together in silence. The day was pleasant and mild, the sun warming our backs as we rode. A nice ride it might have been, had we not been on such urgent business. Whitewood Creek wasn't far, and I was a little thankful for it. The normally talkative Jane was sullen and quiet. It was almost like keeping Hour as company.

Even though her tongue was clamped, the rest of her was active and on alert. Her eyes were sharp to the trees, and her ears seemed to prick at every tiny noise. I supposed that was the scout in her, always hearing more than the regular folks. Mostly what I heard was nature noises. Birds in the trees, smaller creatures in the underbrush. I was about to say as much to her when a sudden sound made her tense all over. Jane put one finger over her lips to shush me before I could ask what it was.

A scream echoed off the stone walls around us. It was a woman's scream. I tensed, and my pony fidgeted beneath me. Jane's horse was still, but the agitation made it chew on its bit and snort. Our horses stamped in place for a long minute before going further.

We moved a few feet off the trail as the sound of thunderous hooves moving in a synchronized storm cloud approached us. There we saw the stagecoach before it rounded the bend. The driver was slumped forward, and the horses were wild and out of control—a stampede of black legs and frantic hooves tethered to a stagecoach bumping helplessly behind.

That's when we heard the whoops and hollers of Indians somewhere in the distance. A whole war party must have been following, or at least it sounded as if they were. Once, Hour's mother told me the trick to the war cries was to sound them loud and frightening and never at once. Three riders could sound like twenty if they echoed their voices right through the gulch.

My heart pounded, rushing blood to my head. I

pulled Dora's derringer out of my pocket, and I pointed it to the trees beyond, ready to fight. There weren't nothing there, and my hand trembled in anticipation of what might spring forth any second. Jane put her hand over the gun, nearly slapping it out of my hand before I could aim at anything at all.

"Don't you even fuckin' try to shoot that."

"But . . ."

It was all happening so fast. We were standing just off the road that the stage was following. With a wild yelp, a group of Indians at least ten deep came up behind it, rounding the bend. The stagecoach was heading toward us with the Indians right behind them, painted up like something out of a nightmare. They had rifles and were waving them in the air. I could tell the lot of them were Lakota, but I didn't recognize any faces.

Jane pulled her own rifle from her saddle holster and aimed it from atop her horse. The stage was almost to us and would pass us soon. It was only a matter of time before we were surrounded by the war party hot on our heels.

"When he goes down, turn and ride like hell after that coach, you got it?"

"After who goes down?"

I never got a verbal answer. With a well-aimed shot, Jane fired her rifle and took down the Indian leading the pack. The man and his horse fell to the ground as if hitting an invisible wall. His arms and legs splayed out on the ground in an unnatural way, and he didn't move once he hit the dirt. Behind him, the others stopped in their tracks behind their fallen warrior.

The smell of gunpowder filled my nostrils, threatening to burn out my insides if I inhaled too deep. Electricity flowed through my body, and, for an instant, I was sure I could breathe smoke if I was so inclined. That minute, that perfectly quiet minute when the world turned sharper than it ever had, passed before me as though it might never end.

It did end though, and all of a sudden, things were happening far too fast. All of the events moved like the world had been sped up too quickly to see properly. I never had a reason to believe that time sped up or slowed down before. Time had just always been constant; an hourglass turned over and nailed to the floor with the pellets of sand constantly and evenly moving at the same pace all the time.

Suddenly, time shifted, and I was filled with a new reverence for the heroes and legends if they had to act like Jane did right then. She turned her horse immediately and tore after the runaway stagecoach. The sense flooded back into my head, and I followed suit. It felt like sprinting through a bog of mud.

We raced after the coach as it banged and rattled against the will of the stampeding team. Our horses overtook it easily since they had only the burden of their own riders to bare. The coach's frame had been hit several times by rifle fire, and the driver was slumped over in the driver's bench. There were six terrified people inside the coach looking frantically at one another. Desperately, I wanted to look back to see how close the Indians were to us now, but I was too afraid of losing my balance.

Jane's horse reached the nose of the front horses and, with one deft hand, she grabbed the reins and slowed the horses to a stop. I halted my horse too, wondering why we were stopping with attackers on our heels, but when I turned around, I saw that there were no Indians behind us, save the lead warrior lying in the middle of the trail. Jane was down from her horse in a blink, barking orders to all of us.

"Get that luggage off the coach now. Everything but people and mail gets dumped here. I said now!"

I hopped off my pony and ran to help unload the bags from the stagecoach with the others. Three women and three men bustled about, doing whatever they were ordered with pale faces. I don't reckon a pint of blood flowed through the lot of us with the way our faces looked. A shot rang out as a bullet ricocheted off the side of the wagon. A few of the women screamed and everyone ducked inside the stage coach. I joined Jane, who had climbed up to the driver's bench to check the wounded man. It weren't as protected as the coach but not as blind either.

"Stay in the goddamned coach and unload it from inside!" she yelled down to the passengers.

There were scuffing sounds and more thuds from bags hitting the packed ground beneath us. One chest was launched off to the left side and rolled into the brush off the road. We slumped low, using the wagon as a shield to check the bleeding man beneath us. He had been shot in the chest and there were no signs of life from him. He was dead. I was fairly sure of it. Another bullet ricocheted near us when Jane tried to reach down for the reins that had fallen into the coach's rigging. It weren't close enough to grab at fast like, and another round of shots ended her campaign. She sat up quickly and looked me in the face.

"Where's the shooting coming from?"

"They're in the fuckin' bushes," she replied.

"Why?"

"'Cause they ain't fuckin' stupid."

"What do we do?"

"Yer gonna stay low. I ain't about to have you lookin' like John Slaughter here."

Jane pointed to the dead driver. Now that I knew the man's given name, it made his death suddenly more frightening.

"Deadwood is only twelve miles yonder. With a lightened load, we can make it. Injuns ain't gonna follow us into the town proper, no way."

"What about Dora's horses?"

"Leave 'em. We ain't got the time."

There was a sudden silence of gunfire, and Jane took the opportunity to swing down and gather the reins to the team in one big movement. In another second, she was up in the driver's bench, whipping the horses and yelling for them to make tracks. The team was strung out and jerky, so they responded immediately with a jolt of motion.

A smattering of yelps sounded from the passengers as we took off down the trail as fast as the horses would carry us. Bullets continued to rain on us but not in the constant torrent they had before. If the Indians had gone to ground, it would have taken some doing to mount up again and commence chasing us. Nevertheless, I held my head down. John Slaughter's dead body was close enough to smell, even with the wind passing us the way it was. That sight was enough to keep me from sticking my head up to see if we were being pursued.

Never had twelve miles seemed so far and flew by so fast in all my life. Jane was as focused as a person could be as she spirited us away from the danger behind us. After about five miles, the danger seemed truly behind us seeing as how the gunfire had ceased. I never got up the nerve to look back, but there were no more whooping war cries, and the only sounds of horse hooves came from the exhausted team pulling us. Truth be told though, it wasn't until we rode into town and saw the saloons on either side that we all hollered for joy.

Our entrance into the busy thoroughfare of Deadwood was one fit for the books. Dusk was fast approaching, and there were quite a few people about. Most moved from our path due to the speed with which we raced through the street. The others moved because Jane was yelling at them. When the team halted, it was in front of the Bella Union where Sheriff Bullock was talking with a few other men. They halted their conversing when Jane stopped the coach, calling for a doctor. Most of the men looked as if someone had walked over their graves. The good sheriff eyed us carefully without the fanfare of the shocked.

"We got a man shot here."

The passengers disembarked, and a gruff-looking man from among them climbed his way to Jane to check out the injured John Slaughter. I assumed he was the sawbones we were expecting, so I stepped down and gave them room. Before I got a good foot underneath me, a dry hand clasped my shoulder. I looked up into the face of Sheriff Bullock. I had never met the man, but he was known for two things: having a substantial mustache and hating it when people cussed in public.

"What happened here, boy?"

"I'll tell you what happened," interrupted a woman who had been one of the passengers of the stagecoach. "We were attacked by Indians coming in from Cheyenne, and this woman saved us."

The woman was thin and shapely with disheveled red hair that looked too red to be real. She talked loud and looked men in the eyes the way Dora or Jane might, but her vocabulary, hat, and finery said she was born a higher class than a Madame. Her dress was garish, like that of a prostitute's, but of far better quality. I wasn't quite sure what to make of her.

"Is that so?"

"Yes, it's so. My companions and I were heading here to join the theater, but we were attacked on the road. I think our poor driver might be dead."

"And you are?"

"Miss Adeline Freis."

"Thank you for your account, Miss Freis," said the sheriff dryly.

All eyes went to Jane and the doctor on the driver's bench. A decent gathering of people had made their way out to the thoroughfare to see what all the commotion was about. The gentlest of silences fell over the crowd as they waited to hear the verdict of the fallen driver.

With a sullen shake of his head, the doctor told one and all that the poor man had passed. Heads were bowed and hats were removed. Had a man died from cheating in poker or after a fair fight, perhaps the feelings would have been mixed about his passing. As it was, John Slaughter was instantly and unanimously grieved on the spot as a hero by everyone.

When Jane jumped down from her perch she had the dead man's blood smeared on her. She dusted her hat, shook her head in remorse, and replaced the old thing on her head. The sheriff looked her over and nodded. They had a recognition that told a story of two people who knew the measure of one another. I wasn't sure how or why, but it was there.

"Jane."

"Sheriff."

"All they say is true?"

"I haven't a clue, Sheriff. What all did they say?"

"That you saved them from Indians."

"Yeh, I s'pose that's true."

"I should give you a commendation then."

Jane started to shake her head but didn't get a chance to. Just then, the crowd parted for one angry woman dressed all in finery. She parted the people before her like a corseted Moses before the Red Sea. The shouting and hollering would have frightened those Indians had they still been chasing us. Dora DuFran was in a state, and she was barreling right for us.

"Jane! What in blue blazes?!"

"Oh Dora, get your back down. We are among the livin'."

Dora looked me up and down, and upon seeing I was in one piece, squared her shoulders at Jane. Without a second glance my way, she held out her hand in my direction. I knew in a second what she wanted, and the great Madame didn't want to have to ask. I slapped that derringer in her hand without protest, and she took it as was her due.

She drank in the scene around her and appraised everything as she scanned. I could almost hear her calculations as she surveyed the people and animals present. Sheriff Bullock scowled at her, obviously trying to figure out what to say to such a woman.

"Yeah, and where are my horses?"

Jane and I looked down, remembering we ditched the horses back where the Indians were hiding. More than likely, those ponies had become property of the Lakota-Sioux by now. They hadn't gotten the stage-coach, but my money was on them running off with the horses and whatever bags we dumped by the road-side. When Jane looked back up again, she was actually smiling. How anyone could smile in a moment like that, after a chase like that, I will never know, but Jane did. She turned to the sheriff in front of all the people present and addressed him.

"Thank you for the offer of commendation, Sheriff, but it appears that my exploits have put me in the debt of a certain Madame. Could I possibly ask that the good city of Deadwood pay the price of two fuckin' horses in lieu of a commendation?"

Sheriff Bullock scowled at the vulgarity but nodded.

"Thank you," said Jane as she grabbed my shoulder and flung me toward Dora. "Come now, kid, it's been a hell of a day, and I think Dora owes me a goddamned drink."

8

THERE WAS QUITE THE party at Diddlin' Dora's that evening. Everyone wanted to meet the infamous Calamity Jane and her sidekick who had saved the lives of six passengers from certain death at the hands of warring Indians. The saloon was at top capacity, about filled to the gills, with miners, dancing girls, and gawkers. Singing and drinking went on long into the night, but unfortunately, I only knew about it from my room in the back.

We hadn't been back long before word spread about the harrowing rescue. Grown men patted my back and offered to buy me a drink, an honest to goodness one. I couldn't think to do anything but smile and bask in the praise. That's how Hour found me, grinning like a stunned fool among a horde of people. Missy was right behind her, whispering something in her ear. Whatever she said made Hour look up from the floor directly into my eyes. Tears were forming around hers as she walked determinedly up to me.

For an instant, I thought she might hug me, but then I remembered Hour didn't hug much. For her it was like being trapped. The thing was, she was crying and searching my face to see something she was having a hard time accepting. Her little head shook back and forth over and over again. I reckoned it wouldn't be long before she started flicking her fingers around her head like she did when she was real far gone. I didn't understand until Missy came up behind her.

"I told her what happened. Better me than to hear it from someone else and not understand, I reckoned. I tried to explain you weren't hurt or nothin', but she got real upset."

Tears rolled down Hour's cheeks and she looked down at my feet, still shaking her head. I hadn't thought for a second how scary the news might've been for her. I was all she had aside from Pa, and Pa was so sick. She sidled up to me, pressing her side against mine, and took my hand. Her little hand was so small and cold. I squeezed it a little for reassurance, but she tugged it away when I did.

"I'm sorry. I'm okay, really."

She grasped my hand again, and I figured this time she wouldn't let go. I knew there was no way I was going to be able to celebrate with all the fine folks singing my praise. The vision I had for my near future was one where I sat in that sawdust home of ours, reassuring Hour, and playing with her kitten, Fred. It didn't take a dime-store psychic to see that. Luckily, Dora sent in Joseph during the evening to bring us a special supper, so the entire evening wasn't a total bust.

By morning, all the nerve from the day before had left my person. So anxious and jumpy had I been from my adventure that sleeping had been a real issue. Every time I drifted away, I'd see Indians in the darkness or hear a sound that made me jump. What sounded like a stampede in my sleep was merely Fred chasing a nearby mouse. When the morning light came through the window, I just felt tired and scratchy all over.

In place of the temporary courage I had mustered, an anxiety had taken root. Hour and I hadn't known a life of leisure, and being left to our own devices without work to do was an odd feeling. My encounter with Jane and the Indians only cemented the antsy feeling in my legs. The only real solution I knew for an issue like that was to work. Hour did best when greeted with routine anyway. We needed to work and keep busy in order not to drive our minds mad.

The saloon was deserted when we made our quiet entrance. The dining hall had a few tired-looking girls with circles under their eyes eating in silence. Dora DuFran sat at the head of the table drinking black coffee and reading the paper with her mouth like a straight line. Nancy May, the main cook, was bustling about in her apron and seemed to be the only one chipper as usual. I watched her purposefully drop a bowl near the face of one particularly tired girl whose head was resting on the table. The clang startled the girl who grabbed her head with a sour look at Nancy May.

"Don't be a-gawking at me, Rebecca. That'll learn you to drink as much as the customers," said Nancy May with a mother's chiding tone.

We crossed over to the side of the table closest to Dora. Hour sat at the table as Nancy May brought her a bowl of oatmeal without being asked. She tucked into it immediately. It was no secret the cook had taken a shine to Hour. Whether it was because she mistook Hour's quiet way for politeness or because Nancy May had no children of her own, I didn't know. Maybe she was a mothering type without any little ones to mother. Either way, the show of affection at that moment was the perfect transition to the conversation I wanted to have with Madame Dora DuFran.

"Miss Dora?"

"Yes, Jimmy?"

Her voice wilted as she spoke my name. The strain of the previous evening had taken its toll even on her.

"I was thinking how kind you been to me and Hour, and how kind Jane has been to us too. I don't rightly know what we would've done without your help. All of you, really."

Dora laid her copy of the *Black Hills Pioneer* on the table and looked me in the eye with a sideways, skeptical kind of glare. The message was plain as her eyes were tired.

"Stop dancin' around the thing, kid. I ain't up for a dance partner so young as you. Spit it out or be done with you. Go on. Out with it."

"Well, I was wonderin' . . . if me and my sister could help you out a bit around here. Earn our keep. You all been feedin' us and the like, and we'd like to help."

Dora's face went from skeptical to surprise in an instant, then back to skeptical.

"You ain't done enough yesterday helping Jane save them people?"

"I didn't do much, tell you the truth. I just rode along and tried not to get shot."

She hooted with laughter and slapped the table hard enough to startle the other girls from their post party haze. They all looked up half frightened, half frazzled.

"You're a funny one, Jimmy Glass."

"Thanks, ma'am. Frankly, I just want to have somethin' to do to keep my mind occupied while we wait for Pa to recover. We'd really like to help. I'd also like to not hafta worry about Hour alone in that room all day too. She's good in the kitchen."

Dora appraised me once again and dubbed me honest. With a wave of her hand, she called for Nancy May to join us in the dining hall. The round woman did as instructed without hesitation.

"Nancy, you got yourself a helper today. Little Hour is gonna help you in the kitchen."

"Fine by me. I sure do like this little one," said Nancy beaming at Hour who was still spooning oatmeal in her mouth. "Got me a bunch of potatoes that need skinnin' and washin'."

"Good. And Jimmy Glass, you're with me. Got Irish Kate upstairs cleaning the girls' rooms, but I sure could use a hand cleaning down here in the saloon. I

lent Joseph out to the new doctor today since Jane is . . .
well . . . *indisposed* at the moment. It's good for him to
keep busy too. Keeps him from gamblin' over at The
Gem. Eat some breakfast, and then, you're with me."

Without needing to say so, I was pretty sure the
word *indisposed* meant that Jane was passed out drunk
by the necessary outside somewhere. I didn't say as
much. It wasn't my place to say at all, especially after
everything she had done yesterday. So, I tucked into my
breakfast and met Dora in the saloon as instructed.

The saloon in Diddlin' Dora's appeared as though a
small, confined tornado had entered through the front
door and proceeded to turn over chairs, tables, and
various kinds of alcohol with no regard. I was ordered
to mop the floors and right the wronged furniture as
I went. There was a spot near the bar counter that I
noticed when I fixed a tipped-over stool. The spot was
wet and looked to be a decent amount of drying blood.
A cold feeling wrapped itself around my spine, so I
chose to leave that particular mess until last. Unfortunately, there was no hiding from it, and after the rest
of the place had been mopped, I begrudgingly took a
rag and mop bucket to clean the crusting blood. It was
nearly black.

Dora moved like she were powered by something
unearthly. She moved constantly, either writing down
something that needed to be ordered or giving orders to
one of her workers. The Madame seemed exceptionally
strict about the girls' hygiene. She fussed at several of
them in turn about washing their nethers every day. It
was true not all the girls on Dora's line were as pretty

as Lil' Missy, but she prided herself in keeping her girls and her house clean.

By the time I had made it to the bloodstain, Dora had decided to take a break in the saloon with me and poured herself a glass of whiskey. She eyed me as I scrubbed the patch of dark blood. I tried to hide my grimace, but it were a hard thing.

"Nothin' serious, kid. One of the gents called the other a cheat, and threw a punch to the face before anyone could say boo. Knocked out a tooth, but that's all. Let me know if'n you find it down there. Feller might want it for a souvenir."

I swallowed hard, but kept scrubbing. Dora laughed a little in the silent air.

"You don't know much about jokin', huh, kid?"

"You mean that story ain't true?"

"Jimmy Glass, most stories ain't true. Now, there's at least some truth to mine. Two fellas did duke it out there over a cheatin' hand, but I don't reckon anyone lost a tooth. Just takin' your measure a bit."

I sat up and looked into the Madam's eyes. They were warm even though they were laughing a little at my expense. If I could remember what my mother looked like, I would have pegged her for eyes like that.

"How do you know?"

"Know what, kid?"

"How do you know when someone's tellin' you a lie? Seems that everyone 'round here likes to joke and tell tall tales. How do you know when someone's fibbin'?"

Dora took a deep breath and threw back the rest of her whiskey.

"Well, that's what the gamblers like to call a *tell*. Most folks got one, but ain't nobody seem to get the same one."

"How do you go about figurin' out a person's tell? I ain't used to things like that. Out in the creek, everybody's sort of just gettin' by. Not a lot of room for jokin' and tells and stories."

"I could see that, but the longer you work around these sorts of folks, the more you get used to marking people with their tells. It takes watchin' a person to see how they tick."

"What's my tell?"

"Oh honey, you're a boy of twelve. Everything you think, the second you think it, is written all over your face."

My face must have reflected the horror I felt inside because Madame Dora DuFran laughed at me hard enough to bend over.

"Oh kid, don't worry. Men ain't as good at hiding things as women. Us gals, well, we were sorta born to hide our feelings. It's how you get by. You'll learn to keep things close to yer chest, but you ain't learnt it yet."

"What about Jane? What's her tell?"

"Jane? Jane is an odd duck if there ever was one. Heart of gold, that woman. She thinks she was supposed to be born a man, but I don't think so. Most people see the gruff drunk that she is or the big boaster she shows and don't know how much things hurt her. That girl feels more than she ought. No, with Jane, you know she's lying when she tries to sidetrack you with one of her stories. She's got a ton of them, and not even Jane know which parts are true and which ain't anymore. Has she told you the one about Custer yet?"

"No, ma'am."

"Good. If she tells you that one, she's trying real hard to cover a big thing she doesn't want to say to you."

"What about you . . .?"

My question was cut quick in my throat because a large, burly man walked into the saloon from the street. It was too early for Dora's saloon to be open to the public properly, but the man looked like he'd already tied a few on before he arrived at Dora's. The scent of whiskey followed him inside like an uninvited date.

The second the man walked in, Dora DuFran tensed. I watched her in her sudden discomfort with an urgent curiosity. Never had I seen this woman startled or even thrown off her game, but now, she looked almost afraid. Not even with a gun in her face did she show one ounce of fear, but now it was different. Of course, she hid it behind a brilliant smile.

"Sorry there, darlin'. We ain't ready for business yet. As you can see, there was quite a party. Please do come back in a few hours."

The man's eyes bore down on her. Dora's hand nervously rubbed her other forearm. When I looked closer, I could see a light scar running underneath her left arm. It looked as if it were caused by a blade or something sharp. An old wound perhaps?

"What's your name?"

"Madame Dora DuFran. I am the owner here."

"I 'member you," grunted the man. "Molly said you'd be here, and if that don't beat all. You actually is here."

"Oh sugar, I think you are mistaken. We ain't never met before."

"No, no. I know you, but you didn't call yerself Dora DuFran then. You was Amy, I think it was. We had us some good times, didn't we, Amy?"

He was swaggering drunk and moving toward Dora in a menacing way. Her flawless smile faltered, but only a little, as she continued to rub the scar on her arm like it hurt suddenly. I immediately stood up and stepped in between them even though the drunkard had a good foot on me at least. All I had in defense was the mop I had grabbed from the floor, but I puffed out my chest all the same, ready to knock the fellow in the gut or in the groin.

The gorilla laughed.

"This yer protector, Amy? Come on, didn't we have a good time?"

With a flick of her hand, Dora flipped up the side of her skirt and produced her little derringer from its holster on her leg. In no time flat, the tiny weapon was pointed at the drunkard's thick skull. He shrank back a little but didn't lower his menacing smile.

"I already told you. My name is Dora, and this saloon ain't open yet. I think it's clear I can protect my own damn self. Now get out before yer head becomes a birdhouse for my garden."

Her voice was crystal clear, and the smile was still plastered on. At that moment, I was genuinely glad to be on her side and not his. For the first time, the man looked afraid. His smile vanished, and all the words he had been meaning to say got lost in his throat somewhere. To his credit, he stumbled out of the saloon as fast as he could.

Dora and I both breathed a sigh of relief when he was gone. She walked back behind the bar, a little jittery in her step, and poured two glasses of bourbon. One she shot and the other she handed me. I wanted desperately to seem tough for her, so I threw back the stuff lickety-split. Regret flooded my body as soon as the alcohol burned its way down my throat, but I held my face together despite it all.

I must not have held it well because Dora laughed at me.

"Like I said, kid. Yer face is an open book, but you held that well. You're a nice fella."

"Thanks. What did that man mean? Molly told him you're here? Who's Molly?"

The Madame of Diddlin' Dora's let out a big sigh.

"Molly is Molly Johnson. Some folks call her the *Queen of the Blondes*. She runs a cathouse down on the corner of Sherman and Lee. She ain't a fan of mine."

"How come?"

"Besides the fact we run competing businesses? Well, she and I came up the same sorta way, but Molly's a tacky thing. I'll give her she's a fine piece of calico, but she's a conniving one. I do my best to help my girls and to help others' girls. No point of livin' if'n we all at each others' throats. What good does that do? Fighting over the scraps of men ain't no way to run things. Plus, I got Lil' Missy off of her. Oh, she hated that one. Molly's got a things for blondes. Has her own little conniving army of blondes over there working for her."

"So you think she sent that fella over here on purpose to upset you?"

Dora stared down into her empty glass, dubbed it wanting, and poured herself another.

"My bet's she got lucky. Some mean drunk that had a past with me came waltzin' in her hall, and she knew just how to get him liquored up and pointed him in my direction. The big bad that went down 'tween him and me was news enough to make the rounds back in the day. It was so long ago, but that Molly got her a shit-sharp memory."

She downed the bourbon and scowled.

"So you did know him?"

"Yeh, I did. I know him."

Absently, Dora began rubbing that scar on her arm again.

"I should've shot him," she said.

"Well, for what it's worth, I think you scared him to death."

"Thanks, kid. You want another?"

The kind woman in front of me held out the bottle and offered me another pour. I nodded and threw back the bourbon once again. To my surprise, the stuff didn't burn as badly as it had the first time around. In fact, it warmed my bones a little. For a second, I wondered if that was what happened to all things that hurt. Was there ever a time, maybe after a lot of practice, you came to need them? Was pain that stuck around a while a thing that hurt more when it was no longer there because you knew it so well?

"By the way, kid, what were you goin' to ask me

before that baboon walked in here and interrupted our conversation? You had a question on your tongue, didn't you?"

"Yes'm. I was going to ask you what your tell was."

Madame Dora DuFran snickered to herself, and smiled back up at me. She took her glass and clinked it against my empty one. Her glass was empty in the next second, and a bit of rose returned to the apples of her cheeks. With a deep bow of her head, with all its bound up brunette curls, she answered me. "Well, Jimmy Glass, it seems you got to see mine firsthand."

9

DREAMS CONTINUED TO FILL my nights with the memories I had left of our old life. They swept over me in the way dreams do when life is anything but peaceful. Of course, Without Cage came in the dreams. Walking in between them, she parted them on either side to hold out her hand to me. I went with her, having no other choice in the matter. Cage just led me and showed me the things she wanted to, the things I guess she never wanted me to forget.

It was us, the family of Pa, Cage, Hour, and me. Hour was Flower the baby then, and home was a reinforced shanty in the woods. The adults were arguing, as they were wont to do, about going into the nearest trading post for supplies.

"You ain't takin' Flower in that papoose carrier into town. I'm not havin' it."

"Her name is *Ojinjintka*. Not 'Flower.' It means more than 'Flower.'"

Cage scowled at Pa as he paced around her, gathering various necessities as he went. Her English improved daily but his Sioux never seemed to. He made sure to avoid eye contact with her, which heated her iron even more. I tried to skirt the edge of the fray, playing with little Flower's hair as she grabbed at my fingers from the cradleboard she was strapped to. Skins wrapped the board holding the baby there tight, and Cage had decorated it with eagle feathers and a painting of a big turtle on the flat side of it.

"Cage, you know white words gotta make it simpler."

"And my name not Cage. Without Cage, that's my name," she huffed.

She stomped her foot hard on the wooden floorboard, and Pa stopped what he was doing to look at her. There was no avoiding the fight now. It had come through the front door and made its presence known to the world. Nothing for it but to let the storm rage.

"Honey, I love who you are and who Flower is, but what I got in my head is a white tongue. Sure, I can learn the Lakota to better say yer words, but them folks at the trading post and beyond, they got white tongues too. In white tongue, you is Mrs. Cage Glass, and that little girl over yonder is Flower Glass. We's gonna have enough trouble gettin' all of us into town to trade as it is, but if you insist on takin' that cradleboard as well, you're askin' fer trouble."

Cage turned on her heel and started yelling in Sioux as she began her own pacing around the shanty. It was all said so fast, even if she yelled a word I recognized, I wouldn't have caught it out of the air. I couldn't make out any of her ranting, but I knew the tone well enough to tell when a woman was cursing at you.

"Cage, please," pleaded Pa.

"No please. No please!"

"It's just for this one trip to town. We need sugar and coffee and . . ."

"You need. You need these things."

"We need cloth to make clothes for the children. Jimmy's growin' like a weed. And we need it for you, so you can have a dress."

Cage narrowed her eyes at Pa with both hands on her hips. It was the wrong thing to say.

"A white dress. You want me in a white dress."

I saw Pa take a few deep breaths. He normally did that when he was measuring a response in his mind. When his shoulders relaxed a bit, he began again from a different direction.

"It ain't fer me. It's fer town. People don't like Lakota. I don't want trouble."

"Then we stay and you go."

For her part, I could tell Cage was making an effort to match his calm. It were a difficult thing for her. I could see the fire raging on in her eyes and her balled fists were stones on her hips.

"That ain't happenin'."

"Why?"

"Because there are other trappers here, there are white people, all sorts. If'n they come across you alone with Jimmy and the baby . . ."

He trailed off, not needing to finish that thought. There was just a common knowledge of what could happen in the wild to a woman. Everyone knew it. Without a protector, evil men were at liberty to do evil things.

In a sudden flash of motion, Pa took up Cage's hands in his and kissed them. The tension in her shoulders melted a bit as he looked into her eyes. He had a way of calming her. Someone once said the real beauty of his charisma was the honesty behind it. Pa never swindled anyone ever.

Even Cage with all her vigor calmed under his gaze then.

"We all go together. Not with the board though. It'll be safer."

"How do I carry her then?"

"In your arms."

Cage threw her hands up in the air in frustration and walked away from him. She stomped over to where I sat crouching next to Flower and unlaced the bits of leather that held her in the contraption. Without hesitation, Cage handed Flower to me to hold and made her way back over to Pa with the cradleboard in hand and a good head of steam.

"This, this here," she said pointing at the painted turtle on Flower's board. "This is Keya."

"It's a turtle, Cage."

"More than turtle. It is Keya. Keya is spirit that

guards life. Keya guards babies. She must be with her Keya or else she will be in danger."

Pa took in another deep breath and let it out. He was obviously searching for more patience than he had at hand.

"Cage, I ain't gonna play along with any o' yer superstitions. You take that papoose board, people will stare."

The fire was pulling back up in Cage's eyes again, and the air turned thick with the impending fight that was sure to escalate. It was like smelling the storm before being able to spot it in the sky. A huge cloud of thunder threatened to tear the shanty apart. I hugged Flower's tiny body as if to shield her from it, but as far as babies went, she was a quiet one. Not even Cage and Pa's eruptions seemed to phase her much at all.

A thought occurred to me then, one that might end this all and make a decent enough peace. I laid the baby on my bed, making sure to stack a blanket up around the edges of her. She was getting to the point where rolling over was a possibility, but enough of a lip along her sides kept her put.

I snuck past the quarrelling pair to the cradleboard, which had been discarded on the floor. My hand searched inside the folds of the skins that overlapped this way and that, looking for a very specific thing. A smile crept across my face when my fingers wrapped around what I was searching for, and I pinched it between my three longer fingers to pull it out.

When the item came free, I laid eyes on a little buckskin turtle with a leather strap making it suitable for wearing. It was decorated with tiny beads and bits of stone, and tenderly painted red in places to look like a turtle. I remembered watching Cage make the little amulet. When Flower was born, she had been so careful to save the bit of her cord when it fell off. It was sacred, she had said, to keep the thing that connected her to her baby. As was her people's way, Cage had put her bit of cord in this buckskin pouch and made a turtle out of it. It was her Keya, she had told me. Pa thought she was crazy when she made it.

I intercepted the argument, holding up the amulet like a white flag of truce.

"Can we take her with this? Is it enough protection, Cage?"

Her mouth was wide open, as I had interrupted her in the midst of a good rant. She looked at the little turtle amulet I held, and the tenderness came back to her face as she closed her lips again. The edges of her eyes softened, and suddenly the storm had passed. Sunny, blue skies opened up above us through the parting clouds. Pa, for his part, looked relieved but still took great caution with his words.

"She can wear it around her fer protection," he said gently.

There was still worry in Cage's face, but she nodded, still looking at the amulet.

Not long after, we were trotting our way to town. I walked beside Pa, who led our mule Betty with Cage, Flower, and a load of furs on her back. Cage held the baby with the Keya around her and the blanket she was wrapped in. Her face was not happy or content, but the cradleboard had stayed at home. She had refused any white clothes, but she had settled for her plainer dress. Compromise seemed to mean no one was truly happy, and everyone chewed on a bitter weed for the duration of the day.

Town had few real buildings. There was a general store and an adjoining saloon that were made completely of wood, but most of the buildings around were nothing more than big canvas shanties. There was no telegraph or mail service yet. One preacher man had set up shop in a lean-to next to the saloon, but he weren't seeing much business. The town didn't even have a proper name. This was a place for trappers and the like to trade and buy goods that weren't available in the wilds of the Dakotas. Nothing more.

We walked Betty to a hitching post and tethered her there among others of her kind and the horses who watered at the trough together. Pa and I unloaded her burden and made several trips into the store to carry everything we had to trade. We left Cage with Flower outside the store near the entrance. She was only a holler away, but when the last of the furs had been unloaded, Pa told me to go outside with her while he spoke business with the clerk.

By the time I made my way outside to her, a small crowd was already there menacing her—her back against the outside wall of the store. At first, there were just three people, ragged-looking trappers it appeared, but then a few more joined in. They seemed to flock to the spectacle like a murder of crows sniffing out an easy meal.

"Who said you was welcome here, squaw?"

"This place ain't fer yer people."

"I think she was part o' that party come by and scalped old Holland last month."

"You better run squaw, and take that papoose with you."

I ran to her in a hurry as her back touched the wall. There was nowhere for her to go, but her eyes told another story. Cage glared at the men as stoic as if she were holding a rifle instead of just reaching for the small knife she had on her hip. No person worth their salt liked to show they were backed in a corner, but backed in a corner she was.

I put my small body in between her and the men.

"Stand back," I said with my boy's voice.

So badly I wished for a man's voice just then, but I summoned up all I could manage. The men laughed at me a little, and some of the menace left the air.

"What you care about this Injun, kid?"

"She's my mother."

Cage didn't look at me, and I didn't look at her, but something connected between us at that moment. There was a recognition that hadn't been there previously. She had always been careful with her affection toward me and had never forced mothering on me since she was not mine by blood, but something had grown in the space between us. Neither of us were the type to discuss the matter, but when I called her my mother to the band of men before us, a binding took place.

The hand that wasn't holding Flower let go of her knife and placed itself on my shoulder. She claimed me for all to see.

Something about this riled them up all over again. Two men came at us. One grabbed at my shirt, and the other grabbed at Cage and Flower. We screamed and Cage wrapped her arm around me hard so they couldn't pull me from her. In the process of protecting me, the other man had seen the Keya amulet come loose from Flower's blankets and yanked it off the baby with a quick snap of the leather that held it.

"No, don't!"

The men let us go, but they ignored Cage's cries for the amulet. Satisfied enough with their new prize and the reaction they were getting from it, they backed off enough to torment her with it. All the fight had gone from her eyes. She held Flower and me to her body, desperately pleading with the men to give her back the turtle.

"You want this thing back? What is it?"

"Looks like Injun black magic to me."

"Do you use this, squaw, to curse little white children?"

Cage didn't say anything. Maybe she knew it would do no good. Every word she said would fall on deaf ears. But those eyes of hers longed after the delicate amulet in their hands.

"Give it back!" I cried on her behalf. "It's for the baby."

Cage squeezed me closer to her.

"It's fer the baby, is it? You hear that, fellers? Black Injun sack magic fer the baby."

The gruff man threw the turtle down and began stomping on it.

"No!"

They all joined in. Some spat on the sack, others kicked dirt and grit on it. Within a few tearful seconds, it was nothing but rags. The urge for tears welled up inside me, and I hugged close to Cage as the men closed in on us once again.

"If'n you cried for that bag, just wait 'til you see what we gonna do to you."

A long shadow suddenly eclipsed Cage, Flower, and me from our left side. At the same moment as the shadow appeared, the clicking sound of a cocking pistol silenced the party around us. The men's attention turned away from us and to the tall, lean figure of my pa standing a few feet away with a gun trained right at the head of the lead man. I was so happy to see him, tears fell down my face. Relief filled Cage's eyes. The men were not nearly as pleased.

"Now, what exactly were you plannin' to do to my wife?" said Pa to the main fellow.

His eyes were level and his tone was mean. It was the stern mean that was meant to speak down to and frighten lesser men. The men before us backed off a little, and the one in front rose his hands in surrender.

"Nothin', cuz. We was just foolin'."

"I ain't your cuz, and it didn't sound like foolin' to me."

"Come on now. We didn't know she was your squaw."

"She ain't. She's my wife. Them's my children. Now, you is gonna back away, and let us leave. You do that, and no one's gotta get hurt."

The men nodded and backed away slowly with all hands in the air, but they didn't leave. This standoff wasn't going to end gently. They kept their ground, not saying anything but not letting us out of their sights. Pa cocked his head in my direction.

"Jimmy, you go get tha store man to help you load Betty. Do it now."

"Yes, sir."

I tried to go once, but Cage was still holding me tight to her. Pa inched closer to her and whispered just loud enough for us to hear alone.

"Let him go, Cage. I'm here. They don't want him."

Reluctantly, she unraveled her arm from my chest, and I ran inside to the store. The man who owned the store refused to help me load our goods in the middle of a standoff, so he sent his black boy from the store-room to help me. The poor kid's dark eyes were as wide as dinner plates when we walked out to the scene I had just left. I felt plum sorry he had gotten wrangled into a mess that weren't his.

We worked as fast as we could, loading Betty up with all that Pa had bought with our furs. The boy and I both trembled with terror as we worked. No one was talking, and not one person moved an inch other than us. This was a battle of wills, and had Pa not had his gun, we would have already lost the fight.

When we had finished, Pa thumbed a nickel at the boy as he ran back inside. He and Cage edged their way to the mule slowly, never turning their backs on the men before them. For an instant, Cage's hand reached out to the mutilated amulet in the dirt in front of them as if to grab for it. One touch from his free hand told her not to even try for the thing. I helped her and the baby onto Betty's back so Pa could keep his gun trained.

"Lead Betty on ahead, Jimmy. I'll bring up the rear."

And so it went that way. I led our mule away from the town with Cage and Flower and all our goods on her back. Pa brought up the rear by walking backwards, still aiming his pistol at the men outside the general store. The men never advanced nor did they back down. All of them watched us with silent menacing faces as we slowly made our way out of town. I would never forget how long it took or how deathly quiet everything in the world was on that terrifying journey home that day. We never went back.

10

TO THE UNTRAINED EYE, life looked to be a peaceful thing for us in the waking world of Deadwood. Hour liked the chores Nancy May gave her to do in the kitchen. Their time was spent rather perfectly, seeing as how Nancy May loved to gossip on and on, and for Hour to speak any words at all was a feat in itself. Time moseyed by them easily as the cook babbled on to the quiet girl peeling potatoes. The key was to stop Hour when she had peeled enough. Otherwise, if left alone, the girl would probably have kept peeling until she was too hungry to continue.

Likewise, my life at Diddlin' Dora's was one of routine and happy days. I didn't mind the work at all. Mopping and moving cases of whiskey was a mighty upgrade from all that I normally did in the shanty by the creek. There, I was mother to Hour and cook to Pa. At least at the cathouse, there was always something happening and someone to talk to. The girls were thankful for my help, and they often doted on me like I were a cute puppy or a little brother. I didn't mind a lick if Lil' Missy wanted to pinch my cheeks and say sweet things to me. Not to mention having a house full of cats was always amusing to watch. They'd tumble after one another and not think a second about pawing a man's unattended whiskey glass off his table.

One customer found himself without a date when he angrily kicked at one of the girl's cats. The black and white cat had made a nuisance of herself, seeing as how her owner was perched in the man's lap. With one adept paw, the cat knocked his whiskey to the floor, and the fellow was none too pleased. He hollered and kicked at the animal, not landing one blow. Joseph poured him another drink on the house, but he had lost his date, who ran off to see about her precious pet. After that, more men than not learned to hold their tempers and treat the furry inhabitants as amusement so as to not upset the girls.

The thing of it was we'd been here over a week. Sometimes, it felt a lot longer. So much had happened in the space of that week, it seemed as though it should have fit into a solid month, if not two. Regardless of feelings, it had been a week, and there were no reports on Pa's progress since I saw him with Jane.

Jane was busy elsewhere, it seemed. When she weren't at the pest tent, which was a rarity, she was at

Dora's, drinking her fill. Not once all week had she tried to sleep in her cot in the storeroom we were supposed to share. I eventually just moved Hour and Fred to it, seeing as how it made not a lick of sense that she sleep on the floor rather than use an empty cot. A few times, I had caught sight of Jane in the saloon and tried to ask her about Pa, but she'd ducked my questions and gone outside. The thing was, I knew where she slept. I'd seen her almost every morning passed out drunk against the necessary behind Dora's.

There came a point I couldn't stand not knowing anymore. I grabbed Hour after lunch and headed to the outhouse. I asked my sister to bring her swear jug, knowing full well Jane couldn't duck the likes of Sheriff Hour so easily. At least, that was the nickname most of the girls started calling her because of her ruthless pursuit of pennies from people who swore. Between the cats and Hour's swear jug, Diddlin' Dora's was certainly cleaning up its ways.

"Why are we leaving? We going home?" asked Hour when we were alone.

"No. We are going to go see Pa."

We found Jane, just as I suspected, unconscious next to the outhouse. I kicked up some dirt and nudged her boot to get her attention.

"Jane, wake up. Please, Jane, wake up."

The woman asleep before us moved a bit and moaned. She tipped her hat up to look at me with a face that could melt wax. Sour things tasted sweet by comparison to her gaze. I immediately regretted this decision, but there was no turning back at this point.

Forward or bust.

"Whatch'ya want with me, Jimmy Glass?"

"We wanna see our pa, please."

Jane looked at me harder and then turned her foggy gaze to Hour beside me. Hour stared at the ground as was her custom. Jane smiled at the sight of her.

"Well, I see you got that jug o' yours, so I'd better be on my best behavior," jested Jane.

"How is our pa? Is he better at all?"

Jane focused on Hour, trying to gather her attention, but her eyes were fixed to the floor.

"Have I ever told ya'll the story of how I got my name?"

The question was directed more to Hour than myself, probably because I knew she was stalling. Still, the sentence did make Hour look up and into the eyes of the infamous woman.

"I 'spect it ain't nearly as pretty a name as we came up with fer you, but it's quite the tale. Do you wanna hear it?"

Ever so slightly, Hour nodded her head.

"Well then, I'll try to give it all the grandeur it deserves despite my current condition. I was scoutin' fer a while in Fort Russell, Wyoming, and remained there until the spring of 1872." Jane was at one end of an invisible rope and we were at the other, with nothing but words, she began reeling us in. "You see, that's when we were ordered out to the Mussel Shell, or Nursey Pursey as the Injuns say. There was an Indian outbreak there. In that war, all the stiff-collared generals were there. You never seen so many high noses. This campaign lasted until the fall of 1873, and it was during this campaign that I was christened Calamity Jane."

Like a child in school, Hour was fixated on every word Jane uttered. She sat there in the dirt, holding her jug, and listening attentively. The fact that the air smelled of all manners of foul things given our current position didn't seem to bother either of them. Jane was quite the storyteller, and soon, I found myself raptly listening as well. It was like she cast a spell over the two of us. We dangled on her line.

"It was on Goose Creek, Wyoming, where the town of Sheridan is now located. Captain Egan was in command of the post. We were ordered out to quell an uprisin' of the Indians and were out fer several days and had numerous skirmishes durin' which six of the soldiers were killed and several severely wounded." In her excitement of the telling, Jane came alive with the story. Her arms flew this way and that with more vigor as she spoke. Only in the hard blink here or the fidget of an arm there, could a person see how much the drink had disabled her.

"Then on returnin' to the post, we were ambushed about a mile and a half from our destination by a war party. They were out fer our blood as much as we were out fer theirs." The stillness of the pause she left filled us with all the anticipation Jane had bet on. "When fired upon, Captain Egan was shot. I was ridin' in advance, and hearin' the shot, turned in my saddle and saw the captain reelin' and startin' to fall. I galloped back with all haste to his side and got there just in time to catch him. I ain't fibbin' a lick, and I probably couldn't do it twice in a lifetime, but if I hadn't reacted the way I did, he and that waxed mustache of his would'a been goners. I lifted him onto my horse and succeeded in gettin' him back to the fort." Jane looked pretty pleased with herself.

"Captain Egan was a funny fellow, and on recoverin', he laughingly named me Calamity Jane, the heroine of the plains! I swear to you this is true, and I have borne that name until this present day."

Some might have thought this a tall tale, but I had ridden with Jane when she saved the stagecoach full of people. To write her off as a skilled liar would have been too easy a feat. Perhaps they were all fabrications. Fabrications that enraptured and engaged my unusual sister, but fabrications all the same. The thing was, I had seen Jane in action. Even if what she said hadn't happened, my guess was it could have. She had the talent of a hero and the tongue of a storyteller. So good was she that I forgot my mission long enough to give up and take my sister back inside.

Joseph was waiting for me when we walked back into the saloon, dazed and defeated. Hour made a beeline to the kitchen to get ready for the afternoon duties, and I was to help Joseph stock up the saloon. A large shipment of bourbon had arrived, and it needed unloading. After drinking in my appearance, he looked at me with a question on his face.

My first impression of the man was that he was a kind fellow, but one that was led around by the nose when it came to his wife, Dora. After a solid week of knowing him, I learned other truths. Joseph was bossed around at length, but not for any other reason than he wanted the fine lady to succeed. He was, in fact, a kind fellow. He was also a soft-spoken man who quietly sat back and watched the goings-on in the place. Joseph absorbed more than anyone gave him credit for, and I had seen how much the great Dora DuFran leaned on him in the quieter parts of the day. To dub him the weak one of the two would have been a grave error in judgment.

Joseph stared at me the way he did when reading the insides of person. I wondered if he'd ever taken it in his mind to be a fortune teller, for he was a good enough reader of folks to do the job without much effort. Weren't much to the task as far as Pa told it to me. The future was easily seen by those poking around in a person's face.

"Missy said you was supposed to be gettin' Jane to take you to see your pa this afternoon. I reckoned I was gonna have to do this load myself."

I looked up at him with a solemn gaze. Jane was my friend, and I owed her so much, but the failure of my mission to see Pa was heavy in my chest. Where was he now, I wondered. Was he still a sick patient in that bed in the pest tent, or was he being prepped for his own pine coffin somewhere unknown to me? Surely Jane would've have told me if he died, wouldn't she?

"Yeah, we got a bit sidetracked, as it were."

Joseph handed me a few bottles, and I set to stocking them in the cabinets beneath the bar's counter the way Dora had shown me. The labels had to be facing out and the bottles staggered. That was important, or so she said, because the bartender needed to be able to see the brand they're pouring right away. Nothing was worse for business than the hurried bartender pouring three fingers of the good stuff for a low-paying miner. Our diligence made the bartending easier, and with the bottles staggered the way she showed me, taking inventory was a quicker job.

"You're worried about your pa," said Joseph.

I tried really hard not to look as forlorn as I felt at that moment.

"Yessir."

"I 'spect Jane told some big story of hers to distract you?"

"Yessir."

"Was it the Custer story?"

I halted my work and looked into his eyes. They seemed to know something I didn't, and this wasn't the first time someone had mentioned Jane's Custer story to me. She hadn't recited that one, but there must have been something significant about it to make such a mark.

"No. It was the story about how she got her name."

Joseph laughed a little under his breath and handed me a few more bottles.

"Oh, that one. That's a good one. Probably not a lick of truth in it, but it's a good one."

"None of that happened?"

He shrugged and pulled out a few more bottles for me to stock. I took them and went back to work, but I kept eye contact with the man.

"Maybe, maybe not. Jane's told it so many times it probably is the truth to her at this point. I heard the real way she got her name was because she was so ornery. One cowpoke or another said to offend a woman like her was to court calamity. Hell, they could both be the truth for all I know of it."

"I'm just worried she told us that so she didn't have to tell us our pa's dead. He looked real bad when I saw him before."

"She ain't told you the Custer story yet?"

"Nope."

"Well then, don't worry too much. Your Pa's still alive."

"What's the Custer story gotta do with any of this?" Joseph scratched his head.

"It's her best story and one she reserves only for something she can't bear to say. Kind of like her 'big guns' if you will. When Jane has nothing to say to you but a story about General Custer, you know then that your daddy's gone."

The two very conflicting feelings of relief and dread washed over me like a terrible tide, red in nature and color. My pa's state of being was an unknown thing. He was alive, but how long? Would he come back to us? What would the world look like if he didn't?

Another thought seeped in as well. Why was Cage coming to me in my dreams, reminding me of old things? I never dreamed of her before. How was it that this began right when we moved to Deadwood, when Pa got sick?

"You know anythin' about ghosts, Joseph?"

"I don't reckon. Never seen one myself. Have you seen somethin'?"

"No. I don't think so. I been seein' a dead person in my dreams," I said quietly.

"What're they doin'? Bein' mean?"

"No. It's Hour's mama. She shows me stuff. Stuff that happened a long time ago about Pa and Hour. I can't make out why."

He contemplated my words a while, and I let him have the silence to do so. Resting his elbows on the counter, Joseph stared past me and toward the staircase. It was a deep look befitting a smart man. I was pretty sure whatever he had to say after all that staring was something well thought about.

"Well, I don't know nothin' about that sort of thing," began Joseph. "But my Grammy was a superstitious old coot. She always said the dead came to us when we needed them. Sometimes they come to help their loved ones cross over. Sometimes they come to watch over their family in times when they really need it. My best guess is that yer family sure needs lookin' after right about now."

I nodded, not having any other words to offer up. We went about the rest of our work with our heads down and our mouths shut as was more fitting of men to do. A sick unease was rising in the pit of my stomach though, and the only thing holding my lunch in place was the knowledge that, for the time being, my pa was still among the land of the living.

Whatever that was worth I knew not, but hell, at least I knew it.

11

EVERYONE WOKE THAT MORNING to the sounds of screaming. It wasn't the good kind of screaming either, where people whoop and holler with excitement. The sound in question was the kind of screaming most connected to something terrible. High pitched and frantic, it was. What scared me the most about it was the voice making all the ruckus was female and familiar. It was soon accompanied by another shout adding to the noise. One that was in the room with me.

I sat straight up from my bedroll and immediately looked around the storeroom for my sister. My heart calmed by a measure or two when I spotted Hour sitting on the floor with Fred the Kitten and staring at our closed door. It skipped a beat again when I realized she was wailing and tense all over. She shook her head violently this way and that, as if telling whomever was out there that this sort of sound wasn't allowed. Fred was batting at a dust ball nearby as though nothing at all were wrong.

I jolted up and over to Hour who was now struggling not to scream and hit her legs. Her focus was on the floor as she gritted her teeth but kept crying all the same. She tried to hit at me when I knelt beside her, but I grabbed her hands.

"What's happenin'?" I asked her.

"Something bad. Missy's crying," she replied with a pained voice.

"Okay, okay. Take it easy. You're fine."

I looked around the storeroom for anything that might satiate her mind. Anything to get her to stop focusing on the trouble on the other side of the door. Off in the corner sat her swear jug, so I made to collect my sister and deposit her next to it. Her little body was stiff as it curled into a ball in my arms, making the act of carrying her a hard one.

When I sat her down, she nearly rolled over onto her side. I supported her weight with my side as I grabbed the jug and spilled the pennies on the floor in front of her. Her focus honed in on the money splayed out like pebbles along the riverbank.

"See the pennies, Hour? They need ta be sorted," I said gently.

"Sorted?"

"Dirty ones from clean ones. Think you can manage?"

She stared down at the assortment, reaching out with shaky fingers.

"Yessir. I can," she said.

I moved around Hour carefully and collected Fred. She chewed playfully on my thumb as I sat her in Hour's lap for safekeeping. No need leaving the room only to have the damn kitten follow and cause Hour to become frantic all over again.

"I'm gonna check it out, the ruckus outside. You stay here in case there's trouble. If you hear someone you don't know coming this way, take Fred and hide in the cupboard yonder, okay?"

"Okay."

I didn't want to leave her, but what choice did I have? Something awful was happening, and what kind of man would sit back on his haunches and not help out? These folks had become my friends, they had taken me and Hour in, and I wasn't about to turn a yellow streak now.

Upon entering the main part of Dora's, I could see that most of the clamor was coming from the kitchen. I raced back through the dining hall and into the kitchen where Nancy May was cradling a bloody and weeping Missy. Her lips were busted clean open and tears mixed with drying blood around a swollen cheek. It was swollen up to the size of an egg already and turning several different shades of blue. My hands immediately balled into fists when her watery eyes looked up at me. An entire world of hurt shone in those eyes of hers.

She buried her face into Nancy's chest once more and continued her crying jag while several girls flitted around her like birds trying to tend to her wounds. Anger forced hot blood to rush in my ears to the point I could barely hear a thing. It must have been so because I didn't hear Madame Dora DuFran come up behind me until she spoke.

"You're with me, Jimmy Glass."

I turned to look at her. Her normally jovial face was angry and stern. That mouth of hers, which normally smiled all the time, was tight in a straight line across her face. The Madame wore no makeup and looked meaner than hell.

The thing she said to me, it wasn't a question or a command per se. It was a fact, like one person seeing the same bits of themselves in another. I was with her. She knew this. I was her man, no questions asked.

"You're damn straight I am, Miss Dora."

The Madame of Diddlin' Dora's held two rifles next to me, and upon my word, she handed one to me. I had fired a rifle a few times with Pa in the past. It was usually to hunt squirrels. This rifle was a might bit heavier than the one Pa had at the shanty, but I held it like I knew what I was doing. At least my anger would allow me to act like it long enough to figure it out.

One of the girls, a scrawny brunette named Ruthy, stopped when Dora grabbed her hand.

"Get all the girls out of their rooms, you hear me? Run all customers, if there be any left, out the back door quiet-like. Get them girls to come down here and stay put. Here, take this."

With that familiar flick of her hand, Dora produced her tiny derringer and handed it to Ruthy.

"If he gets here before I do for any reason, aim at his trunk, you got it? Don't get fancy. Lead poisoning to the gut will take any man down, no matter how big."

"Yes, Miss Dora."

Dora turned on her heel and left the kitchen. I followed behind her, trying to match her determined stride. I didn't know who was responsible, but I was anxious to see him pay. When we passed through the saloon and outside onto the walkway, I became confused. My mind had figured we would go upstairs toward the girls' rooms to take the man down right away.

"Ain't we gonna get the man who hurt Missy?"

"Yep."

"He out here?"

"Nope."

"Then what're we doin' out here?"

"We're gettin' Jane."

Jane was where we expected to find her, curled up in the open by the outhouse in the alleyway. There were two emptied bottles near her boots, and she stank of Indian whiskey. Dora didn't have time for cordial manners or kind concerns. She kicked Jane's mule-eared boots without delay. A scent flurried up to our nostrils of mud and urine.

"Jane, wake up."

There was a great show of groaning and mumbling. Dora kicked her again. This time, Jane woke with a start, producing her revolver pointed directly at Dora DuFran's heart. For an awful minute, I reckoned Jane was going to pull the trigger, but after a few hard blinks, she recognized her friend and lowered her gun.

"What in the hell do you want, Dora? If you are 'bout to go after me with yer mop bucket again, you can just . . ."

"I need your help."

The tone in Dora's voice was stern and uncompromising. Jane appraised her, looked sideways at me for a second, and noted the rifle in my hands. I couldn't tell for sure, but she appeared to still be drunk.

"Jimmy get into some trouble?"

"No. I need help with a customer who ain't payin'."

Jane waved her hands in a dismissive way at the both of us before she slumped back to the earth. Her hat tipped down over her eyes.

"That all? Get Joseph."

"I loaned Joseph to Charlie Utter to ride shotgun to Cheyenne."

"Well, get Sheriff Bullock then."

"The sheriff had him a nasty fight with some fella outside The Gem Saloon last night. They both all bloodied up. Come on, Jane. I need yer help."

"If it hadn't escaped yer fuckin' notice, Dora DuFran, I am—at the present moment—on the incapacitated side of my fuckin' brain."

"Jane, it's Missy. She got quite the lacing last night."

Jane's demeanor changed as she sat up and looked right into Dora's eyes. Suddenly, this wasn't a thing to swipe at anymore like so many annoying flies.

"Who beat on her?"

"It's my fault, Jane. Frank Bellingham came by here drunk a few days ago."

A deep hurt ran across Dora's impenetrable face. One that came from a scare long ago. A weakness that ran from her arm, down through her heart, and up to her eyes. Dora rubbed the scar then to emphasize the memory of the hurt. Jane's face got fierce like I hadn't seen since we were shooting at Indians by Whitewood Creek.

"Frank the Bear Bellingham came by, and you didn't tell me?"

"I thought I ran him off. He was drunk and confused. Molly sent him my way as a prank to get back at me for stealin' Missy from her, but I never thought he'd come back. Last night, after I went to bed, he come by the saloon lookin' for me. Missy thought he was just another customer."

A lot went unsaid after that. More than was said to begin with, I reckoned. We all knew the way of things in Deadwood. The mean and strong got their way, no matter how deranged, more often than not. In the silence sat all the indignities Missy must have endured the night before.

"Where is he now?" asked Jane, angry and focused.

"He's up in Missy's room. Sometime this mornin', he kicked her out all bloodied and locked himself inside. Anyone goes by gets shot at. Please help me, Jane. I ain't a good shot."

Without hesitation, Jane stood and grabbed the rifle in Dora's hand. We marched back toward Diddlin' Dora's like an angry mob behind our leader Jane. Tempers were high and blood boiled in our veins. I had never felt so alive holding that gun and marching off to war. It may not have been a true war, but it was the only one I had known. The Indian scuffle with the Overland Stagecoach was a battle, sure it was. But I hadn't prepared for it, and it terrified me to be a part of such a thing. This was different. This was vengeance. This was a debt of justice to be paid. I hadn't had anything against the Indians at the time, but this man, who hurt our friends, was going to pay if I had anything to say about it.

Upon entering the saloon, the first thing a patron might see would be the bar on the bottom level. The second thing would probably have been the wooden staircase to the right of the bar that led up to the second-floor hall of rooms. This was where the girls stayed. It was also where they entertained customers for the evening. From the landing, you could see a long hall with ten or so doors. Each girl painted her door a different color. When I'd asked about this, Joseph explained that Dora believed in letting the girls' personalities shine through a bit. I was curious what exactly went on behind those doors but I wasn't quite sure I was ready to find out.

"Which door is Missy's?" asked Jane when we reached the top of the stairs.

"Two down on the right." It was the pink one—the exact color I would have chosen for her myself.

None of the girls were anywhere to be seen. Ruthy had done her job and spirited them all down to the kitchen. A few cats eyed us suspiciously as we walked by. They stuck to corners and hid in cupboards to better observe without being detected. The air vibrated. Something was amiss, and they could sense it better than anyone.

A line of ruby carpeting ran down the length of the hallway, muffling the sounds of our footfalls. We fell silent. When we reached Missy's door, Jane put her ear up to it. We had been careful not to make even the slightest of sounds for fear of being gunned down before we even made a stand. He'd already made bullet holes in the door which carved ricochet marks down the hallway walls.

Jane asked us to step back from the door slowly with a hand gesture. She took two half-steps backwards, held her rifle tight, and kicked the door hard with the force of a mule. The wooden door flew open and splintered in the places where the lock and the hinges had tried in vain to keep it in place. Jane moved in with a quickness I didn't think she'd be able to muster in her drunken state and pointed the rifle at a heap of an unconscious man laying half on and half off Missy's bed. The man stirred only a little at the intrusion and didn't seem willing to give his attackers the time of day.

I had remembered the man being large, like a gorilla or a bear, but seeing him in the light of the morning brought the reality of his size down on me. I pointed my rifle at his hulky body as well, but my hands trembled a bit to do it. Dora stood just behind me, as stoic as a statue, at least in appearance. I could practically hear her heart thudding next to me. It was the drumbeat to our own personal war right then and there.

"Frank Bellingham, get yer lousy ass up out of that bed this instant, or I *will* shoot you in the back like the yella shithead you are."

The huge man moved a little and rolled over to a sitting position, his shaky eyes on Jane. His lids were heavy with sleep and alcohol, and he looked at the barrels of our rifles like they were more amusing than threatening—a few flies buzzing against a horse maybe. With a long yawn, he stood up and crossed his arms over his chest.

"What's this all about?"

"You beat up one of Dora's girls."

"So?"

"So, you ignorant wretch, you have until the count of five to get yer ass out of this room, pay the Madame, and apologize to Missy."

Frank scratched his head and started laughing. It was the laughing more than anything else that made me and Jane ready our rifles. The unmistakable sound of a bullet being chambered forced that massive man to cease his laughing. But it wasn't enough to wipe his smile away. At that moment, more than anything else, I wanted to shoot that smug look clean off his pock-marked face. Visions of shooting him and then beating him with my bare fist until there was nothing left of him but a mass of bloody meat taunted me.

I started breathing smoke behind my rifle when Dora laid a tender hand on my shoulder from behind. It was the sort that a mother would use, patient and kind. My pretend battle eased off my eyelids.

"Steady, kid. Wait for Jane," she whispered to me and only me.

"One," began Jane.

"I ain't apologizin' or payin'. That little whore wasn't good enough to pay for. I can get better down in China-town for a dime."

"Two."

"You can count all you like, whore. I ain't leaving this place 'til I'm good 'n' ready, and I ain't payin' your whore friends neither."

"Three."

At the count of three, Jane pointed her rifle down at the man's leg and fired. The giant crumpled onto the floorboards, hollering in pain. A bright bloom of red appeared on his left thigh. Meat and flecks of bone poked out from the skin into the air through a window of pant fabric. Frank looked at the wound with a shocked face. It would have been extremely comical if the rest of us hadn't looked so surprised ourselves. We all gawked with open mouths, like fish caught from a river, in Jane's direction. She moved closer to the wailing man and stood over him menacingly.

"You! You said the count of five!"

"Yeh, did I? I don't recall. I never can remember such details while in the presence of cocksuckers. Now get yer sorry ass up before I give you a matching pair."

Now the big man was frightened. Those drunken eyes of his were wide, and the faint smell of urine permeated the air nearest to him. I weren't certain if it was from Jane's recent nap at the necessary out back or if the Bear Man pissed himself. Frank stood quickly and unevenly, and Jane gave him room to do so. He hobbled and groaned in pain as he tried to put weight on his shot leg. His giant body crumpled to the floor again and again. It took him three tries to stand tall and stay that way. She didn't even point the rifle at him anymore. It was held loosely by her side as she relied on the man's terror to motivate him. I, on the other hand, refused to lower mine even an inch.

Frank went to grab his personal effects from the side table, and Jane drew her revolver from its holster with her other hand. The movement was so smooth and swift, it looked to be more out of habit than a thought-out command. The Bear Man froze and put his hands up, leaving his money, gun, and belt on the table. He growled in pain.

"That ain't goin' with you," said Jane.

"You whores robbin' me now?"

"You owe this establishment. That there is payment for yer shitty fuckin' behavior."

"You can't do this."

"Oh, I do believe I am the one with the fuckin' gun, so yeah, I can. You best be grateful I ain't takin' more payment out of yer hide. Move it."

Jane's words were thick with sarcasm and hatred. With a sour glare, Frank Bellingham limped his way out of the now open doorway. He clutched his leg as he dragged it down the hallway and toward the staircase. The three of us followed behind him, me with my rifle trained on his back, and Jane with her revolver. Her rifle was balanced between her hand and her shoulder. Jane looked calm, as though that rifle were actually a fishing pole, and she was going for a leisurely stroll to the creek. I was so tense my neck hurt from the strain of it all.

"Should we just shoot him now?" I whispered to Jane. "He's gonna just come back, ain't he?"

"Shootin' a man in the back in a coward's game, kid. Don't ever let me catch you playin' that hand. Understood?"

"Yes'm."

Frank made it to the staircase and tried to descend it one step at a time, careful to not put weight on his injured leg. After a few steps of overcompensating, he stepped wrong and slipped. The large man fell down the remainder of the stairs in a comical state of yelps and screams. Enough blood had been pouring from his wound that he left a little bit of himself here and there on the way down to the ground level. We followed behind him. Dora suppressed a laugh. Jane did not. Her cackling rang through the saloon like a bell on Sunday.

He pulled himself up, frothing at the mouth with rage. I couldn't think to do anything but stand tall and keep the rifle trained on the giant man. Jane took to laughing out loud again at his comical misfortune, which, in turn, lured some of the girls out of hiding. When I glanced over, a handful of Dora's girls were staring at the sight of a bleeding Frank Bellingham, angry and frothy in front of a laughing Calamity Jane.

"I am gonna get my pig sticker and come right back fer you," threatened Frank in between clenched teeth.

Jane only smiled and trained her gun back on his face.

"No, you ain't. As soon as you leave this here place, I'm goin' to collect some of my biggest friends, including this lovely lady's husband, and we're gonna run you right outta town. Trees 'round these parts can bear some awful fruit from time to time. You best get movin'."

The man's vigor stayed but definitely lost its edge for the time being. Jane looked as cool as a block of ice, more comfortable than I had seen her since the Overland Stagecoach mail incident. This was her element. That was a plain fact.

Frank Bellingham turned and limped out of the saloon with his back turned to us. I had him in my sights the entire way. The thought of Missy's battered face made my finger want to squeeze that trigger. The impulse to rid the world of that man cut deep into my bones, but Jane had said that was a coward's game. Men with no honor shot men in the back, and I wouldn't be thought of like that. I let that terrible man go, trailing a bloodied leg. I watched him push his way out of the door and disappear into the bright noon of the day. It was then that I let myself breathe once again and relax.

Dora put her hand on my shoulder and gently pried the gun from my hand. My arms ached from holding so tensely for so long. She patted my back, and one of the girls, I was too dazed to tell who, brought me some water.

I was the one who saw him come back in minutes later. Jane had her back turned to everyone. She had bellied up to the bar while Dora poured her a glass of fancy bourbon, on the house of course. He had threatened to go get his bayonet after all. We never knew if the blade he brandished had actually been his, retrieved from a saddlebag somewhere, or if it was one he stole from the first pedestrian he came across. Either way, Frank Bellingham blew into Diddlin' Dora's like a terribly quiet breeze brandishing a knife. He moved so swiftly, at first I thought it was a daydream, like some terrible vision after everything we'd been through.

When I blinked, he was still there, running straight for the back of Calamity Jane, my friend. The coward's game. It was his game. Dora hadn't seen him yet to warn her friend. She was looking down at the glasses she was filling with bourbon. My hand itched for the rifle but remembered Dora had taken it from me. The only thing I could do was warn her.

"Jane! Look out!"

The infamous woman didn't hesitate a lick, not for even a second. She turned with her gun already drawn from her holster. Her left hand cocked the hammer over and over again as she fired three shots into the Bear Man's trunk. She hadn't even waited to see who he was or where he was coming from. Instinct spun her around to face her target spot on.

Frank Bellingham collapsed dead on the floor of the saloon. Self-defense in the eyes of the law, what little there was in Deadwood. We hadn't resorted to a coward's game, even in the end. The only coward was the one leaking blood on the floor. I felt glad knowing that fact.

Jane puffed out a rib cage full of air and threw back a few fingers of bourbon. Some of the frantic girls ran back in to see what had happened. Ruthy screamed at the sight of the dead man in the saloon. Dora collected them all, like a gathering of chickens, and herded them back into the dining hall and away from the scene. Somewhere from outside, a group had formed and rushed into the saloon to see what had happened.

"What's goin' on?"

"This man attacked one of my girls and when asked to leave, attacked Jane here. She shot him in a fair fight. She's a goddamned hero. Go get the deputy to clean up the body."

Two of the men ran off to do just that, excited to do something important involving a murder. A gaggle of looky-loos stayed behind to gawk at the scene. Gossip started quickly as someone recognized the man and ran off to spread the word Frank Bellingham was dead. As far as I could tell, he wasn't a popular type, so the news wasn't likely to spread too far to anyone he knew. Only famous outlaws or infamous people like Wild Bill warranted a full blown gossip mill.

In all the commotion, I didn't hear Jane sidle up beside me. She made her presence known with a pat on my back. I jumped in my own skin a little as I turned to her, wild-eyed. The sight of blood and death had been staining my vision. Facing a friend was a shock.

"Hold up. Easy now," she cooed to me like I were a wild thing.

"Sorry. It's just a lot of blood, and . . ."

"It's okay, Jimmy Glass. It's a bad day when you get used to the sight, lemme tell you."

"You all right, Jane?"

"I'm as fine as ever. I came over to thank you. Now,

I owe you one, kid. Just let me know how I can repay it, okay?"

I nodded to her numbly, not really considering the gravity of her words.

OUR LITTLE SECTION OF the world was becoming a hotbed of news and happenings. No one much cared about the death of Frank Bellingham. The man had no family that spoke to him and no real friends to speak of, retribution was certainly not coming our way. This allowed all of us to breathe easier knowing the drama had passed. I certainly had drunk my fill of the famous lifestyle, and for the first time, I had an inkling of why Jane drank so much. So much attention threatened to be exhausting.

Joseph came home and fixed Missy's door so the poor girl could recover in peace. Doc came around to see about her, and Jane or Dora would change her bandages, but other than that, she allowed no one to visit her. It was sad such a spark of a girl could fade so much so quickly. I wanted to visit her so many times, but fear kept me away. I was afraid of rejection and of making myself a pest to someone who had surely seen enough of men for the time being.

By the time I made my way back to our little storeroom, Hour had arranged the pennies in several lines starting with the cleanest, shiniest pennies to the ones that were nearly black with dirt. I had been gone longer than I planned so I came bearing gifts: a plate of mashed potatoes, some milk, and a bit of bread. She looked up at me when I set the tray near her. Her face seemed calm enough so I sat next to her.

"You okay?" I asked.

"Missy?" she asked. "She's gone?"

"Gone? What do you mean gone?"

"Like Pa. She's gone. I won't see her."

"No, Hour. She ain't gone. She's up in her room. Got beat up a bit, but she's okay. And Pa ain't gone neither. He's here."

"No. He's not," she said, looking around the room as if to emphasize his lack of presence.

"You're right. He ain't in here, but he ain't dead. Pa's down the road a piece. He's in the pest tent gettin' better, just like Missy's in her room."

"Like Mama?"

The question hit me in the chest. It was rare that Hour spoke of her mother. She had been so small when Cage passed.

"Yer mama died. You remember?"

"Yes. She's gone. Pa's gone."

"No no, Hour," I said reaching out for her hand. "Gone and dead are different here. You know that right? They ain't the same."

She shook her head slowly, and I didn't know what to say. How could I explain a thing like this in a way that might work for her? What sort of story might a man weave to explain the way of death? Even if there was a way, my young mind wouldn't be able to find the words. Maybe if she could see it for herself.

It was evening time before I got the nerve up to confront Jane about seeing my pa. After the craziness of the Frank Bellingham episode died down, I remembered her pledge to owe me a favor. I wanted to see my pa, and I wanted Hour to see him too.

Jane was drinking in the saloon at a table with a group of men asking her to tell the story of how she killed the Bear Man yet again. She waggled her empty glass, and one of the men took it from her. He sped away in earnest to bring her back a fresh one. A great bow of her head signaled her thanks as she began her telling her story where she had ended it.

"And then, I says to him, 'One more word from you and I'll make it a matchin' pair!'"

Raucous laughter all around.

I snuck as quickly and quietly as I could to the side of her table, but she marked me on the spot. It wasn't a total surprise. When Hour and I played quiet Injuns back home, I always lost.

"Fellas! This is my brave accomplice, Jimmy Glass! A drink fer Jimmy!"

More drunken cheers rang through the saloon, and

someone handed me a shot of whiskey. I looked around at the surly men and the one tough woman in front of me and threw the stuff back as quickly as I could. That familiar burning hit my throat, but I managed to hide it in my face. Another round of cheers and several rough hands patted my back, making me almost cough the whiskey back up.

"He was with me at the stagecoach too. I can't tell if'n he's brave or just stupid to follow 'round the likes of Calamity Jane!"

More laughing and toasting and slapping of my back. My head was swirling with all the praise and booze and sudden camaraderie from strangers. I tried to stare straight forward and focus. Jane was so good at distracting me, but I needed to concentrate. I had to get Jane alone to talk about Pa. I couldn't wait again or be sidetracked, no matter how much I enjoyed being considered her brave accomplice.

The opportunity presented itself when she excused herself to go outside for a bit of privacy. I knew where she was headed and could intercept her on her way back. The outhouse was in the alley. If I waited out front of the main doors to Diddlin' Dora's, I could get a moment alone with her. Jane was having too much fun to set down for the night just yet.

Jane left the saloon and headed the way I suspected, so I followed her outside and posted up against the wall. The night was a little brisk, a signal that fall was around the corner with winter trailing close behind it. A few cowpokes passed me, taking in the night air. They debated which whorehouse was the best in Deadwood, but came to no agreements. One liked Dora's the best, but another praised the blondes at Molly Johnson's.

When they were out of earshot, I spotted Jane sauntering back up the walkway and heading straight for me. She slowed when she saw who it was and what my face inevitably told her. I was upset and needed to talk.

"You look bothered, kid."

"I am, Jane."

"Is it about Frank Bellingham? I won't rope you into those stories if'n you don't want the attention. It ain't fer everybody."

"No, it ain't that."

"Well, out with it, kid. I ain't got all evenin' to guess at yer feelings."

She crossed her arms over her chest the way Dora did. Thing was, Jane's bosom wasn't nothing compared to Dora's, and the stance looked mighty different.

"We are friends, ain't we?"

She seemed taken aback by that but recovered quickly.

"Well, I reckon we are."

"And you said you owed me a favor, right? For the help with Frank Bellingham."

Her look turned crooked as she steadied herself for the unknown.

"Yeh, I did."

"Then I want to cash in the favor. I want you to take me to see my pa."

Jane breathed out a long sigh, and her shoulders relaxed. Her face looked as if a huge weight had been lifted. Relief relaxed her all over.

"Whew, kid. You gave me a right bad scare there. I thought you were gonna ask fer somethin' crazy awful, the way you had yer face all screwed up."

"You mean, you don't mind takin' me?"

"I'll take you if'n that's what you want. It ain't a pretty sight though. Worse than you saw before."

"Then why have you been duckin' me when I asked?"

"Because I knew how hard it would be fer you to see it. Not to mention how Hour would take it. I didn't want her to see that and lose all the ground she's been coverin' at Dora's. She's better, ain't she?"

"Yes'm."

"I just reckoned seein' the likes of yer daddy right now would do more harm than good."

"Jane, I get your side, but we gotta see him. He's our pa."

The tough-as-nails lady looked down at me and screwed her face into a chagrinned expression. I could tell the idea didn't set proper with her, but she knew she had to let up. He was our pa after all. We had a right. Jane nodded to me, her hat bobbing with the motion.

"All right, kid. You win."

"When can you take us?"

"Hold yer horses, Jimmy. Listen, I still reckon takin' Hour is a bad idea, but you're her brother and have say o'er her. I'll take you tonight, and after seein' your pa in his condition, if'n you still wanna take her along, we'll do that tomorrow."

"You mean, you'll take me tonight? What about yer party?"

She waved her hand in the direction of the saloon as

though she were swatting gnats.

"You mean with them cowpokes? Hell, they'll be around tomorrow and the day after, and I reckon, the day after. Come on, Jimmy Glass. Let us go see yer pa."

Jane beckoned me, and I followed her out into the flame-lit evening. Most people didn't try to see it, but even in the most lawless of places, it could be beautiful. The moon was big and almost full over the makeshift streets of Deadwood that night. It had rained a little previously, and the wet mud of the thoroughfare sparkled with moonlight. Everything else lit up warm and orange from lamps, making the contrast of the two stark and lovely.

I breathed in the scent of horses in the livery yonder and the incense wafting on the wind from China-town. Somewhere, a group of rowdy men shouted with laughter with the tinkling rhythm of a piano's keys behind them. Down the street a piece, a woman's voice serenaded the night like some sort of angel.

Once the pest tent was in sight, a whole new scene unfolded itself. There was nothing jovial about that place, and the only sounds were those of pain and woe. A human in pain was a more terrible noise than any I knew of. The smell of urine and feces and blood filled the air. When I breathed in through my nose, all I could sense was rust and something else metallic and wrong. Perhaps that was what death smelled like when it came to call.

Outside the tent, Jane pulled two handkerchiefs from a gunnysack filled with them. We tied the rags around our faces like bank robbers and entered through the flap that acted as the front door.

It was much as I remembered from before. There were rows and rows of cots with men and women in various stages of the disease. Details were harder to make out with everything cast in the dim candlelight. Evening in the pest tent looked different. Things were softer somehow, in that you didn't have to see them in the hard light of the day. There were bedpans on the floor, no denying the odor, but you didn't quite see the awful things inside them. Disease was disease, but I reckoned it was easier to look at without the sun forcing the details on a person. I wondered, as I had on many occasions, how it was that Doc and Jane could stand to come here day after day. They did so willingly and without payment.

Jane led me through the tent, but she didn't have to really. After my first time here, I remembered where my daddy was despite the lack of lighting. Even if I hadn't carved the place in my memory, my waking dreams took me there often enough. Down the rows of cots, turn right, and then six more rows until you made it to his spot.

There he was, but not as I remembered and not how he appeared in my thoughts of him. The sight of the man in front of me did not register with my mind. This was my pa. It was the correct spot, and Jane said as much to me, but the man before me was so much altered I barely recognized him. His soft burnt hair, so much like mine, was nearly black from sweat and dried blood. His skin was thin-looking and uneven. The bumps on him had festered and burst into oozing scabs that looked painful on his thin body. Thin, so thin. I hadn't been away from him that long. He shouldn't look that thin and frail. His eyes were half open and staring blankly at the ceiling. Air moved in and out of his opened mouth, but the breaths were short, and there was too much time in between them. I called his name, but he didn't respond.

"He stopped eatin' a bit ago. We tried forcin' broth, but he just throws it up. That's why he looks so skinny."

"I was wonderin'."

I moved closer, unable to really feel my face. I wanted to find his hand to hold it.

"I wouldn't," said Jane as she eased me back a step. "Surest way to catch this is by touchin'."

I waited for something but wasn't sure what exactly. Perhaps I expected him to come to and look at me, or maybe he'd say something meaningful to give me some hope. It was a stupid thought because nothing happened. He opened his mouth a little to flash a set of exposed teeth, but nothing came out. Jane and I just stood there in silence, watching a man struggle to breathe.

"He gonna die?"

"I reckon so," said Jane with an apologetic tone to her words.

"Anybody as bad off as him ever come back?"

"I'd be lyin' to you if'n I said there hadn't. That's not a reason to get hopes up though. I don't want you to hope too high about this because high hopes fall pretty hard. Your Pa is dying, best I can tell. Me and Doc, we do all we can, and maybe he'll recover, but I wouldn't lay a bet on it."

I nodded. It was a blessing, being told the way of things as they were. Somewhere, underneath the terror and sorrow, a tiny bit of me was thankful for that. It wasn't a feeling that would surface any time soon, but at least it was down there, ready to be felt when the time was right.

We left the pest tent, heads looking down at our feet the way Hour's might've. The rags on our faces had been thrown into a laundering bin, and we washed our hands in an old horse trough that had been repurposed for the pest tent's needs. There was so much to say between Jane and me and no way to say it, not properly anyway.

"You know, I knew Wild Bill," said Jane out of nowhere.

I looked over at her, but she was still staring at the ground in front of us. Walking back to Dora's was a slow journey at our current pace, and neither of us minded that much.

"Yes'm, I heard that."

"He was a good man, that Bill. Everyone liked him. People said things about us that weren't true. Things his wife would've died inside to hear. Rumors are a funny thing to start, and I can't honestly say that I didn't start my fair share of 'em in various stages of drunkenness."

We were quiet for a bit. I wasn't sure about the true nature of ghosts. I heard a preacher once say when you love someone, a piece of their soul forever walks with you. Joseph's grammy said ghosts came around when their families needed them most. Something joined us there in that silence. I don't claim to know if it was the ghost of Wild Bill Hickok, but that explanation sounded just as good as any.

"Bill was smart and funny and kind in all the ways I wanted to be. He sorta brought out the better side of anyone he cared to get to know. I ain't ever loved a person that wasn't family. Romantic love it weren't really, as best I can figure, but I loved Bill. He was a good friend to me. The trouble was his gamblin' streak. Made a lot of enemies that way. One reason I don't gamble. Got enough bad blood on my hands without addin' to it a goddamned gamblin' habit. When that shithead, Jack McCall . . ."

Jane trailed off for a second and caught her breath. I watched her struggle to choke back the makings of a tear.

"When he murdered Bill, I was too drunk to go and get him. I should've killed him . . . me. I should've done it. Not some court and hangman, me. It should've been me. I was Bill's friend. It was my right."

We had made it to the porch in front of Dora's place. The group inside was still ranting and rowdy as Jane and I leaned against the wall, heavy with death and regret, the ghost of Wild Bill hovering near as I could tell.

"The fuckin' point being that there are only a few people that get to tug on your insides like that, and anythin' you do or don't do fer them is on you when they die. I ain't ever gonna be over Bill, and it's up to you what you wanna do 'bout your pa. I won't intervene anymore. I shouldn'ta ducked you to start with."

"What do you mean?"

"I mean, you saw what his condition is at present. He ain't got a lot of time, kid. If'n you want to take yer sister fer a farewell, that's yer business. I will help with whatever you need."

We finally managed to meet one another's eyes. Hers were tired and frayed at the edges, and I'm sure mine were hot and swollen from the tears I hadn't managed to shed as yet.

"Thank you, Jane, fer your help. You said you'd owe me one, and you paid up and then some. We're even, and I appreciate it."

I stuck out my hand to shake on the accord. Jane's face softened all over, and she clapped her rough hand on my shoulder.

"Ah shit, kid. That weren't no kinda favor I e'er heard of. That's just what friends do fer each other."

13

THE SCREAMING STARTED BEFORE Cage could even show me it was another dream. Immediately, my instinct was to tense, but when the foggy layer lifted, I relaxed all over again. There was nothing to do now but resign myself to whatever the dream had in store. Cage would show me what she wanted to show me. Whatever her reasoning was, there was no getting around that.

The scream came again. It was a desperate thing, that scream, like an animal trapped in a snare. Flower wasn't yet three years old, but already she acted different from most children. The quiet baby had turned into a reclusive child who hated to be held. It was the one thing all mothers wanted to do for their babies, and

Flower hated it with a passion.

I was fishing when I heard her. That panicked scream I only knew to be Flower's sent me running for home without even pulling up my line. The mad dash to our home took me only minutes, but she was already out of the house and headed for the trees. Cage was right behind her, reaching for her, calling soothing words in her Sioux tongue.

When she grabbed Flower, the girl screeched and pulled away from her mother. Instinct made Cage grab her daughter again and try to hold her close, but she yelled and broke away, slapping at the air in front of and around her. By the time I reached them, Cage had given up and let go of her daughter, tears streaming down her face. Her arms hung limp at her side as she watched Flower run over to a nearby tree and sit on the exposed roots. She rocked back and forth there, hugging her arms around herself. A tiny weeping sound came from inside her.

"What happened?" I asked.

"Nothing happened. I don't know why she cried."

Cage looked defeated and tired, yet she looked to her daughter with a visible longing. Every part of her vibrated with the ache to hold her baby, but she stayed put. My own want to comfort Flower told me to go to her as well, but I followed Cage's lead. In the past, Flower hadn't wanted me to hold her any more than she wanted anyone else.

"Why is she like this? I don't understand. Why does she hate us?" I asked.

Cage stiffened a little, then released a calming

153

breath.

"She does not hate us. She is closer to the spirit of the eagle than most people. My daughter, she is blessed."

The way Cage said the words, I couldn't tell if she was telling it to me or telling it to herself. Perhaps she was saying it so we both might believe. Either way, she wiped the remaining tears from beneath her eyes and nodded to herself.

"But why can't we hug her? Why does she hate it?"

"You cannot hug the eagle. Eagles are meant to fly. She feels trapped."

We stood together watching my sister from afar. She whimpered to herself as she rocked to and fro, upset over something unknown to us. I hadn't felt so helpless since I watched those men trample her Keya amulet in front of us in town.

"What can we do? She needs our help."

"I don't know. I've tried everything. The eagle must fly," replied Cage.

I resented this helplessness. Flower was my sister, not an eagle; I was meant to protect her. She was mine to care for, mine to watch over. Anger rose up inside me at my own useless arms, unable to help her the way she needed.

Finally, enough was enough. I couldn't watch her suffer from afar anymore. I'd try anything and every-thing if it meant she'd stop hurting. If jumping around like a fool made her feel better, that's what I was resigned to do. I'd stand on my head and recite a riddle if that'd make her smile a little. I went to her.

"Jimmy, no," Cage called after me, but I was already on my way.

Her rocking slowed as I reached her, but the whimpering increased as her little body stiffened. She expected me to touch her, and she was bracing herself for it. Slowly, I sat next to her on one of the roots coming loose from the ground, but I didn't reach out to touch her. For a while, we just sat there next to one another as she relaxed by degrees. Once, I put my hand out to touch her knee, but she tensed all over again, so I didn't go through with it.

This didn't make sense to me. I never struck Flower, ever. No one had. She had been such a good baby, there weren't any need to be mean to her. Why was she so tense?

I tried humming a song she liked and clapping but got no response. When she was a baby, she used to laugh when I made a popping sound with my thumb in my cheek. I tried it then, but again, she didn't seem to care.

I thought about what Cage had said, that Flower was an eagle spirit feeling pinned down. How did you make an eagle calm? How could I get Flower to relax again? She couldn't speak to tell me.

We sat there a good long while, Flower and me, and Cage watching from the house. Flower and I sorta settled into a cadence there, just breathing the same air together for a while. It was peaceful, the way we were. Everything was so calm in fact that I nearly missed her moving her foot. The movement wasn't absent like someone might do when they weren't thinking about it.

She was watching her foot and moving it deliberately.

I didn't say anything at first, just watched her drag her big toe in the dirt. Before long, I realized she was using her foot to trace a line in the dirt around the root she was sitting on. Flower was drawing in the dirt. Her little shoulders relaxed down and away from her ears the more she drew until she was almost herself again.

Taking a nearby stick, I pushed one end into the dirt near her foot and drew a slow swirl. Flower's foot stopped tracing as she watched me. Her big eyes grew wide with interest in this new game I made for her. I drew another swirl, and she smiled just a little at the pattern. Quickly, I found her a similar stick and offered it to her.

"You wanna draw with me?"

She didn't look at me, but she did nod her little head. With a quick motion, she snatched the stick from my hand and set to mimicking the swirling patterns I had drawn for her. It didn't take her long to master those, so we tried others. Circles, squares, hearts, and the like. Flower mastered them with a flourish. She wanted more, so I drew fish and birds and bears for her. I recited their names, but she didn't repeat them just yet. Right then, the drawing was the fun thing.

I didn't hear Cage approaching until she was directly behind me. The only thing telling she was there was the gentle brushing of her dress against my back. She didn't try to interrupt or even join in on our game. She seemed to merely want to get a closer look at what we were doing. Taking note of Cage's presence, I reckoned I should draw something new for Flower to try.

"Try this one."

I wiped the previous design clean with my foot and began a new one. It started with an oblong circle with a half circle and four angles at each end. There was a small gasp behind us when I added the details of the segments of the shell and the eyes on the head. It was crude, yes, but when I finished, a turtle was clearly drawn in the dirt before us. Flower studied it intently as though trying to etch the thing into her mind.

"That's a Keya. It's your Keya, Flower," I said, the way I had with the other drawings.

Like the others, my sister rejected trying to say the name. She merely set to work trying to recreate my drawing in the dirt next to her. Her first attempt wasn't half bad, and I told her so. Flower was content and she was happy. I had won the battle.

A delicate hand rested on my shoulder. When I looked up, the matching hand held out a small knife in a buckskin sheath. The thing was in Cage's palm like an offering to me. I stood with a confused look on my face. She took my hand without hesitation and laid the knife in my palm.

"What are you doing?" I asked.

"This is my gift to you."

When I gave the knife a second look, I knew it better. This was *her* knife. It was her favorite knife. The blade I held in my hand was the same one she finally laid on the grass when she decided to trust my father all those years ago. It was the same one she reached for when the men threatened us in town. I searched in her eyes for some explanation, but they were deep pools that told no tales of the swimmers who got lost in their depths.

"But why? I don't understand. This is yours."

"You gave me a gift, Jimmy Who Watches."

She motioned to Flower, who was ignoring us and engulfed in her new game of drawing Keya over and over again.

"But . . . but Cage . . ."

Cage shushed me and closed my fingers around the present. It felt warm in my hands, a beacon of love and intent and untold things yet to happen.

"You need this, and she needs you."

14

THE RISING SUN IN Deadwood brought with it a town humming with excitement. A group of Lakota had been relieved of the ponies they had stolen from various white settlers in the area. Deadwood's livery was filled to capacity with recovered horses. Word had it that Dora's horses we had left during the stagecoach shootout were among them. The thing was that most of the horses had been running wild among the Indians so long they bucked and fought at being forced to be stalled once again. Joseph and Dora had returned that morning, after identifying their recovered horses, covered in sweat, hay, and irritation.

While the wild ponies were becoming the talk of the town, I focused on readying Hour to go see our pa. Trying to explain a thing like this to any little girl would be a hard thing, but trying to explain it to a girl like Hour was pert near impossible. She kept insisting on taking Fred, the kitten, to see Pa.

"Why, Hour?"

"It'll help him. She helps me."

"Hour, I want you to listen to me, really listen, okay."

"I can hear you."

"Pa is dying. He probably won't be with us much longer. We need to go say goodbye. Do you understand?"

"He's gone or dead?"

"Yes. Well, no. Listen, he will be dead. We need to see him, you hear?"

"Yes. I'm takin' Fred," she said resolutely.

"Hour, that ain't a good idea."

"I'm takin' Fred."

There were times, terrible times, in my life that I just wanted to slap my sister. I tried to have so much patience with her, but when my world was collapsing around me the way it was today, I struggled to scrape up the strength to deal with her. It was such a chore to care for her in those moments, and I cussed myself later for it, but I wished against all the stars in the sky that she was a normal girl. Maybe she could be one who liked ponies and pretty rocks. Hell, I wouldn't have cared if she liked playing cowboys and Indians and fishing in the creek like a boy, as long as it wasn't a struggle to get her to look me in the eye.

I pinched the spot between my eyes with my thumb and forefinger, trying to squeeze some proper words

together beneath my anger that would make her understand. I didn't hear her get up. The blood was pulsing
so hard in my ears I didn't hear nothing but my own
frustrated heartbeat. All the same, when I opened my
eyes and the fuzziness in my vision cleared, they fell on
an empty room. I stood in alarm and looked around for
my sister.

"Hour?"

My head spun this way and that, but there was no
hide nor hair of my sister or Fred the cat. The door that
led to Dora's saloon was wide open, and I didn't waste
a minute putting together where she had gone in my
head. I raced out of the door.

"Hour! Get back here!"

In the hallway, there was no one to be seen. Instinctively, I went to the dining hall and then to the kitchen.
If she went anywhere out of habit, it would have been
there. My heart caught in my throat, and I was forced
to swallow it back down when I discovered no trace of
Hour or Fred the cat. The saloon was next, but the only
one there was Ruthy. She was busy righting some tables
and chairs that had gotten banged around the night
before. The girl had a sour demeanor and bags under
her eyes large enough for a week-long trip to Denver.

"Ruthy, has Hour come through here?"

"Hour?"

"My little sister? Hour?"

"Oh yeah, the peculiar one that ain't talkin' much."

"That's her. Did you see her?"

"Yeh, she come through here just a second ago.
Holdin' that kitten of hers. I was meanin' to ask her how

she got the thing to sit so still in her arms like that. Mine won't be still fer me fer nothin'. Just the other day . . ."

I didn't have time for this.

"Quick, where did she go?"

"Out that a-way."

Ruthy pointed the saloon door that led out onto the street. I said thanks and made it to the door in a hazy cascade of worry. My heart still thudded so hard, I began to see the world as though looking through a tunnel. Hour was my sister, my responsibility. It would be my fault if anything happened to her.

The quick breeze hit my face with an agitation that filled some ancient part of my body with a new sort of dread. There were times, like with the stagecoach, when trouble seemed to sneak up and surprise you in a quick blast of events. Then, there were times that you could smell the happenings coming a mile away, like when the sky turned all green and hard before a bad storm came. I walked out of that saloon into a frenzied wind that kicked up things this way and that. There weren't an order to it. It smelled wet and foreboding and made the hairs prickle on the back of my neck.

When I spotted Hour, she was already halfway across the wide thoroughfare holding that kitten in her arms. Her determined stride was taking her to the pest tent, or where she best reckoned the pest tent must be since she hadn't been there herself. Laying my eyes on her put three little muscles in my ribcage at ease, and I exhaled the relief. At least I could see her now. I knew where she was, and she was all right.

The second after that thought marked my mind, yelling—the bad kind—came from the far end of the thoroughfare and down a street. It was accompanied by a group of horses furiously whinnying and the sound of hooves against wood. The frenzy peaked with a smashing noise and the screaming of men. I moved to the edge of the walkway outside Dora's and craned my neck to see what the commotion was about. Several men leaped out of the way of three wild horses stampeding from the livery and bucking their captors away.

Two of the horses forced their way out onto the open thoroughfare, frothing with rage. One got caught up in a merchant's stall, grounding the poor beast in the dirt. Of the freed horses, there was a brown one and a painted one. The brown one went one way, and the painted one went the other. In a moment of sheer, terrible understanding, I watched as the painted horse raged its way down the wide road and headed straight toward Hour, who had stopped her progression in the very center of the road. She was standing stock-still in the middle of the thoroughfare staring wide-eyed at the crazed horse barreling down at her, her kitten squirming in her arms.

All I could think was that she was mine. My responsibility, my sister, my only family soon. Hour was mine, and I had to protect her. Everything happened so fast.

I sprinted into the thoroughfare and grabbed my sister, but her body wouldn't be moved. She stood, as if in a trance, gaping at the stampeding animal. I wanted to say something, anything to get her to understand she had to move. A charging animal didn't care. It would run her down, and Fred with her. The thing was, no words would come to my mouth. Not a one.

I heard screams. People yelled for us to get clear and take cover, but Hour was frozen in place and wouldn't be moved. The only thing left for me to do was to get between her and horse. I moved in front and hugged her, covering her tiny body with mine in the hopes of taking most of the damage myself instead of her. The hooves were beating their way closer now.

She was mine. Mine. Mine. My responsibility. God, I was so sorry for every bad thing I had thought about her minutes before.

The ground beneath us shook, and I braced for impact.

Mine. Mine. My life. My sister. My only family left.

"Hey!"

A gunshot splintered the air. The drums of the stampeding hooves halted, and I turned to see Jane standing like some sort of beacon in between us and the rearing horse. She was holding a gun straight in the air with her other hand up as well, shielding me and Hour from impending doom. The horse screamed and snorted but came down and to a stop just in front of Jane. For a brilliant second, I wondered if this was really happening or if it were a dream.

The painted thing fidgeted angrily and snorted pure fire at Jane, who began slowly lowering her revolver and cooing to the beast.

"Whoa, whoa. Easy, girl. Easy now."

"Jane?" asked Hour, as if coming out of her trance.

Our savior turned her head and looked at me.

"Get her the fuck out of the road. Now!"

At last, my sister was pliable. I led her and the frantic kitten struggling to get out of her arms away from the horse and back onto the planked sidewalk. As soon as we made it to the front of Dora's, Hour released the kitten, and it scampered almost comically through the open saloon door and back to our room. A number of people had heard the screaming and came out to see what the commotion was about. I held Hour's hand and squeezed as we watched Jane.

"Whoa. Whoa, now there, honey. Take your peace now. Whoa."

Jane slowly lowered her gun to the ground in front of the grunting beast, but kept her other hand high in the air as if its presence kept the creature from starting up its running again. It worked more or less. The painted horse stamped the ground and complained, but she stayed there as Jane came back up to approach her with two hands emptied of weapons.

As Jane approached the horse, we spotted three livery hands sneaking up behind the wild horse with lassos and whips in hand. Quietly, Jane shook her head to them, and they backed off, waiting for her next signal.

More people gathered along the sidewalks, watching Jane ever so slowly approach the animal with deliberate steps, outstretched hands, and a calm voice. By the time she was close enough to grab the bridle, she didn't have to. The painted terror was calm and leaned into her for comfort.

Jane signaled one of the hands to give her a lasso,

and she gently placed the loop around the horse's neck. There would've been an applause had everyone not been terrified of sending the creature back into a hysterical state once again. I heard Dora whisper to someone out of sight behind me.

"That's her horse now."

"Who'd want it after all that?" replied a man's voice.

"She will. Ain't nobody that horse will belong to but her. Trust me."

The hands led the horse back down the street toward the livery. There was no sign of where the brown one had gone, but there was a terrible streak of destruction in its wake. Jane marched right over to me and Hour and fell to her knees, taking my sister in an embrace I knew she'd hate. The thing of it was, Hour didn't flinch and didn't pull away. She let Jane hold her. Her little body was tense but she allowed it.

Jane finally pulled away, holding Hour's tiny shoulders in her hands. Frantic tears had streaked wet paths of clean down Jane's tanned and dirtied face. Those crystalline eyes of hers stared, searching into the little girl's eyes. I wanted to say something but had no words.

"You can't be doin' that, little one. I know you got a different way of seein' things, but you gotta run! You hafta git outta the way. Protect yourself. You hear me? That horse coulda hurt you so bad. *So* bad. Please, Hour Glass, tell me you hear me. Tell me you understand."

Hour was staring into Jane's tear-stained face much like she had with the horse. Neither of us could tell if any of this was sinking in. But then, to the surprise of everyone, Hour responded.

"Jane?"

Jane's face brightened as she brushed some of the little girl's hair from her face.

"Yes. Yes, honey. I'm here."

"You swore," said Hour, and she held out her hand.

The tension, the sheer gravity of the situation melted then. Jane started to chuckle so suddenly, snot came from her nose in a bubble. A bunch of the girls who had been recently plagued with little Hour and her swear jug snickered and giggled. Dora DuFran, the jug's biggest contributor besides Jane, laughed so hard she doubled over as far as her corset would allow.

A laughing, tear-stained Calamity Jane reached into her pocket and produced a copper penny. She placed the coin in Hour's hand and closed her tiny fist around it, smiling from ear to ear. Hour nodded to her and then looked away as though their transaction was now at an end. Jane hugged her again, lighter this time, regardless of her diverted gaze.

"You're right, kid. I s'pose I did."

15

WE DIDN'T GO OFF to see Pa that day. Hour, despite her outward appearance of indifference toward the happenings with the wild horse, was shaken in a way only I could detect. After we were deemed safe to go back to our normal day, Hour made a beeline for the back kitchen and Nancy May's presence. Structure and routine was key with Hour, and she did best when she had a set schedule for the day's events.

I followed her back to the kitchen to an awaiting Nancy May. She had a look of pure relief to see us. Evidently, the girls had made sure the news traveled quickly to her ears. Nancy wrapped little Hour in her arms, burying my sister in a mound of warmth. Hour squirmed uncomfortably, as she usually did in a hug.

I knew something had clicked for Hour when I saw her little hands tremble as she went to the kitchen and washed them in the basin. After drying them, she walked over to me and held the shaking hands up for me to see.

"They ain't stoppin'," she whispered plainly to me. "How do we make them stop?"

Nancy May's eyes grew as big as saucers. She had never been present when my sister had said so much before. I held her hands to try to steady them. They were ice cold.

"I know, Hour. I think kitchen duty is covered for today. Ain't that right, Miss Nancy?"

Nancy May caught on to me fast. She was a quick-witted woman.

"Yes'm. It's true, honey child. All caught up on the chores here. You just go have you a rest."

"Rest?" Hour whispered to me.

I knew it wouldn't do right now to have my sister without a task. She was obviously shaken up, but sitting idle wouldn't be a fitting solution either.

"You got a new penny to add to yer jar, ain't you? And I bet poor Fred is gonna need some love and affection after her big scare. Think you can take care of that?"

Hour looked down at my knees and nodded.

"I bet Miss Nancy will give you a bit of milk fer the kitten."

"You bet yer buttons. Come here, child, and we'll get you a saucer. Then, we'll go find yer kitten, Fred. Show me some of them pennies."

Nancy May looked over her shoulder at me as she

led Hour away and nodded. I nodded back. I had been watching Nancy over the time we'd been here. She was a tough cookie, like most of the people I'd seen survive it out here. Jane, Dora, Nancy. They all were tougher than most folks even imagined being. Deadwood was a wild place. Wild and lawless. People died all the time. People killed other people. Life was a cheaper thing here than in places with laws and police and borders.

So why change themselves for a little girl? Why did a hard woman like Dora or Jane or Nancy bend to and coddle a helpless girl? Why did men like Joseph DuFran and Charlie Utter do the same? In a place where life didn't matter much, why did one strange little girl's life matter so much?

I went back to working around the saloon like normal. The idea of getting Hour to Pa was gone now. She was a wreck, and I was none too ready to go outside and relive the trauma we'd just endured. Work was a good idea. Hour would nurse her kitten, and I would clean vomit off the floor by the bar. If nothing else, I needed the space and quiet to think on our near-death experience.

Ruthy worked near me, setting up the tables like Madame Dora DuFran wanted them. She wasn't a pretty or smart girl in the sense most thought, but she had an instinct about her that I appreciated. I didn't want company, and she didn't push hers on me, even though I could tell she wanted to talk. She humbly did her work next to me and allowed a calming silence to sleep in the middle.

I had finished mopping up the sick and righting the

barstools when I noticed a flash of blonde on the railing above. When I looked up, I saw the battered face of Lil' Missy peering down at me. It felt like ages since I'd seen her, and even longer since she'd tried to come out of her room. The only news I'd heard of her was that she had finally started eating normally again, but that was all the talk on the topic.

With a small nod of her head, she beckoned me upstairs and then promptly turned and disappeared down the hallway. I put away my mop and bucket and climbed the staircase without a word. This was something I hardly ever did. There wasn't a reason for me to come upstairs and bother the girls. It was a place of mystery and lace up there in that hallway. The only time I had been invited before was to aim a rifle at the Bear Man.

When I reached the top, I found Missy not there, but her door was slightly ajar. An invitation, I reckoned, but when I reached the door, I knocked to be polite anyway. With a timid voice, she invited me inside.

Missy was in a big nightgown, one that looked a little too big on her shoulders. Her blonde locks were pulled up with a ribbon and the bruising on her face was looking better. Yellowing parts were beginning to heal and turn fleshy again. One eye was still swollen but not all the way shut like it had been.

"Hey," she said like it was an experiment.

I reckoned she hadn't talked to most anyone. Was she trying out her voice on the likes of me? What had I done to make her trust me that much?

"Hey."

"Um . . . I . . . I saw . . . what happened . . ."

Missy pointed to her window. I went to the window and looked out. The view was of the alley, but if you craned your neck to the right, you could've seen the whole thing with Hour and me. With such a ruckus, how could anyone not look? Apparently, she had watched it happening. I pulled my head back inside.

"We're okay, and all . . ."

I was cut off by a sudden embrace. Missy, the most beautiful girl I had ever seen, threw herself into my arms and hugged me. Suddenly, one of the worst days of my life got a whole lot better, and I wrapped my arms around a bruised angel. She felt small under my hands, even though she was bit taller than me. Taking it all in, I became intoxicated with the smell of warm cinnamon all around her.

All too soon, a chill breezed between us. She had pulled away from me.

"Sorry," she said looking worried.

I felt a stupid grin pull at the edges of my mouth.

"Don't be sorry."

"I just . . . I just wanted to thank you."

Missy looked on the verge of tears.

"Fer what?"

"You were one of the people who . . . who got that bastard."

Habit had me look around for a second for Hour and her swear jug, but then I remembered where exactly I was. Being near Missy put me in a daze.

"Oh that. It wasn't nothin', really."

"Don't say it wasn't nothin'. That's what stupid

people say when they ain't got nothin' better. It was brave."

Her eyes were so serious, not like how she normally was. The lightness of her was missing somehow. Missy was always so sweet and fun. Never serious and full of tears like she was now. I wasn't sure what to say, so I shifted my feet in place and stared at my hands a lot. That gaze of hers was intent though, and there was more she wanted to say.

"I been meanin' to tell you that. The thanks part. But I've been so scared to leave my room. Silly, ain't it? I used to feel cooped up to be in here too long, and now, it's the only thing that feels safe. I go out there and everything starts swirling around, big as life. Bigger even."

"You had a bad shock. You'll feel better soon. I know it."

"And I see that man, that *beast* of a man, every time I shut my eyes. Every time I sleep, there he is waitin' fer me. Like he ain't dead. I know he's dead, but his ghost is hauntin' me."

"He ain't gonna hurt you no more," I said, trying to sound soothing.

"I know, I know. But my mind doesn't seem to. Anyway, I heard a commotion outside, and when I looked 'round, I saw the whole thing with you and that sister of yours. I saw Jane save you from the horse, but before, I was so scared. I was scared you was gonna die and then I'd never get a chance to thank you. And then there'd be two ghosts hauntin' my dreams."

I smiled. She was worried about me. The prettiest

girl on the earth was worried about me.

"Well, maybe that would be good. Then I could fight the other ghost and make him leave you alone like he ought."

She smiled for the first time in days and hugged me again.

"Miss Dora says to take my time getting better. She says it'll all be waitin' fer me when this has passed. What if it never passes, Jimmy? What if I'm 'fraid of men forever, and every night is a nightmare to me? How could a person stand it?"

"I don't know, Missy. Am I 'nuff to be called a man?"

The girl looked at me fondly. Maybe not like she'd look at a grown man on a horse, asking to take her away, but it was a look beyond that of just a friend. I weren't no boy with that look.

"Yeh, I reckon."

I moved to the edge of her bed and sat down. Patting the spot next to me, I invited her to join me. To my utter delight, she sat without hesitation and laid her head on my shoulder. Cinnamon clouded my vision, and I began gently stroking her hair.

"Okay, no funny business. I promise. Tell me whatever's on your mind. Anything at all. Confide whatever you got, Lil' Missy. I'm here to listen."

The most miraculous part was she did.

She had ridden to Deadwood with Molly Johnson's wagon of girls. One of the girls had been pals with her back at Belle Fourche and told her Deadwood was the next up and coming place to make a little money. Thing was, when she got there, there were already three blondes working for Molly and they held onto their places in the brothel with teeth and nails dug in. Missy was more than relieved when Dora found her outside Molly's joint and offered her a job.

Missy's real name was Melissa Elliot. Her parents had gone at the same time during an outbreak of yellow fever. Ever since, she'd been working her way up through the ranks in saloons and brothels all over. She was only sixteen, but she had traveled about more than most grown men I knew. She loved it with Madame Dora and wanted to stay on with her as long as she could.

It weren't long before she got me talking. I told her about how I never really knew my mom, and what a strange woman Hour's mother had been to me. She wasn't bad or good, just odd in her Indian ways that I didn't understand. How she named my sister Flower and told stories of ancient people who revered children like her. Being unusual wasn't something to fear. It meant she was closer to the spirit of the eagle, and we weren't to force her to live here like we did when all she wanted to do was fly. My words filled with sadness when talking about the woman's passing.

By the time we got to the part where I had to take care of Hour myself, Missy and I were laying on the bed next to one another, her head cradled on my shoulder, her legs bent up around my knees. Occasionally, her cat Puddin' climbed up to play around on our entwined bodies, but for the most part, it was just the two of us. I knew of what men and women did together, and the parts of me that knew that sort of thing without my brain knowing it were whispering ideas to me. The thing of it was, my heart didn't want to oblige.

We were friends, she and I. Real friends. I wasn't about to ruin that minute or the many minutes that followed it by trying to turn it into something it weren't or shouldn't have been. Minutes turned into hours, and before we knew it, night had settled into the little room with us, like an old friend and not a ghost.

The day had begun with one of the worst moments of my life. I thought I had lost my sister forever. But the strangest thing happened afterwards. I spent the best afternoon of my life talking with a girl I had only met not a fortnight ago. Perhaps it was what love felt like. I was so young, I had nothing to compare it to. We confided such secrets and such tiny, trivial things in that room, she and I. Was that love? I didn't know, but I wanted the afternoon to last forever. In any case, it helped to exorcise the spirit of the Bear Man to leave her be for a while.

Outside that door was the real world. No wonder Missy wanted to stay inside here. In here, secrets were kept, company was invited, and hugs were always welcomed as hugs. Nothing was owed and nothing was paid but words. For her, outside meant customers to cater to and fears to overcome. For me, it meant a sister to care for and a dying father. We didn't want to ever leave.

The time came as sure as it ever did. I knew Hour would need me when Nancy got busy with the dinner rush, and there would be a lot of questions about me coming down from Missy's room if there was a crowd in the saloon to watch me do it. When I stood up to go, Missy grabbed my hand and held it for a long minute. She walked me to her door. We hugged, and I told her everything would be all right. I breathed in the spicy smell in her hair before we separated, a scent I planned on cherishing for a long time, but she did me one better before she let me go.

Just as I opened the door, Missy reached out and grabbed my face with both of her hands. That girl, the most beautiful thing in the world, kissed my lips right there and then. It lingered for only a second, a breath in an hourglass, and then it was over.

"Thank you, Jimmy."

I left her room, and she closed the door behind me. The world seemed to rotate a little, and I wondered if I was in danger of falling down. A quick shake of the head allowed me to right myself and walk straight through the hallway and down the staircase.

There weren't anyone in the saloon yet except Joseph, who was arranging the liquor the way Dora liked to get ready for the rush of after-dark customers. It was a blessing he didn't notice me walk through the saloon. I tried to be as silent as one of the damn cats, and apparently, I was doing just that.

A few of the girls were eating dinner in the dining hall. I found Hour with two plates of food waiting for me at a table. She wasn't fond of eating in front of a bunch of people, especially not without me. It was something she'd never liked. When I approached, I smiled at her, and without a word, I picked up the plate I knew she had made for me and followed her back to our room to eat.

Missy's kiss was still warm on my lips. I would leave it there for safekeeping in case I wanted to remember it again later.

16

I FELT CAGE COMING before my eyes even had time to shut completely. She was like gray smoke snaking her way to where I laid my weary head down. My lungs breathed her in deep as she crashed over my person. Her whispers of things long since passed encompassed and pulled down on me until I not only fell asleep, but tumbled down deeper and deeper into a memory that would never go away. I didn't want to go to that place. Memories of it were a seething torrent hiding just below what seemed to be the calm waters I pretended to swim in. There was no use resisting it of course. Cage had her ways, and she would show me what needed showing.

Before I knew what was happening, rain fell on

my face. It was a warm sort of rain, the kind that fell in the summer. Normally, playing in the rain of the late afternoon would be a thing of fun, but when I looked around me, a foreboding sat heavy with the moisture in the air. I didn't want to be here. I didn't want to remember this.

Flower sat under the shelter of her favorite tree, a girl of maybe four years old. Modesty hadn't found her yet, and she sat splay-legged, like a boy might, across the roots that jutted up from the ground. Her eyes stared forward in a sort of trance. She neither moved much nor did she draw with her stick. Only someone who really knew could see the concern painted on her face.

Moaning came from the shanty we called home. It was the sound of pain, the call of the dying.

Pa pushed back the canvas flap and hurried out into the rainy afternoon with me. The look on his face was tired, and he held an empty pail in his hand.

"Jimmy, I need you ta go keep Cage company, okay? I'm gonna take Flower to go get some more fresh water fer her. She keeps throwin' everythin' up."

"What's wrong with her, Pa?"

"Don't likely know. Might be the Yella Jack. There was rumor the fever been goin' 'round. Just watch her, okay?"

"Should we take her to see a doctor?"

His weary face looked defeated.

"No doc 'round these parts will tend to an Injun. You know that. Please, just fetch her whatever she needs."

"Yes, sir."

"Come on, honey. Come with Pa to get some water."

Flower rose and walked away with our pa without question. They didn't hold hands like a father and daughter might, but she stayed close to his hip. I watched them disappear into the rainy mist before turning to go in the shanty.

When I opened the flap and stepped inside, the smell was that of bile and sick. It felt stiflingly warm inside our home, as if the added heat of Cage's fever was acting as a furnace. Without thinking, I rolled the front flap back and made to tie it off in the hopes of creating a bit of breeze for her.

"No, please do not, Jimmy," said Cage through chattering teeth.

The short glimpse I got of her made me want to turn away immediately. It weren't a proper thing, Cage looking that way. I let the flap fall shut as it had been before. There was one of our chairs perched next to her bed, so I sat in it and made myself look at my stepmother.

Her black hair was loose and wet with perspiration. It curled and snaked around her head in matted tendrils. The skin hung from her bones on her face, sallow and waxy. Those dark eyes of hers popped out by contrast when she looked up at me, red-rimmed and desperate. She shivered something awful despite the fact I could feel how hot her skin was sitting a foot away from her.

"Another blanket?" I asked.

Cage shut her eyes and nodded.

I grabbed the quilt at the end of the bed and draped it over her. It was their wedding quilt made by Cage's mother and sisters and given as a gift the day they married. The very center had a star pattern with various diamonds and triangles of reds, yellows, and oranges. I tucked it up underneath her chin, and she breathed its familiarity in deep.

"I see things," she said.

"What things?"

"There on the walls. Beetles. Dark bits crawling around. Do you see them?"

I followed her gaze but saw nothing unusual. It was just the canvas walls as they always had been. No spiders or beetles.

"No, Cage. I don't see nothin'."

She mumbled something in Sioux.

"Cage, Pa went to get some water. You're gonna get better soon."

"It's Keya, I think."

"What's Keya?"

"The bits on the wall. Little Keya. They come to me."

"Cage, there ain't nothin' there."

She turned her eyes back on me then, a sudden urgency in them. Her hand shot out from underneath the quilt and took mine. Her skin was burning hot as she squeezed my fingers together.

"Jimmy Who Watches, know they are here. They watch. I will too. Know that."

"Cage, you're hurtin' me."

She was so frightening to look at. This wasn't Cage,

not my Cage. I wanted nothing more than for her to stop and bring my Cage back. Fear filled up my belly, and I didn't want to be there. I didn't want to have to be brave.

"The Keya, they speak . . ."

"Cage honey, let go of Jimmy. You're hurtin' his hand."

The sound of Pa's deep voice broke her from her reverie a little, and she released my hand back to me. Cage's eyes went out of focus a little then, and she turned away from us. I wanted to run away, to cry somewhere, but I held my spot long enough for Pa to come up behind me and place his warm hand on my shoulder. The sound of sloshing water echoed when he set the bucket down next to the chair.

I stood and watched him dunk a rag into the fresh creek water and ring out the excess. He laid the rag on Cage's forehead with more tenderness than I was accustomed to seeing in him. Still, the shock of the rag's presence startled her and caused her to flinch a little. Pa whispered soothing sounds to get her to calm.

"Sleep now. It's gonna be all right."

Cage nodded slowly, her eyelids heavy.

"Tell Jimmy . . . I . . . I am sorry."

"You ain't gotta be sorry. Sleep now."

He and I stepped out of the shanty to leave her to her rest. I looked around for Flower and found her back in the spot she had occupied previously. She wasn't drawing in the dirt or rocking or anything. The girl just stared forward.

"She said she seen bits on the walls," I told Pa. "She

said there was Keya crawling everywhere. What's that mean?"

"Cage's just feverin', son. When your fever's bad 'nuff, a person sees all sorts of things that ain't there."

"Is she? Is she gonna die?"

"I don't rightly know."

We both turned to look at Flower together, two men contemplating a strange little girl. Flower didn't so much as move a muscle. For a second, she lifted that far away stare of hers to meet our eyes. We three were locked there in a shared gaze, connected by something we couldn't explain. Maybe she understood us then, maybe she didn't. Either way, just as quick as the moment came, it left, and Flower was back to staring at the dirt in front of her.

"She won't draw or nothin'," I observed out loud.

"Nope."

"I wonder why."

"My bet is she knows somethin' we don't. It seems to be the way of things with her."

Cage passed sometime in the night. It shouldn't have been that way, but there it was. My sister and I slept in our cots on the other side of the shanty as we always did, and Pa bedded down on the floor next to their bed to give her room to fever. The moaning lessened enough where we all slipped into our individual dreams, but come morning's light, Cage was still. She had gone quietly as we dozed, like a late night visitor, tiptoeing her way around our bodies on her way out without wanting to wake us.

The sadness she left in her wake was consuming.

So much so I couldn't seem to feel it all completely right that moment. The loss settled into my bones and promised it wouldn't leave me any time soon. Without my asking, it had become a part of me in the night. I couldn't even find it in me to cry just yet. It all was too much, and maybe a dream. Perhaps this was a terrible dream or a mistake?

Sorrow shook its dark head at me. I knew Cage wouldn't be coming back. This was life now, and it would never be the same again.

Few words passed between us. There weren't anything to say. We wrapped Cage head to toe in their wedding quilt, the star pattern fanning out from her chest and shining up to her head. All of us took a last moment to see her face before we covered it, never to look upon it again.

Pa had Flower and I help him pack not only a few things, but all of our things. He had bought an old cart a few months back that he hooked up to Betty. We loaded the few meager possessions we had worth keeping into it, and Pa tore down the canvas around our shanty. Cage's body was the last thing to add to the cart, and we laid her among our supplies with all the care we had in us.

"Are we movin' away, Pa?"

"Yes."

"Why?"

"This place is haunted now."

"Ain't we gonna bury her?"

"No son. We gotta take her to her people."

Her tribe of Lakota moved around as they were

wont to do. Their summer place was not too far away from us. Pa lifted Flower onto Betty's back and we made our way solemnly through the woods.

The birds had the nerve to sing. That seemed like a mean thing for them to do to me, but they did anyway. I reckoned maybe birds didn't care none when one of ours died any more than we cared if one of them died. Still, the world went on past us, as it always tended to, as we journeyed to Cage's people. No words passed between us. Flower had just begun to talk in strings that made sense, but none of us wanted to try.

We reached the meadow where the tribe normally camped and were relieved to find them still there. Our slumped backs and sour faces told them the reason for our visit before any words were spoken. It was a good thing as they spoke little English and we knew only a bit of broken Sioux.

Without hesitation, a scaffold was erected at the edge of the camp with poles and saplings. The women chanted and cried over her body as they placed it, still wrapped in her star quilt, high up on top of the structure. It seemed everyone from the tribe came to pay their respects. Eagle feathers and beaded bags were tied to the scaffold poles, and there was a constant song being chanted from those who seemed to know her best. For our part, we stood a piece away from the memorial, bearing witness to the event.

"They ain't gonna leave her up there, is they?" I asked Pa. "They wouldn't leave her for the buzzards out in the open, would they?"

"No. This is their way o' saying farewell. Cage

told me once it was to coax their spirit to find its way. Tomorrow they'll bury her."

I nodded and looked over at Flower. She watched the ritual too, but it was impossible to know what she was thinking. I wondered if the gravity registered with her. Would it have registered with me when I was her age?

People cried and wailed beneath her body without abandon. My white sensibilities said to look away from them. That sort of behavior was for private and shouldn't have been seen, but then again, this was the Lakota way. It was Cage's way. Her people grieved out loud for all to see while we hid ours in our bones. Ours was there to suffer us in silence, but who's to say which was better? Maybe crying it all out bled the bones of sorrow. Maybe it didn't live with you forever like that.

There was an older couple, Cage's parents as I knew them, who sat at the base of their daughter's scaffold. The woman wailed as the others did, but as she did, she cut into her arm with a knife. No one seemed to stop her as she did this. In fact, it looked to be something everyone silently deemed suitable. Cut after cut was made on the top of her forearm as she wept and chanted. The man next to her did the same. He did not cry, but he cut small pieces from the skin on his arm while chanting along with everyone else. I pondered if the cutting eased their pain at all.

"What are they doing, Pa?"

"It's a grievin' thing. Parents of a dead child sometimes cut themselves like that. It's just their way. Them's her folks."

My eyes trained on the couple and then the other Lakota around them.

"What do the children do?"

"What?"

"The children. What do Lakota kids do when their mama passes?"

Pa looked around at the children around us.

"I s'pose they cry."

Standing there, I nodded to myself. Something got decided in me, and I was determined to have it done. I left Pa's side, and he didn't say a word. From my belt I retrieved the knife Cage had given me, the one I carried with me everywhere. It was small and didn't have much of a blade, but it was true and sharp. It slipped from its buckskin sheath easily. Stepping forward, I ran the blade down the length of the heel of my right hand. Sorrow must have numbed me for I barely felt the knife as it opened my skin. A tiny line of red opened into a steady dripping of blood.

The Lakota around her scaffold fixed their collective gazes on me, but to their credit, her funeral song went on. It made me happy because I didn't want to interrupt it. This was meant to be an addition, not a distraction.

I closed the remaining gap between me and one of the pillars holding her in the sky. My eyes shut as I bid her farewell in my silent fashion and wiped my hand on the wood of the pole. A red smear stained the place where my hand had been. It was my way, my token left for her. Having done the deed, I made my way back to Pa and Flower, my gaze on the ground.

"Why'd you do that?"

"I didn't much feel like cryin'."

Pa nodded, and we three paid our respects in the silent way we were accustomed.

We should've stayed that night. The tribe invited us to stay and camp with them for the evening, but Pa insisted we needed to be moving on before dark set in. The three of us would camp in the woods somewhere because these weren't our people, not anymore. I wondered if it was that so much, or if it was the way the women looked at Flower. They were longing looks, the way mothers longed after babies. Perhaps Pa feared they would take her and claim her as theirs. Either way, he lifted Flower onto Betty's back, and we headed away from the camp and on into the unknown of the evening light.

"Where are we goin' now?" I asked Pa when we were out of earshot of the Lakota.

"To the Black Hills. There's talk they've been finding gold there."

"We ain't trappin' no more?"

"We can do what we have to. Minin's a good way to earn."

"But the Black Hills? Cage said they is sacred to the Lakota. It's a holy place. She wouldn't like you goin' there to mine."

"Son, those were her ways, not mine." His voice broke off a little as he said it, and he swallowed something big down in his throat.

"And she's gone now."

17

I WOKE FROM MY dream already in mourning.

Death wasn't like they said it was. They are the people who tell the tales and spin the legends. Stories tell you that when in dire need, when someone is dying, their loved ones are there every second of their dying days. Stories say that fellas die in the arms of their women, and children stand over their father, crying tiny tears as he slips away gently into a good night. In those stories, no one ever laughs or tries to distract themselves with work or gets kissed by a pretty girl while their daddy is suffering. No one sleeps through the passing of another mere feet away from them.

I figured that when the time came, the gravity of it all would be well known to me. There would be no room for laughter or thoughts of friends. There would be only sorrow and deep lamentation because in the moments before he died, I would know how to feel and I would know how to act. The words that needed speaking would come to my head without issue. Only the silent sorrow of mourning would be in my heart because, after all, there shouldn't be room for anything else.

The day Jane came to us, her head hangdog and low, I was helping Hour get dressed. Our plan was to try to see our pa again, barring any more runaway horses. I even convinced my sister to leave Fred at home after explaining that the ordeal would be too trauma-tizing for the little creature. Funny how fast that place was becoming home to me. The shanty near the creek seemed ages and ages away. I was using a broken comb to tidy Hour's black hair when Jane entered the sawdust room in the state she was.

"Jane?" said Hour.

Jane knelt down to be closer to eye level with my sister. I stood and steeled myself for what I suspected was the purpose of this visit so early in the morning. Normally, Jane would be passed out drunk outside somewhere, but here she was and as sober as she got.

"Hey there, poppet. You feelin' better?"

Hour nodded.

A little thing it was, this interaction, but so monu-mental at the same time. My sister struggled with these sorts of social things, but here in our new home, she was getting better. She was thriving. Here, she could talk to strangers and respond to them. The isolation of the shanty loomed over us as well as the news I knew to be on Jane's tongue.

Calamity Jane, pioneer woman in the buckskins as a man, stood up and looked into my eyes. I had never seen her afraid, but she was as close to it as possible at that moment. My chest began to hurt in a deep place where it was only possible for organs to ache. This was it. This was the part that was going to test my measure of a man. I had to be a man, but more than a man right here and right now for me and my sister. Standing up taller, I tensed my limbs with balled up fists for hands at my side, and I waited for the words that would alter my life.

Jane's mouth fell open a bit and shut again. She seemed to be struggling to find the words. I wanted to yell at her. A part of me wanted to yank her ears to force the news out of her mouth. I wanted this moment to be over already, but she stood there all the same, searching my eyes for the words to say to me.

"Jimmy. Um . . . I uh . . . have . . . have . . ."

Jane trailed off, and I felt like I might just bust from the inside out.

"Have I ever told you the story of my time with General Custer?"

My heart fell into my shoes. I was ready for anything but this. They warned me, Dora and Joseph, they had both warned me that when Jane couldn't say it, when it was too much, when my daddy was gone, she'd resort to the Custer story. It was her last defense. Still, I hadn't expected it. Somehow, the diversion hit me in the gut harder than the actual news. Falling to my knees like some sort of coward, I began to weep. It was a silent thing. The tears came in spurts and mucous-filled coughing fits. I collapsed in on myself. All the afore-mentioned strength and preparation had melted away with the mention of one dead General.

The first thing I noticed after a while of sobbing was the pressure of two hands on my shoulders. When I finally managed to collect myself, I looked up to find the hands belonged to both females in the room. Jane's rough hand was on my left shoulder, deep pools of regret and sorrow in her eyes. Hour's hand was on my right shoulder, but she seemed to only be doing the act because Jane was. She looked into my eyes but all I saw in them was confusion.

With a little shake, I collected myself and stood on my knees in front of Hour. I placed both hands on her shoulders as gently as I could so she didn't feel trapped at all. Gratitude flooded over me when she decided she could look at me instead of the floor. Little miracles lit my way in this dark train tunnel of ours.

"Hour. I need to tell you somethin', and I want you to hear me."

My sister didn't seem to respond. I took a deep breath in and let it out slow to give me the patience I was sorely lacking at the moment.

"I need you to hear me now and understand some-thin' important. Tell me you are hearin' me proper, okay?"

She nodded only slightly.

"Pa died, Hour. He's gone now, just like your mama and mine. He was real sick. Jane and the doc, they tried their hardest, but he didn't make it."

Hour stood stock-still. It was hard to tell if any of this was really sinking in. I didn't necessarily expect tears with her, but I was hoping for something that said she understood. I looked to Jane, but she only shrugged. Sometimes, reading my sister was like reading a book written only in pictures you couldn't make out proper.

"Hour, honey, do you understand what yer brother is sayin' to you?" asked Jane.

Her gaze left my face and went back down to the floor.

"Hour, you need to hear me. Pa is dead. The disease took him. Do you understand?"

"Gone or dead? See him?" she asked in a tiny voice.

"Yes, yes, we can see him," I answered, relieved.

I looked up to Jane, suddenly unsure of what I just told my sister.

"We can see him, right?"

Minutes later we were crossing the thoroughfare with Jane leading the way. Hour held my hand and squeezed extra tight as we passed the place in the road where we were almost run over by the crazed horse the day before. She wore her only decent dress, and me my britches that hadn't any holes. It was only proper to say our farewells.

The day didn't seem right for this sort of thing. Funny how the weather just goes about its business even though your world has been cut in two. It seemed that with this much sorrow, the world around you would have the good decency to look sorrowful and melancholy on your behalf. Nevertheless, the sun went on shining and the clouds were mere wisps in the clear blue sky that autumn morning. There was no rain or wind. The world on a whole was still and happy. Folks around us laughed at jokes, and somewhere in the distance, I could smell food cooking. It all felt like blasphemy somehow, yet there it was. A reminder that no one cared about our little tragedy.

Doc was washing his hands in the trough outside the pest tent when we arrived. The rag he wore over his face was pulled down around his neck, and his apron was stained with sick and blood. The already pale man managed to look positively whitewashed when he saw us approaching the tent, and he moved quickly to intervene.

"No, Jane. It ain't a good idea," said Doc.

"They wanna see their pa and make their last respects. They got a right, Doc."

"The risk of infection is too great. Hank Glass wouldn't want his kids in there."

"I've already been in twice," I said, interrupting the doc.

He looked down at me with a world of sorrow in his eyes.

"With Jane. I wore the mask. We was careful."

Jane shrugged at the good doctor, "What can you do? It's their right."

Doc sighed deeply and reached over to grab the bag of face rags. He pulled three fresh ones for us and we fastened them on properly. I had to help Hour with hers. It took us a long minute to get her situated seeing as how the face handkerchief was confining for her. Several times she fought me when I tried to tie the thing around her neck. Every time, she shook her head vehemently against the rag. When she finally began to squeal in protest, I had to tell her the truth.

"Hour, you hafta wear this. Pa was real sick, and the people inside are real sick too. You gotta wear this or you might get sick like them."

Hour's head shaking got more violent as a reaction. I knew she was slipping. This was all just too much for her to take in. No part of me wanted to force anything on my sister in her delicate condition, but there was only one way I knew to stop this. I felt like a right bastard the second I said it.

"Hour, if you don't, you can't ever see Pa, not ever again. He'll be gone forever. Like your mama. Dead and gone! We'll hafta leave you out here alone. Is that what you want?"

Her head stopped shaking suddenly, and I could see, in that blank stare she had at the ground, tears rimming those big eyes of hers. I wish I hadn't said it. It was wrong and mean and she probably wouldn't speak to anyone, not even me, for weeks because of it. The thing was, I couldn't worry about that right then. Right then, I had to get her handkerchief on over her mouth, or else she'd regret not doing this for the rest of her life.

My sister allowed me to tie the rag around her face, and we all walked into the pest tent in a silent procession.

There were fewer occupied cots than I remembered. I wondered for a moment if that was a good sign or a bad one. Had these people, who once laid here like Pa, died or got better and went home? I hoped they were better. Somehow, the thought gave me comfort that they were home somewhere with their families, and their kids weren't having to do this terrible march.

Pa was where I had left him, except it just wasn't Pa anymore. It was him, but it looked like someone had come in with a body that sure looked like his. On the surface, it had his features, sure enough, but the meat of him wasn't there. When you got up close, there was no Pa in it anymore. It was as if he left long before we got there and just left this husk here. The sight of it should have been sad and frightening, but it wasn't so much. My pa had left this terrible tent already. No longer would he suffer, no longer would he bleed and hurt and smell the putrid scent of decay and sick. All this time, and he was already gone.

No one said anything. I suppose we were expected to say something. In the stories, they said things that mattered. Maybe the doc knew what to say? Or Jane? But no, they stood beside us silent. Looking down at Hour, I noticed that she was looking at our pa. Not the ground, his face. She stared into it, searching for something she couldn't seem to find. I knelt down beside her.

"What do you think?" I whispered to her so only she could hear.

Hour turned and looked up at the doc and Jane standing over her. Something about her gaze clued Jane into her intentions, and with a quick nudge to the doc, they turned their backs on us to give us some privacy.

"Pa's gone," whispered Hour.

"Yeah, honey. He is. He died."

"He flew away."

I gaped at her, a little perplexed by this specific response. We hadn't any religion to speak of. I had heard people speak of angels and souls flying up to heaven and the like, but Hank Glass wasn't a religious man at all. He put on the airs, if he needed to, when in mixed company, but I couldn't remember ever taking Hour to a church.

"He flew away?"

"With Mama and the eagles. He flew. It's all okay."

Let her be, her mother had told us way back when. Don't force children like her. They were closer to the spirits of their ancestors, she had said. She was only a breath away from the eagles. Let her fly. She knows more about flying than we ever will while still drawing breath. Let her fly.

Amen.

18

ON THE SECOND DAY, the weather finally caught up with the news that a man had died and orphaned two children. The clear skies and bright sun of the day previous might have still been present somewhere, but dark rain clouds and the gray mood of a storm covered them like a blanket. The whole of Diddlin' Dora's was quiet because everyone was readying themselves for the funeral, with best dresses and tailored britches stacked high for the ironing.

Dora had placed a sign on her door, warning would-be customers from trying to come inside.

Closed until dinner for family funeral.

A funny thing that was to me. She didn't even know

Pa. None of them knew Pa other than the doc and Jane, and they really only knew the sick version of him. I suppose they knew us, and that was enough of a thing to consider this a family tragedy. We had turned up not even three weeks ago as strangers to them, and now, we were family. A strange sort of world this was, but I was eternally grateful for their kindness.

The details of burying a man seemed an odd thing to consider. With the absence of Pa from this world, there was a cavern in my chest that ached all empty-like. How did one go about the task of burying the thing that left the hole? To even think of all the logistics seemed barbaric and wrong, but there was a coffin to consider and a funeral.

We didn't have much in the way of money. Before leaving the shanty by the creek, I had collected the tiny bit of money we had on hand for fear thieves might make off with it during our current handicap. I met with the undertaker and handed him all the money we had. By the look of the fella's face, I could tell he was used to seeing more. We stood there together for a long minute, staring at all I had in the world.

"Son, this all you have, eh?"

He had a strange accent that some of the miners had as well. Something European I didn't know how to label. I stood up as straight as I could being that I was now the man of the family. My eyes met the man's to discuss business.

"Yes, sir."

"I see."

Another long pause. For a bad second, I thought

about going back to Dora's and raiding Hour's swear jug. It wouldn't yield much, but perhaps it would close the gap.

"Is it enough for a coffin, sir?"

"Well . . ."

The man looked down at me, scratching his chin. He was a tall, lean man who seemed very well put together. His suit was cheap but clean, and his fingernails were meticulously trimmed and tidy. Tufts of strawberry-blond hair stuck out from under his broad hat. Try as I might, I couldn't find so much as one thread out of place on his whole person.

"Yes," he said at last. "Not de finest, mind you, but I have been working de extra hours making simple coffins on account of de pest tent out here. It won't buy you a stone for de headstone, though. Haf to be de wooden kind."

"Thank you, sir. That will be fine."

"For de epitaph, will you write the spelling here on dis paper?"

"Yessir."

"Did your fadder have religion?"

"How come you askin'?"

"To know if I should ask de preacher to come say a word."

"Do he charge?"

Another long silence fell between us, and the tall man examined me from on high.

"No. Is free."

"Then yes, please. Thank you."

"Funeral will be in two hours. Okay?"

"Okay."

I turned to leave, but the undertaker called out and stopped me.

"Hey dere, Mr. Glass."

Something stung deep in my ribs at the title. My pa was Mr. Glass, Mr. Hank Glass. But now, I was Mr. Glass. I was the man of the family, and the man was called Mr. Glass.

"Yessir?"

"My wife, she grows flowers. Not'ing impressive, not here, but maybe she has some for your fadder? Maybe to make de coffin look nice?"

"Thank you, sir. I would be much obliged."

We nodded to each other, and I left to finish the tasks at hand at Dora's. I had to dress and help Hour dress. All through the brothel, the girls bustled about, donning their nicest dresses with hats and everything. Dora and Joseph greeted me with sad faces full of sympathy. To my utter delight, I found Hour with Nancy May. She was sitting stock-still, playing with Fred as Nancy combed her ratted head of raven hair with a proper hairbrush. It was a nicer piece than anything that ever went through Hour's tangles previously. The only thing she'd ever had was back at the shanty, an old hairbrush that was handed down from my mother to Pa to her mother and then to her. The look on Hour's face was one of happiness, or at least as happy as Hour ever looked. Relief overtook my senses to see that someone else had done some of my tasks for me. I wondered about Hour's odd mood only briefly. Easier for all of us that she weren't a mess, I reckoned.

Looking around, I saw that everyone was accounted for, except Jane. Even Charlie Utter and his brother Steve were there for the funeral. They weren't in Dora's place but had volunteered to dig the grave in Ingelside Cemetery for my pa. Craning my head to and fro, I searched the ocean of sad faces as I wandered around Dora's, but there was no Jane. Not nowhere.

"She ain't here, kid," said Dora suddenly from behind me.

"Jane?"

"Yeh, she ain't here."

"She at the pest tent?" I asked.

Dora let out a sigh.

"No, she ain't there neither."

"Then, where is she?"

"Where do you think?"

Dora gave me a crooked look that said a mouthful without opening said mouth. I left her side and passed through the saloon, knowing exactly where Jane would be. I found her as I so often did—drunk with a bottle in her hand and half unconscious against the side of the outhouse. Her hat tipped down to hide her face, so it was difficult to see if she was asleep or just faking it. Approaching her slowly was normally the best tactic, so that was exactly what I did. I made my presence known to her with a small clearing of my throat.

"I know you is here, Jimmy Glass."

"Are you coming to the funeral? It's in 'bout two hours."

Jane shook her head slowly and tilted her hat so she might be able to see me properly. Those eyes of hers were gray and red-rimmed. The scent of bourbon was so strong I didn't need to get much closer to know how very drunk she was.

"My apologies, kid, but I ain't comin'."

"Why not? Everyone's goin'."

"If'n that's true, then why you need an old drunkard like me stinkin' up the ranks?"

"I want you there, Jane. Please."

"I ain't goin'. Bill's there. Hurts too much to be in that place with other people, just talkin' and carryin' on like the fact he's dead don't make a lick of difference. Walkin' past that marker that I know is fuckin' his. Nah, kid. I'm sorry, but I ain't goin'."

"But you hafta, Jane. I thought we was friends and all. Hour will want you there too."

"Hour probably won't care a lick if'n I'm there."

"I don't believe that."

"Sorry, kid. My answer is no. I send to you and your sister my greatest condolences, but I can't go back there, not yet."

Anger made the blood in my veins hot. It pulsed its way around my body until my head felt like it might burst from the pressure. A calm man might look at the situation. Jane had lost her Bill not even a month ago, and the strain had hurt her bad. Not to mention, she had on several occasions saved my very life and the life of my sister. Jane had even nursed our father until his death. This woman didn't owe me a thing, but my heart told me otherwise.

"You . . . you ain't nice like I thought. If'n we was real friends like you say—"

"Is this where you gonna call on that favor I owe you, kid? Is that the next part?"

The sarcastic disdain in her voice was like a cold slap to the face. Her eyes glared at me under the hood of drink. I was struck dumb and silent by it, but after all, she was right, wasn't she? Maybe it hurt more because she was right. I was about to use that to get her to show up, and if that wasn't a coward's move, I wasn't sure what on this earth was.

None of that didn't mean it didn't hurt, and I stomped off away from Jane and her filthy corner of the world to go back to Diddlin' Dora's, where everyone was properly melancholy in the way people ought to be. Jane, in her differentness, could keep her bourbon and her bit of mud and squalor. I still had an army of prostitutes willing to brave the drizzle of the stormy day to look properly forlorn on account of my pa's passing.

We made our way slowly, as processions are wont to do, through the muddy parts of the Deadwood thoroughfare. All the girls were in attendance, as were Dora and Joseph. Nancy May was the type to hate events outside her kitchen, so she volunteered to stay behind and look after Diddlin' Dora's. She armed herself with a double barrel shotgun in case any person got the fool idea to rob the place whilst the owners were away.

Charlie Utter and his brother were waiting at the cemetery over an open grave. Someone, possibly the Utters, had already lowered the casket containing my father's body into the hole in the ground. Charlie and Steve stood stoic and solemn next to it, hats over their hearts. As we approached, Charlie bowed his head to me, and I bowed back. When I peered inside, I saw a bouquet of wildflowers tied together with a ribbon on top of my pa's pine box. The undertaker was right. It did make the whole thing look nicer.

There was quite the gathering surrounding my pa's grave, most had never known him. I did see the faces of a few of the miners we knew from the creek. They actually had known Pa. I hadn't the money for a newspaper bit about him, but rumors traveled quick in the camp, and the sight of old friends warmed me.

Hour stood next to me, her face staring intently at the hole in the ground. She didn't seem upset much by the idea of the funeral, but according to her, Pa was flying now. To her, I supposed, there wasn't much to be sad about.

The undertaker presented himself then as we all looked around for a person to lead the proceedings. No preacher had come to the site as promised, and I wasn't sure how to go about a thing like this. When he motioned me over, I went, leaving Hour in the care of Lil' Missy standing next to me. Dora followed me on over as well.

"Preacher Smith, he will not be attending," said the undertaker.

"Whatcha mean? I thought there weren't no fee," I protested.

"There wouldn't be, and there is not."

Dora made herself known by nudging into the conversation.

"Talk straight. What happened to Preacher Smith?" she asked.

"Don't rightly know. I went to his place, but he weren't there. Just a note."

The tall undertaker produced a note for us to read.

Gone to Crook City to preach, and if God is willing, will be back at three o'clock.

"It's pert near four," said Dora.

"Yes. I s'pose God weren't willin', or perhaps some Injuns were more willin'. I do hope not. I was on my way to tell de sheriff, but I reckoned I need to tell you. I'm sorry, but there is no preacher comin' for de service."

"What are we gonna do? I don't know what to say," I said, suddenly panicky.

"I am afraid I am a terrible public speaker," said the undertaker.

"What do you say at a thing like this?"

I turned the question at Dora who always seemed to have some answer or another. Her all-knowing eyes looked a little lost, like she was swimming. She smiled warmly to cover up all the uncertainty inside of her.

"We'll make do, kid. Maybe we can take turns sayin' nice things. I know Joseph had himself an old family bible. I reckon he can run back and . . ."

The vivacious woman trailed off when she spotted something over my shoulder. Sight unseen, the thing must have been wonderful because her grin turned from painted on to a real thing etched into her skin. Her eyes softened like all was suddenly right in the world, and for the briefest of moments, I thought maybe Preacher Smith had arrived after all. The thing was, when I turned around, there was no preacher man. There was no man at all. It was Jane. She marched across the cemetery and stood above my father's grave, looking from person to person. When she found my face next to Dora's, she gave me a wink. Never had I been so relieved to see a person in all my life.

"We ain't got a preacher, kid, but I think you got the next best thing."

I nodded, and we rejoined the rest of the congregation. I took my place next to Hour, front and center. Delicately and slowly, I felt a small hand creep underneath mine own and interlace fingers with me. I held Missy's hand without hesitation as she leaned that blonde head full of curls on my shoulder. Jane, for all her informal nature, took off her hat and held it to her chest.

"I ain't the type that should give a sermon, or speak at the grave of a person, but word made it that Preacher Smith ain't a-comin' today, so I'm afraid the lot of you are stuck with me."

A few smiles and snickers infected the crowd.

"Anyhow, I aim to give Hank Glass as proper a Christian burial as I'm able. I didn't know the man well, but I did spend the last few days of his life with him. Illness don't seem like a good death. It ain't brave or glorious like dyin' in battle. It also ain't cowardly like dying whilst runnin' away. It just *is* . . . the way the moon *is* and the sun *is*.

"Hank Glass was a good man. In his illness, Hank Glass ain't spoke to me about life. In fact, I will speak truth now, since that's what is proper. He didn't get the chance to say a word to me, the poor wretch. So how is it that I know he were a good man, you might be wonderin', if'n he never talked to me personal? Well, that would be because I spoke with his children, Jimmy and Hour over yonder. In fact, I do believe there are but a handful of you here today that actually knew the man in question. Most of ya'll are here for the same reason I am, because you got to know these two fine kids."

I wanted to cry. Somehow, someway, I knew Jane wouldn't like me to do that. And after how wrongly I had treated her earlier, I held in the brine pushing its way to the surface. Missy squeezed my hand and added a bit of bravery to me.

"You fine folks here have only spent a couple o' weeks with the two Glass children, and here you are, at a funeral fer a man you didn't know. Maybe that speaks only to yer character, but let's face it, I have drunk with all of ya'll, and there ain't much character between us to spread 'round with a butter knife."

More laughter from everyone, especially Dora.

"Maybe some of ya'll been cussin' too much around little Hour here, and now are in debt to her swear jug that ole Charlie Utter made fer her. Yes folks, you can blame Mr. Charlie Utter right over there for the sudden disappearance of your pennies."

Charlie laughed and shook his head. He daubed his eyes with a handkerchief from his pockets. Steve patted his back.

"Nah, I think the real reason be the character of them two kids. I know I have felt it. Jimmy Glass there saved my life sure as the sun'll set, and Hour brings about the goodness in every person she meets. There ain't a lick of coward in either of them. What can we, as passin' guests in their lives, say made them as they are? Well, the answer's simple. Their pa. All these years on his own, and look at what fine people he brung up.

"You ask me how I knew Mr. Hank Glass was a good, fine man? I know it because I can see the fruit of his efforts in his children. May he reap sweet rewards in Heaven. Amen."

"Amen," said the congregation together.

Somewhere, from some unknown spot in the crowd of prostitutes around me, a girl took up singing a hymn. Others slowly but surely joined in, seeming to know the words by heart. The crowd around me swayed, causing me to sway gently to and fro as well. I didn't know the words, but the sound and feeling of it was comforting, and the tears I couldn't hold back any longer fell down my face without effort.

When I looked up again, I noticed that Jane was gone. No longer did she stand above my father's grave saying the words I wanted to be able to say and couldn't. Craning my neck a bit, I found her a little ways from where we stood. Jane was sitting on a different grave, away from the masses. She was doubled over and weeping against a grave marker. It took me a long minute to understand which grave it was, and when I did I wanted even more desperately to take back everything I had said to her by the outhouse. The grave marker she was crying against said it was Wild Bill Hickok's grave.

19

TWO WHOLE DAYS PASSED after Pa's funeral before I got mind enough to head back to our claim. In the meantime, Hour and I did good work at Diddlin' Dora's to pay our part, even though she said we didn't need to. It was high on my mind to go back to our home though. The time spent in town was a different sort of living, but we belonged at home. I needed to be able to earn a living for Hour and myself, so working Pa's claim was the right thing to do. After all, the claim would move down to me, seeing as how I was his eldest and only son.

Hour stayed with Nancy May the afternoon I set out to secure our spot on the creek. When I told Dora where I was headed, she seemed worried for one reason or another, but I was hell-bent on getting the place back up and running. I promised I'd be back before dark so she wouldn't worry. Besides, I wasn't planning on leaving town yet. There were too many folks to say goodbye to for me to leave just like that. The moving process would be one of many transitions.

With a gunnysack over my shoulder, I set out to make my way through town and down into the gulch where our claim sat. I looked at Deadwood as it passed me by with a sad fondness. It was never so apparent how lonely and quiet our lives were down by the creek until I spent a bit of time in town. I would miss it terribly, but assured myself Hour and I would visit often. It weren't like we were going to California or some other far-flung place.

The time I made was good, and before long, I was loping my way down the steep slope toward creek tucked away in the gulch. The tinkling sound of water was a welcoming one, even if it did make me feel the sudden urge to release my own water. The going here was a little slower as the recent rains had made the mud slick and the falling leaves covering it slicker. I nearly slipped and cracked my hind end in half several times, but before too long, our little shanty was visible through the thick trees.

A smile curled its way across my face as I spotted the canvas roof of the little place I called home not too long ago. The thing of it was, the shanty weren't the only thing I spotted. There was movement nearby. A deer maybe, or a rabbit, I thought, but then, there were two and three. I squinted to peer further, thinking maybe a pack of wolves or something of the like. Quickly I understood the moving figures weren't deer and they weren't rabbits. Men. There were men, crawling all over our home, close to a dozen at first guess.

Air caught in my throat, and I held it there, as to not make a sound. Several of the men had guns, and I did not. I swallowed hard all of those noble intentions I had been carrying with me. Fear rippled through me and made my hackles rise. The thing of it was, I didn't understand what was happening until I saw Mr. Mills. He was holding a rifle and departing my shanty with a handful of dishes. They were the white dishes that belonged to us. I knew him. He was one of my pa's friends who owned a claim not far away. We had him over for supper whenever Pa managed to take down something bigger than a squirrel or a hare. Mr. Mills had attended Pa's funeral, hat in hand.

Then there was Mr. McCreeny. I spotted him too, taking a few sifting pans and shirts. He had been plagued with small pox too, but he recovered. He was our friend and an attendant at Pa's funeral only two days prior. That man, I had seen him weep two days ago. Our friends and neighbors, they were here ransacking the place like it was a dead carcass and they the vultures.

A slimy thing in my stomach turned over to expose its unpleasant underbelly. All the fear inside me turned from yellow to orange to red with the rage of the recently wronged. Weapon or no, I was going to go down there and beat on those men with my fists until they dropped our things. If they didn't, I would die trying. It weren't right, none of it was.

Just before I made to charge down the rest of the distance to my shanty like an outraged Indian, two sets of arms grabbed me and dragged me down to the ground. Immediately, the smell of dirt and moss filled my nose as one of my attackers covered my mouth with their hands. I kicked at them frantically until I had the sense to look at their faces and identify the owner of said hands. My body instantly relaxed when I saw the faces of Charlie Utter and Calamity Jane. When she saw I was going to keep quiet, Jane released my mouth.

"What are you doin' here?"

"Keepin' you from doin' somethin' stupid," replied Charlie Utter.

"How did you know . . ."

"Dora told us you were headed home to start fixin' the place up. I figured somethin' like this might happen. I grabbed Charlie, and we made tracks to find you."

"But . . . but how did you know where I lived?"

"What part of the knowledge that I used to be a fuckin' scout for the fuckin' army didn't you comprehend, kid? It weren't like you was hard to track."

They allowed me to sit up as we surveyed the scene below. That old feeling of anger rose up again, making my eyes glow red hot from within. If humans could growl, I would have.

"Yeh, I reckoned that might be happenin'," said Jane.

"They do work fast, don't they? No goddamned respect for the dead. Not out here," added Charlie Utter.

"We gotta go get 'em," I said with a tone that I hoped meant business.

"Kid, that'd be suicide. There's at least a dozen of

'em down there, all carryin' weapons. I'm a good shot but not that good. And Charlie, he hates the sight of blood."

"Oh, blow it out your ass, Jane," spat Charlie. "I'm fine with it, but do I think runnin' down there half-cocked is a good idea? No, sir. That down there is the opposite of a good fuckin' idea. Sorry, kid."

"But we can't just let 'em . . ."

"It's just stuff, Jimmy. Your life ain't worth a sack of stuff. Come on now, let's get you home."

I wanted to protest. This was supposed to be home. Bowing my head, I allowed Jane to lead me away from my old home. I watched, helpless as my once friends and neighbors picked through the bulk of our things like meat off a bone. I followed Jane and Charlie back up the hill where three horses were waiting for us. They had led a pony there to bring me back on. I climbed onto the little black horse and followed Charlie's lead back to Deadwood.

My head hung low. Even though I reckoned Jane to be right, it still hurt. My life wasn't worth a sack of things. Hour needed a brother now, not a sack of stuff, and I had to live for her, but I couldn't help but think about how good that vengeance would have felt. I could even taste the ghost of it on my tongue. In my most realistic fantasies, I would have gotten quite a lacing in before they overwhelmed me, but it was in the fighting that I felt redeemed.

Jane waited until Charlie's horse was a decent bit of ground ahead of us before she tried to break me from my reverie.

"I hope you have seen the light now. There ain't no way you can go back to prospectin' as a possible career choice, kid."

"Why not? The claim's mine."

"The claim goes to whichever one of them cock-suckers found your Daddy's deed first."

"It ain't right, Jane."

"You, Jimmy Glass, have just spoken the biggest understatement of the fuckin' century, I reckon. If I had me a ribbon, I'd write that on it and pin it to yer chest. That don't make it untrue though. I'm sorry, kid. The claim, she is forfeit."

"But there has to be somethin' we can do."

"We are livin' in an illegal mining camp in a territory rightfully belonging to the Lakota tribe, so says the government. There ain't much recourse here."

"We could go to the sheriff."

"Sheriff Bullock is an honorable man, but his power don't pass town lines. He can't do nothin' about claim jumpers, even though he might want to."

We rode in silence for a few minutes pondering the unfairness of life and what sort of work there was left to me if my pa's claim was no longer mine.

"Well, I could stay with Dora. I reckon she'd put me and Hour up if'n we continue to earn our keep. I don't mind saloon work, and Hour loves the girls."

"Yep, you could do that . . . fer a spell."

"The people at Dora's, they was the real friends at Pa's funeral. Like you and Charlie and Dora and Missy. Ya'll are the good people. If we stay with you, we'd be okay."

"Folks have made a life with less."

Jane was agreeing with me but with a tone that didn't sound as though she was. The more I added, the more she confirmed what I said as a truth, but never did she say it was a good idea. It was a game, this bantering, and it was beginning to be maddening talking this way with her. I wished she'd just out with the thing she thought I ought to do rather than pandering to my words.

"Truth is, Hour does real well in the kitchen . . ."

"And when she grows up, what'll happen to her?" asked Jane.

At last, the tip of her meaning was poking out from her mouth, and the rest would soon follow. Whether I liked it was another issue entirely.

"She'll help out Dora, and maybe replace Nancy May when she gets too old?"

"No she won't."

"What do you mean?"

"Look at yer sister. She ain't the type to survive this place. It takes wiles and grit and a helluva lotta luck. Maybe you're right, kid. Maybe you two can live with Dora forever and ever, you tendin' bar and Hour cookin' in the back, but there are a lot of things that hafta fuckin' line up like girls in a calico line fer that to work out."

"I don't understand."

"In the not-even-three weeks you've been at Dora's, you've been close to death how many times? It ain't you, it's the nature of a place like this. Some of us are built fer it, and others ain't. What if somethin' were to happen to you? How long do you think that sister of yers, in her different sorta condition, could survive?"

"Not long, I reckon."

"I reckon so too. Not to mention, I weren't lying when I said she was purdy and would grow into an hourglass beauty someday. She will, mark my words. Half breeds always tend to. Thing is, a beauty like that won't be content to work the small pay of a kitchen gal, not with the sorta attention she'll be gettin'."

"No, she wouldn't do that. I'll be there to protect her, and you will. We can keep her from it."

"And what if we ain't? What if we gunned down?"

"I . . . I don't know."

"How long do you think Hour will last when she's old enough to be looked upon as pretty by men with the way she is?"

I stared down at the mud clumps my pony kicked up underfoot, not wanting to face the reality Jane was painting for me to see. It was ugly, so ugly, and I wouldn't see it for what it was.

"She ain't safe here, kid. Even if the best scenario possible happens, and she has a class act like Madame Dora DuFran in her corner, she ain't safe here. Not with those different parts of her out there for everyone to see. Anything can happen out here, and most brothel folks ain't like Dora fuckin' DuFran."

Shivers rippled all over my body thinking of my sister like that. I knew the realities of whoring, and it didn't bother me much that Missy did it to earn her money, but when I applied the same thoughts to my sister, the equation changed. Sick rose up in my throat, and I swallowed hard to get it back down again. Those figures and what they added up to were enough to raise all the bile in my belly.

"What're we supposed to do then?" I asked Jane, defeated.

"The two of you need to get outta here lickety split. Hightail it, and soon. You need to go to a place that can teach you proper things and teach Hour how to cope with her ailment. Readin' and writin' and the like. Someone who can help her adapt her ailment to the real world and live on her own. She will always be in danger as long as she's always needin' you to protect her. That girl ain't got a chance as long as she depends on you to act as her guardian. Someday, you ain't gonna be 'round, and then she's no better than a baby bird outta its nest."

"You sayin' we need to go to a school?"

"That's exactly what I'm sayin'."

"How? And with what money? I barely had 'nuff for the undertaker. We got nothin' but the pennies in Hour's jug."

"Leave that part to me, Jimmy Glass. You just get it in yer head that yer goin'."

20

I TRIED TO DO as Jane said, but the idea of going off to school was such a strange concept to me, it was hard to wrap my brain around it. Sure, I knew my letters and numbers. Pa was strict about that. I knew how to read and work figures in my head because he taught me with the world around us. He'd mark words in the dirt, and we'd have to read them. Pa would use rocks and sticks and move them around to show us adding and subtracting. Not many kids knew that much in our part of the land, so I counted myself rather educated.

The idea of going to a proper school with proper teachers was a strange thought. I lived in the world and knew world things. I could skin a hare and fire a gun.

There wasn't a better fisherman in the whole Gulch as me. I could feed a family of three with nothing but a cane pole, some line, and a barbed hook. But proper school? The idea seemed like the kind of thing rich kids from a place like San Francisco might think about doing. Not me.

I suppose that's why I didn't take the whole thing seriously at first when Jane said she'd find a way to send us to school. For the next week, life went as it had been going. Hour worked in the kitchen, and I worked in the saloon. Days came and went, and Jane flitted in and out of Dora's as she most often did. If I were so inclined to find the woman, she could be found at any of her regular haunts: either at the pest tent, passed out drunk by the outhouse, or drinking at Dora's saloon. Nothing about her actions would make anyone think she was working up a plan to send us away.

The dickens of the whole thing was that the words she spoke to me on the sullen ride back to town haunted every thought I had. I was so happy at Dora's. Cleaning and tending bar was a nice job, and people more often than not were excited and happy to see me. All the girls doted on me and paid attention to Hour like she were a little sister. Even Lil' Missy began coming down to the saloon again in her work dresses. Her bruises were healing nicely, and the skittish nature she'd adopted was slowly melting back into that firecracker girl we all knew. The routine of it began feeling like home every time we woke, ate breakfast among all our friends, and separated to go off to work.

Then, the thoughts came. Those awful seeds that

Jane had planted in my mind. They'd take me by surprise when I was least expecting it. One evening, I was stocking the new bottles of whiskey when I stood up quickly, making myself visible to a grizzled miner sitting at the bar. There weren't nothing behind the act. I was just springy as boys were prone to be. The sudden appearance of my face must have startled the fellow, because his first instinct was to draw his revolver and point it at my face. One second I was stocking bottles, and the next, I was staring down the barrel of a loaded gun. I raised my hands above my head, thinking he might be trying to rob me, but the shaking hands and battered union soldier hat on his head told a different story.

Joseph was by my side in a flash with a shotgun pointed at the man's face.

"Easy now, Martin. Put 'er down now. He ain't no grayback. Lower that gun," said Joseph calmly and evenly.

Something twitched under Martin's eye as though realization was fighting its way through the haze to reach him. Old eyes in a young face blinked hard.

"Martin Castor, lower your gun now. This boy ain't your enemy."

Jospeh's voice was getting louder and stern. Several people had stopped their conversations to see what the hubbub was about. Even the piano player halted his jaunty tune.

Martin Castor blinked a few more times and clarity lit up inside his eyes. He lowered his gun with a face like a man waking from a terrible dream. After returning his weapon to its holster, I lowered my hands back down, but my heart was a jackrabbit in my chest. Martin shook his head back and forth and met me with a contrite, embarrassed face.

"I . . . I am sorry there, kid."

"It's okay," I lied.

Martin slid from the bar and stumbled out of Dora's. The ghost of shame was his only drinking companion, and it followed him out of the door and into the cool evening. Joseph leaned over to me after he replaced the shotgun in its holster under the bar's lip.

"He had a bad war, Jimmy. It ain't you."

I nodded and went back to work. The thing of it was, Jane's words had infected every second of that altercation. Her words were as good as theirs telling me how cheap life was and asking what would happen to Hour if that man hadn't come to his senses? What if whatever rebel enemy he thought he saw in me in that second stayed? What if his sanity hadn't come back, turning me into Dora's bar boy again? If that man had shot me, what would become of Hour? Things here could change that quick. One bullet and my sister was helpless.

Missy sauntered down the staircase right about that time. It might have been an hour later, but I was so lost in my own ideas that time flew past me. Either way, the blonde in the maroon dress made everyone perk up and take notice. She was so beautiful, even with her bruises still there, with her bouncy blonde hair all woven up in a pile on her head. Moving like some kind of cat, she pranced from one haggard-looking man to another.

With a twisted ability that I never would have thought me capable of, my mind suddenly turned Missy, the belle of my dreams, into Hour. In this vision, Hour was Missy's age, but she moved about the place as elegant and beautiful as a picture. Her black hair pulled up the way Missy's was, her crystal-blue eyes staring straight ahead.

When the men pawed at Missy, I saw Hour as the one they were touching. My beautiful sister would hate that. She would hate everything about the life of a whore. I pictured her trying to flirt as the others girls did, but in the end, she would cry as some grizzled miner covered in dirt hauled her upstairs to her room.

I shook my head and swallowed down the toad in my throat. The woman was Missy again, just Missy. It wasn't Hour, I told myself. She wouldn't do that. Dora wouldn't let her do that. Dora and Joseph and Jane were nice. They would protect her.

A tiny voice in the back of my head whispered Jane's words to me yet again.

"What if we ain't here?"

As if called by her own words in my mind, Jane stepped through the saloon door, spotted me, and made her way over to the bar. She ordered a whiskey from Joseph and threw it back right then and there. Joseph poured her another without her having to ask. A routine of muscles, as it were.

"You been thinkin''bout what we discussed, kid?"

"Yes'm."

Jane tossed the second whiskey down and looked at me with the crooked, appraising way she did. I got the feeling Jane sized up people on the regular. So much so it was habit.

"You have the look of a man with a plagued mind," she said.

"Yes'm."

"Then you have been considerin' what I said."

The memory of seeing Hour as Missy clouded my eyes, and as if Jane could see it for herself, she nodded to my understanding.

"Yes'm. I still don't know how you gonna pay fer it, but I think you might be right."

"Well, I know I'm right, and I know how to pay fer it."

"That's nice, Jane," interrupted Joseph. "Is the thing in question your considerable bar tab you owe us?"

Jane scowled at Joseph.

"I figured riddin' you of fuckin' vermin like the man who beat up Lil' Missy were a good payment. Got yer goddamned horses back too."

Joseph smiled and poured her another shot of whiskey.

"Just takin' you down a notch there, Jane. When Dora ain't 'round, it's my job, you know."

Jane lifted her glass and toasted Joseph.

"Here's to you and your fuckin' handler."

"Cheers."

As soon as Jane's whiskey was gone, she slapped a page of newspaper on the bar. It was a proof of some kind. I read the writing, but the words didn't enlighten me the way Jane thought they ought.

Charity Benefit Held This Thursday!

Come join the fun at the New Theater. Drinks, Dancing, and Entertainment! All for a good 'cause to raise the money needed to send Calamity Jane's daughter away for a proper education. Jane has cured the ill and fought the savages for our great town. Come one, come all to help her daughter!

Joseph and I read the paper and then read it again. We looked at one another and then back to Jane, as though any moment she might sprout another head. Hell, maybe that head would explain this all instead of just gaze at us with a smug smile on her face and whiskey on her breath.

"The New Theater?" began Joseph.

"It ain't got a name yet, so I figured people would know it if'n I said it were the new one."

"So Hour's your daughter now?" I asked.

"For all intents and purposes, she's my fuckin' daughter for the event. Folks'll be more inclined to donate to Calamity Jane's daughter than the daughter of a Lakota. No offense intended, Jimmy Glass. I ain't got nothin' against Hour's mama. Them's just the facts of white folks."

"Jane, how did you do this?" I asked.

"Remember that lady in the stagecoach? The purdy one with the high talk, loud as a fart in church?"

"Yeh. Freis was her name?"

"Miss Adeline Freis is one of the owners of the new theater. I told her my wants, and she offered to host the benefit. She was real appreciative on account of me makin' sure she didn't end up another scalped body on the road. Not only that, but she offered to provide some of the entertainment with her actin' troupe."

Joseph and I gawked at the buckskinned woman with our mouths opened like some sort of fish that found its way on land and started serving drinks in the saloon. Of all the things I expected out of the day, a benefit for Hour weren't one of them. Jane snickered at our faces and slapped the bar hard to accent her amusement.

"If'n you could see your faces at this moment!"

"Jane, it says drinkin'. Where are you gettin' the booze?" asked Joseph.

A sudden light flashed in his eyes as though a realization was heavy on his heels.

"Well, your lovely wife is gonna be donatin' them for the benefit. None of the girls though, Joseph. I already spoke with the refined Miss Bennett, the aristocrat of Deadwood, and she will be in attendance. Best not to have the whores around while a lady's present."

"Jane, have you talked to Dora 'bout that? Did she agree?"

His face showed a warning. Apparently, he knew Jane well enough to be wary of which of her words were true and which weren't.

"Madame Dora DuFran will only be too fuckin' happy to donate to this worthy benefit of mine," said Jane with a grandiose wave of her arms and a loud, booming voice.

She was also backing away with a smug grin slapped

across her face. I was reminded of a saying my pa used to say. Something about a fox in a henhouse. Her arms were spread wide, and she bowed over and over again as she backed her way to the door. In one hand rested the whiskey bottle we had been pouring from just seconds before. Neither of us had seen her swipe it out from under our noses.

"Jane, I'm warning you . . ."

"Relax and cool yer goddamned heels, Joseph DuFran. She'll agree to it. You'll see."

"Jane?"

"Don't worry! It's gonna be a great time."

And just like that, Jane disappeared behind the door and out into the darkness from which she first appeared. Joseph and I were left alone to deal with an irate Madame Dora when she found the bit of paper on the bar an hour later.

21

THE BENEFIT FOR HOUR'S education turned out to be quite the event. It seemed as though the only people who knew or cared to know who Hour actually was lived within the vicinity of Diddlin' Dora's, and not a one of us was going to spill the beans about Hour's true mother. One of the biggest problems was Hour had to attend so Jane could parade her around for authenticity's sake. I tagged along and helped to serve the drinks since Joseph stayed behind at Dora's place to keep it running.

Why wasn't I a headliner next to my sister? Jane said people were more likely to pony up the cash for a sweet, lone girl than to fund a boy who was nearly a man and working a man's job. I didn't want to lie, but she explained about how simply staying quiet weren't the same as lying. If I had to claim Hour as my kin during the party, the explanation would be that I was Jane's stepson. That felt close enough to true to agree to, and thus, the benefit began.

The New Theater, as we called it, since it hadn't a name yet, was one of the prettiest places I'd ever seen. There was a big open room where the benefit was held, and in the middle of the room and off to the wall sat a large, half-moon stage. Curtains the color of wine and heavier than a head of cattle hung like weeping clouds from the rafters above. Everything smelled clean and new. The folks running the place moved about like they were straight from a story, painted up like heroes and reciting poetry. There were so many ruffles on their clothes I figured we could have made an extra shirt apiece with all the excess fabric. A strange bunch to be sure, but their smiles never faltered.

My head moved on a swivel, trying to see all the decadence. Hour was different. She had a tendency to fixate on one miraculous thing at a time. In fact, she was capable of fixating forever on something as mundane as the fringe of the curtain. I was thankful Jane and I had talked her out of bringing Fred the Kitten with her. That little cat was becoming like a security blanket to Hour, even though I had never heard tell of a security kitten. One look at those curtains billowing down to the ground, and I could just picture trying to pry a terrified kitten down from the top.

The theater crew was wonderful to us. One of the ladies wrapped some strands of colored pearls around

Hour's neck and told her she was the guest of honor. When Hour resisted the necklace, she told her they were magic beads that gave her super powers of courage. Something about the phrase stuck in her head and something about the pearls did give her confidence. She walked around and looked at people for just long enough to seem like she were any other little girl. There were no words coming from her, but the way she walked about unafraid in a herd of new faces was a sight to behold. As long as the beads were around her neck to finger with her tiny hands, Hour was all right.

Miss Adeline Freis took what looked like an old spittoon and tied a theater mask onto the top. The mask was painted gold with a carved face that looked stupidly happy. A large yawning mouth curled up almost to its eyes, and the way it was fixed on the spittoon, patrons had to feed their donations in the creature's grinning mouth. Most found it fun, but it looked downright weird to me. The drunker people got, the more entertaining feeding the mask was, and the more money found its way to our education fund.

Every type and class of person was in attendance. I served whiskey to cowpokes, bourbon to landowners, and brandy to the upper class. Jane hadn't been fibbing about Miss Bennett either. The grand lady was in attendance in a black-and-white-striped dress that would have paid for mine and Hour's tuition several times over. Her dark hair was curled and spun up into a fine black hat atop her head. Folks whispered about her claim striking it rich, and her wealthy family back in San Francisco. She dropped her hefty donation into the smiling mouth of the mask with a gloved hand, only to be immediately approached by a very drunk Jane. The entire ordeal had taxed her more than the usual, I figured, so she was drinking even more than usual.

"Miss Bennett, so good of you to come," said Jane as she approached the refined woman.

She removed her hat and placed it over her heart like a man would, and she shook the lady's hand with her free one. Miss Bennett, to her credit, obliged Jane with a friendly smile and a handshake in return. From afar, Jane looked like a person who was stable and in good spirits, but once you got up close and personal, you could see how drunk she was. Miss Bennett observed this much as well and instantly affected a sourer exterior. Her smile stayed glued to her face, but it was a strained one at that.

"Miss Jane. Thank you for the invitation. I am so glad you have taken such an . . . interest in your daughter's education. Where might she be?"

"She's right over yonder. I'll fetch her fer you. Be mindful, she is a bit quiet."

"Of course."

Jane escorted Hour, whispering gentle things in her ear. Hour thumbed the colored beads around her neck like a nun with a rosary. I wanted to rush over, to hover over my sister and protect her from any embarrassment or from just being the center of attention as I knew she wouldn't cotton on to being. A voice inside me whispered to trust Jane, so I did nothing but watch my timid sister approach the fine, wealthy woman. Miss Bennett bent low to address her.

"Hello there. What is your name, darling girl?"

Hour stared at the floor unwilling to answer or look up. She was agitated. I knew because her fingering of the beads got faster and a little jerkier. It was a thing most wouldn't notice, but I did. Soon, she would start shaking her head back and forth. I was supposed to be protecting her. My feet itched to run over and whisk her home.

"Her name is Hour, Miss Bennett. I'm afraid she ain't much fer talkin'. You see the reason I wish fer her to be get some proper schoolin'."

"Hour? Such an odd name but lovely. Truly a name that is hard to forget," said Miss Bennett, still trying to sound loving around my sister.

"Yes'm. She is a picture. A little learnin' and she could do most anythin'."

"I do see why you'd like a proper education for her."

"She don't look much like you, Jane," shouted a man from the crowd.

I had been wrapped up in the conversation in front of me so much so that I hadn't noticed I wasn't the only one. A small crowd had circled the women and Hour. Apparently, the exchange of a lady of high class and Calamity Jane was far more interesting than anything else at the present. Jane squinted into the crowd, looking for the man behind the question.

"Is that Billy Castor?" asked Jane.

"One in the same!"

All at once, I saw the transformation. There were two distinct Janes I had discovered. The Jane I knew best was the rugged, kind-hearted drunk who slept in the open and saved people with a lick of notice. Then, there was the stage Jane. She appeared whenever Jane had herself an audience. Her voice got louder, her gestures grander, and in a flash, she was a show all to herself. With the brilliance of a smile, the show woman arrived in full color.

"Well, Billy, she ain't lookin' much like me, huh? You are right there, and let's thank God fer doin' her the favor of not takin' after her mama! Whew-ee! God done blessed me extra to not curse my child with a mug like this."

Jane gestured to her face, and everyone laughed. Lots of people slapped their knees and slipped extra dollars into the wide mouth of the grinning mask. Miss Bennett's smile was becoming even more pained the longer she stood in the middle of Jane's limelight. The rowdy attention was not a thing she fed from like her mannish counterpart. Hour never looked up from the floor. Every shout made her jump just a little.

"Why she ain't talkin', Jane?" asked another man from the ever-growing congregation.

"Why would she wanna to talk to you, Charlie Hopper? That mess you call yer face is even uglier than mine! It be one thing if you were a conversationalist, but we all know you work at the livery because only horses would keep your company."

More laughing. The man named Charlie Hopper laughed too, and several people around him patted his back. One bought him a drink. More drinks were passed around, the clinking of glasses and the sloshing of liquor filled the air with a din of drunkenness. Miss

Bennett, having obviously tired of the scene, discreetly bowed and vanished into the crowd.

"Tell us about General Custer, Jane!"

A little muscly bit in my chest tensed without my say so. I forced it to settle and my hands to calm as I poured some more drinks.

"Ah Teddy, ain't you tired of that ole story yet? I swear you ain't got the memory God gave a beetle."

"You ever gonna wear a dress again?"

"Steve Utter, is that you? I ain't answerin' any of yer fool questions, and you best be glad there's ladies present or I'd give you 'nother walloping to teach you some manners."

Everyone laughed at that, except Steve Utter, who looked genuinely nervous. He took a drink of the whiskey in his hand. Charlie Utter patted him on the back so hard he coughed up half of it, which started up the laughing once again. Some kind soul brought him another drink.

"Who's her daddy, Jane?" shouted someone.

"Is it Wild Bill?" added another.

If you didn't know Jane, you wouldn't have seen it. There was a tiny flinch in her eyes, undetectable by most everyone, but I saw it. Not only me, but Dora, who was tending bar next to me, saw it too. Without missing a step, the madame gracefully moved out from behind the bar and started for her friend.

"Do I ask you what manner of mule you fuckin' consort with, Tom Billings?" retorted Jane, the show woman smile still slapped on her face.

The crowd laughed again, and Tom Billings looked

only mildly insulted. It was all in good fun, but the fun was beginning to turn cold. Dora glided into view just as Hour tugged on Jane's sleeve. My best guess was that she was hitting Jane up for a penny for swearing. Sure enough, Jane smiled and fished a copper from her pocket. With a grandiose wave of her arms, Dora DuFran took center stage among the motley assortment of folks present.

"Ladies and gents, thank you for making this benefit a smashin' success!"

A thunderous applause arose from the well-intoxicated crowd.

"Your charity to help Jane's girl is truly an inspiration. I think we proved what fine people are livin' here in this ole minin' camp."

More applause thundered about us. I just stared at Hour in the middle of it, wanting desperately to take her away from all this. She fidgeted in place, not taking her eyes from the floor.

"I have the terrible job of tellin' y'all that the benefit is now over. We need ta get this youngin home and in bed."

There was a smattering of booing, and one person hissed.

"Now, now. Cool your heels, fellas. I also have the fine job of tellin' y'all that the after party will be with me at Diddlin' Dora's down the road. And I'm sure most of you fine gents can tell, a party at Dora's doesn't end just 'cause the sun comes up!"

Cheers and whoops and hollers sounded high in the air. I caught a glimpse of Miss Bennett, sour face in hand, ducking out of the front door before the crowd made their move to the after party. Miss Adeline Freis ducked behind the bar with me as the massive herd of people filed out of her theater and headed for Dora's. Jane and Hour soon joined us, and I was relieved to be done with the whole affair. Just before she followed the crowd outside to lead them like children to her saloon, Dora leaned over the bar and addressed Jane.

"I hope you got what you wanted Jane fer all the free whiskey I served up tonight."

"Oh hush up, Dora. You'll more than make it back tonight. Just charge 'em extra. They're all too drunk to know the difference."

She opened her mouth to say something, but shut it again, looking thoughtful. Dora's scowl said volumes, but she didn't want to admit Jane's idea was a good one.

"Run along now, Madame. Them ducklings need their mama to show them the way to the whores. Go on, now," said Jane, waving her hand.

The look of pure distaste on Dora DuFran's face was the funniest thing I had seen in days. Miss Adeline Freis bit her lips to try not to laugh, but I couldn't help but snort trying to hide my laughter behind clasped hands. Jane's smile was wide and smug.

"You make it nigh on impossible to love you, Jane," spat Dora DuFran.

"That's one way to look at it. Another would be I'm nigh on impossible to hate too."

Dora huffed, turned on her heel, and stormed out of the theater.

22

NO ONE COULD POINT to a time on the clock when the party died at Dora's that night. It went long into the night and then into the morning for sure. Laughter, drinking, music, and the like. Such rowdy fun was had, and Jane positioned herself squarely in the center of it.

I knew this fact merely because I heard the evidence through the door of the storeroom. Hour slept well enough through the din, but I couldn't. Admittedly, the thought occurred to me to go and join in on the festivities. A break from the terrible weight of my grief would have been welcome. However, the fear of leaving my sister—the only family I had left—to sleep by herself after everything we had been through left my belly feeling yellow. I wouldn't leave her.

It was Fred who noticed the smoke first. There was no telling when I gave up my wakeful vigil in the wee hours of the morning, but in that time, something sinister entered the saloon. When I woke and searched the room, I found Hour crouched in the corner of the storeroom and Fred yowling at our tiny window, begging to be let out. A dark, slithery smoke snaked into our room under and around the door. Somewhere in the air, I could smell the raw scent of burning.

I went to the door and threw it open. Smoke billowed inside the room, dancing along the ceiling. It raced into my chest and I coughed. Seeing a new way out of the danger, Fred leapt from the window and raced out of the room. His departure made Hour's state worsen, and she pulled in on herself in the corner, whimpering.

Gripping my sister's shoulders, I tried at pulling her from her corner. Her rigid, little body wouldn't budge, so I tried wrapping my arm through hers and yanking on her elbow. Hour was surprisingly strong when she set her mind to resisting.

"No no no no no," she wailed as she took her arm back.

There was commotion beyond our room—the echoes of boots on floorboards racing here and there. Panicking yelps of girls as they made their way to the front door. Grunts of barely sober men stumbling behind them. In the din, I heard Dora yell at someone to fetch help.

Hour wouldn't budge, so I left her to see if I could

cut the snake off at the head. Where there was smoke, there was fire. If I could help put out the blaze, this could all be over. All I needed to do was follow the heat.

Joseph was in the kitchen with another man I didn't recognize throwing buckets of water on a growing flame that was licking up the walls near the stove. Beneath the fire, the wood turned the same dingy black as the stove itself. I couldn't help but wince and cover my eyes when the heat of it slapped my face.

"Get outta here, Jimmy!" yelled Joseph as he threw another bucket of water into the roaring mass in front of him.

The man I didn't know handed him another bucket, but their efforts weren't enough. Fire was a living thing, and it was growing too strong for two mere men to control. It was turning into a beast, and the beast reared its ugly head to the ceiling and beyond.

"Jimmy, get Hour. Get the hell outta here!"

My legs flinched at first, wanting to help the men, but thinking of my sister got them running again. I made my way through the dining hall and to our hallway, coughing up smoke and cinder all the while. When I reached our room, the smoke was thicker than before. Hour still huddled in her corner, knees up to her forehead. She coughed into herself.

The building shook a bit. Some force of nature told the folks sleeping on the second floor to run from this place, and they did so at the same time: a stampede of girls and customers moving quickly and in unison down the stairs and out into the morning fresh air. They might as well have been cattle for how it rocked the saloon.

Even the walls of our storeroom home shook and the wood beneath us trembled.

Though no soul meant to cause the shelf to fall between me and my sister, it happened all the same. The shaking of their combined fear toppled a shelf of sundries that crashed onto the floor. It barely missed the curled ball that was my sister, and she whimpered louder for it.

The air thickened with smoke. Blackness made seeing harder and harder. The clear picture of the little girl in the corner dimmed, obscured by the haze. I coughed again into the sleeve of my shirt, trying to call out Hour's name.

"Hour! Hour, can you see me?"

She said nothing and showed no sign of moving. I crawled on top of the over-turned shelf, a feat in itself seeing as how it weren't at a steady angle smashed against the wall the way it was. I took to crawling on my hands and knees to get to Hour. By that time, I was coughing a good bit, and she was shaking her head back and forth with a violence I knew I could calm.

"I need you to come with me. Hour, can you hear? Come with me. It's a fire. You gotta come with me!"

She made no move, no change to indicate she heard me or wanted to go.

"Come on! We gotta get outta here. It's a fire. Fred's already out there. So's everyone else."

My sister just kept shaking her head. The smoke around us thickened more, and I coughed hard trying to breathe it in. When I reached out to her, trying to grab her arm to pull her along, it was like grabbing at a stone. Hour locked up. There would be no moving her, not without the leverage to get under her and lift her dead weight in my arms. How I might achieve such a feat while working around the broken shelf, I didn't know. But I had to try.

"Please look at me, Hour. Please snap out of it!"

I pulled myself forward a bit, and tried to see a gap big enough for me to slide into. Another coughing fit knocked all of the energy from my body, and I slumped into the shelf below me. I tried to get back up, but the smoke had a hold of my lungs and twisted them like a rope. Reaching out ahead of me, I felt my sister's elbow and tugged as hard as I could.

"Hour please. Please come with me," I said, choking. With every breath I wasn't getting, a bit of energy left my person.

Suddenly, I was moving backward and away from my sister. Something stronger than me had a hold of my feet and dragged me back toward the door. My body scraped along the hard wood surface of the shelf, making me bleed in places on my arm. I saw the dim silhouette of my sister's huddled form vanish before me.

"No no no! Hour!"

Before I knew it, Joseph had his ample arms wrapped around my chest, and he was pulling me from the storeroom. I fought against him as best I could, but years of hauling crates made him stronger. He wrestled me out of the storeroom and into the hallway where another barrage of smoke met us.

"No! Joseph! Hour's still in there!" I screamed through a coughing fit.

"I'll come back in fer her. I can't get you both."

I pulled against him, kicking and hitting where I could. My sister was in there. The only family I had left was shivering in that tiny room alone.

"Go get her, not me! She don't understand. She won't run!"

Joseph locked both arms under mine and around my chest so I couldn't kick at him anymore. He dragged my squirming body backwards out of Diddlin' Dora's and out into the street where a motley array of folks were gathered watching us. The cool, clean air sent goose flesh across my body. The back of my boots hit mud, and a new set of hands held onto me. I was beset on both sides by women, Dora to my left and Missy to my right. Their eyes were wide, and their faces smudged with old makeup and soot. I struggled to stand, but the women wouldn't let go of me.

"Hour! My sister is still in there. Let me go!"

Joseph left me and ran back toward the smoky entrance to Dora's saloon. He threw himself inside, only to be knocked back by the heat. He tried again, but the smoke was so think, he couldn't get three steps in without bending over from the cough.

I struggled once more against the women, but they held fast to me. The fresh air had given me new energy, but not enough against two strong women. I wanted to go after my sister. She was still in there. She wouldn't move to save herself.

"Let go o' me! I need to get to her!" I screamed with tears falling down my face.

"You gonna get yerself killed in the process," said

Missy.

Joseph tried again and again, but the heat and smoke was too much. Even crawling on his belly didn't work. Panic hit me in the chest over and over again. My limbs twitched to run back inside. Everything moved far too fast for me, like a fish I couldn't grab a hold of. My mind couldn't keep up.

A wagon filled with men and water pulled up at that moment. They moved with an impressive urgency toward the back end of the building where the kitchen fire had begun. When Joseph spotted them, he gave up his efforts and stumbled back to us.

"I'm sorry, Jimmy. I can't get past the bar. I'm so sorry."

"No! No, it can't be!" I said, trying to break away from the women and crawl back toward the saloon. "I can't lose her too!"

Joseph grabbed my torso as I got to my knees and held me there. Dora and Missy surrounded us. I reached out to the smoke-filled brothel, crying for my sister and clawing the earth beneath me. Wet brine poured down my face so much I could barely see through it. Snot and all manner of things covered my cheeks and mouth.

"It's okay, Jimmy. Them's the vol'nteers. They'll get the fire out. Then we can get yer sister," offered Missy with no real conviction in her voice. She too was already crying.

Dora and Joseph offered no words. All they could do was solemnly stare on, trying not to look into my eyes. Their silence was all I needed to know. Somewhere behind us I heard the gentle rhythm of a prayer. Hour was lost. No one could survive in smoke like that.

It was then I saw the figure in the blackness. Perhaps it were a figment in the eyes of a desperate boy, but it made the whole world slow down again. I blinked hard against the tears and breathed deep to clear my mind. She was still there, the specter of a woman amid the smoke inside the saloon.

She hadn't the form of a person. Not really. However, there was no mistaking the curve of that face, the long raven hair, and the sturdy arch to her back. The woman turned to look at me with a face I knew so well, a face that had been taking me back again and again in my dreams.

"Cage?" I whispered, but no one heard me.

The image of her began to fade into the blackness. I ached to call out to her. To tell her Hour was inside. To beg her to save her daughter. Everything around me was speeding up again, getting louder. She faded anyway without a word, and my heart sank back into the knowledge I was alone, completely.

"Where's Jane?" asked Dora suddenly.

"Around back by where she normally is, I reckon," answered Joseph.

"No, she ain't," said Dora. "I checked there when I got out. Figured she'd be out here."

It was at that moment we heard the knocking of boots against hard floorboards. A normal sound by most accounts on any other day at Diddlin' Dora's, but on a morning where the saloon was a home to only ghosts, it sent everyone's hearts to beating again. That meant movement, that meant life, and that meant a chance.

The knocking quickened as if someone where running.

I wiped the tears and snot from my face with the back of my hand, staring at the door, waiting for something to happen. Anything. The quiet prayers behind us stopped as well. We all held our collective breaths waiting for what was next.

The dense smoke parted as a figure busted through it and out into the thoroughfare. Only after she left did the choking blackness return to stand vigil where she had been only moments before. Jane pushed her way through the doorway, her face ducked down and her eyes shut. In her arms was the stiff body of my sister. Hour clung to Jane. Her arms wrapped tightly around Jane's neck, and her legs locked around her body. The buckskinned woman held her tiny body close as she stumbled to her knees next to us. Jane turned her head to the left and coughed a good bit of smoke from her lungs. She spat wetted cinder to the ground. We rallied around them.

"Hour? Can you see me? Are you okay?" I asked, trying to see her face.

There was no moving her. Hour's face was buried in Jane's chest and her limbs were locked tightly around her body. She didn't respond at all, and it worried me to no end. When I saw the gentle rise and fall of her little back against Jane's protective arm, I relaxed into the dirt below me. Hour was breathing. She was alive. That's the best I could've hope for.

23

IT TOOK A WHILE for the volunteers to put out the blaze and clear the building. Remarkably, a good bit of the place was still in working order. The fire had begun in the kitchen, a fact that would surely plague Nancy May to her dying day, and it spread to the dining room, storeroom, and parts of the saloon. The rooms upstairs were spared.

When we went back inside, everything smelled of smoke. The pictures and paper on the wall were gray and singed around the edges. Nearly everything in our room was destroyed, though we managed to salvage Hour's penny jug and her colored beads. Fred too was spared. We found him outside cowering under a broken wagon wheel. In the end, hearing the kitten meow was the only thing that would convince Hour to let go of Jane.

The first thing Dora did was run back to her private room and check her safe. She smiled when she returned to us with the knowledge all the money was intact, even the funds raised for our schooling.

We all milled about without words that day. Even Jane moved silently. So many times I tried to run up and thank her, but she wasn't having it. All I got was a wave of a hand in my face and a strange look. Maybe it were too much for her. It certainly was for me. We agreed on silence and slept in close quarters that night in the rooms spared by the fire.

Fire or no fire, our traveling day was still on the horizon. We were to ride with Charlie Utter to the school Jane had picked for us. I tried to convince them to let me stay. Surely, there was much to do to rebuild.

"You nearly lost yer sister to that fire on account of her nature," said Dora when I begged to stay. "Best thing is to get her to folks who can help her with it. We raised that money to get you out, and out you will go."

The money raised was enough to send Hour and me off to school twice over. At least, that's what Dora had told me. I didn't know a thing about school or how much it cost. All I knew was the bit of prospecting my pa had taught me, and the saloon work I learned at her place.

When told how much it was, I tried to give the difference to her. Hour and I only needed enough to get us there and through our schooling. The least I reckoned I owed Dora was some money for the room and board she'd provided us. Perhaps it might pay for the whiskey she'd given for the benefit. The great Madame wouldn't have it.

"You been workin' here fer that, kid. Keep yer money."

"But, you and Joseph, you been so kind. Jane, she saved us."

"Jane won't take it neither. Don't even ask."

I thought on that for a good, long second.

"What if I pay off her drinkin' tab with you?"

Dora's first inclination was to say no. I could tell that in her face, but she stopped herself and looked thoughtful. She considered my proposal while rolling a silver dollar in her left hand. Jane, with all her goodwill, had a tendency to run up quite the tab at Dora's saloon. It was a hot spot between the two women.

"All right, kid, but the rest you keep, you hear me? There's gonna be things you need that ain't paid fer by the school. And no tellin' Jane. Deal?"

"Deal."

We spat on our hands respectively and shook on it.

It was two days before we were to head out. Jane and Dora made arrangements with Charlie Utter to take us to Sturgis where we'd be enrolled in a Catholic boarding school called St. Martin's Academy. Two days was all we had until we said farewell to everything we knew in the world. The idea of a boarding school loomed over me like a beast awaiting in the dark of my nightmares. I knew it was right, but this sort of life was all I had ever known. Anything else seemed terribly odd and frightening. The devil you knew, as it were.

The day before our departure, Jane offered to take me back to our old shanty by the creek to retrieve anything else the other miners might have left. Hour was busy helping Nancy May clean out the old stove, and Joseph had the saloon well at hand, so I agreed.

Dappled sunlight fell on our faces like warming shapes in the brisk air. Summer was over as far as the weather in Deadwood was concerned, and the autumn painter was already getting busy changing the leaves to all manner of colors. The past few days had been blissfully devoid of rain, making the ride an easier one with no mud to contend with, but there were gray clouds in the east building up their bulk and threatening to turn this fine day into a stormy one.

We rode in silence, partly due to my nervous nature when facing the prospect of school, and partly due to the hangover Jane normally suffered from around this hour of the day. I sat atop one of Dora's horses, and Jane rode the crazed, half-Indian horse she had saved me and Hour from. It wasn't just a thing that was said in passing. That horse was Jane's now. No one would touch it, and the thing was wild around everyone else. Under Jane, the horse was so tame he practically purred like Hour's kitten.

We tied the horses at the edge of where the landscape jutted down steeply into the gulch. Below and through the trees the creek and our shanty sat, so we carried on by foot. This part of the land was prone to give way under our steps and early fallen leaves made the floor a canopy of booby traps. It was all too dangerous to go on horseback, so we hoofed it to where our shanty once stood.

I say once stood because it stood no more in a manner of speaking. The thieves and beggars of the land had come through and cleaned us out so thoroughly, not even the canvas that once acted as our walls was left to mark its presence. We nearly passed it by before I recognized the ill-fitting floorboards Pa and I had installed to stave off trench foot. Neither of us had been much of a carpenter, and I had snagged my pant cuffs on loose nails more often than not. Now, those loose nails were all that was left.

Jane didn't say much of anything as I slowly walked the ruins of our former life. A barren tomb of a life if I ever saw one. Everything of value we owned was gone. There was no point looking for Pa's deed to the land. It had been taken first, along with anything of worth that wasn't nailed down. Pots, pans, cups, pillows, blankets. You name it, and it was erased from existence. All that was left were some rotting floorboards and a place that looked much smaller than it had a month ago.

The loss of it all took away my breath. I wasn't so foolish to think it would all be waiting for me, but I thought some scrap might have been left for the children of Hank Glass. His pocket watch for his son or a ribbon for his daughter's hair. There was nothing here. Nothing but some crooked floorboards that we once fussed over and deemed too much of a hassle to redo. A little boy somewhere within me wanted to cry, but the man who enveloped him wouldn't allow for it.

Jane hadn't said a word the whole time. Not a moment's mention or the fleeting thought of a word.

When I turned to look for her, I found her leaning against a nearby tree with her hat tilted down over her eyes. She reminded me of a statue of a person rather than a person. Someone waiting.

"It's . . . it's all gone."

"Yeh."

For the first time since I met her, Jane had blessed little to say. She had been very quiet since the fire.

"They left nothin'."

"Looks to be the way of things."

"I don't get it. They was our neighbors. Some were men my pa trusted, but they left nothin' fer his children."

She turned her head and spat. A fat glob of something or other splat on the dirt a few feet away. I waited for something, anything to come from her mouth that might make all this right, but not a thing was forthcoming. Jane spat again.

"I saw one of 'em at the benefit the other night. I didn't say as much, but I recognized him from the day I come here alone to collect our things. He was there puttin' coins in for donation like everyone else, but all along, he was a thief."

The look I gave was a pleading one. Jane always knew the way of things. There were always words on her tongue to make sense of a scene, to make it sting a little less. When she did speak, it was like she read my mind on the matter.

"Kid, I ain't got nothin' fer you on this one. The day I understand the likes of men will pro'lly be the day I die or thereafter. I wish I could answer you something true 'bout this, there ain't nothin' fer it. All you can do is look forward. Hell, it's all any o' us can do."

The weight of it all was a heavy fog that rolled in over my eyes. I was at a funeral again. This time, it was my home's funeral, and I was mourning something I didn't even understand. Inside the fog, Jane suggested we leave.

"Why'd you let me come here?" I asked her breathlessly.

"Cause you ain't the type to go on word alone. Sometimes you gotta feel a thing, see it, smell it, taste it, before you can dub it true and move along."

I felt my head nod, but I hadn't commanded it to do so. Something somewhere in the back of my brain took the reins and led me and Jane back to our horses without another word between us. Hell, what more could we do?

The next morning was moving day for us. Charlie Utter had readied his wagon for Hour and me, and he had built a small crate for Fred the Kitten to make the journey as well. The thought of asking Hour to leave her kitten here with Dora had come to mind, but I quickly dismissed it. We were going to a new place, and Hour was used to routine. This would all be a difficult adjustment, so I decided Hour got to keep her confidence things. Fred and the colored beads were coming with us, no argument.

A gentle fog hung near the ground even as midmorning brought Charlie Utter's garish wagon to the front of Diddlin' Dora's. I wondered if it had been the same fog that had infected my brain recently. Had it leaked out of my ear in the night and haunted the world of Deadwood or was it left over from the fire? It was a dumb thought, but you think dumb thoughts when you're afraid. I tried not to tremble as I loaded the few meager possessions we had left and an angry kitten onto the wagon with Charlie Utter's help. Hour stood on the floorboards outside Dora's, nervously watching us handling her kitten. Her thumb and forefinger were likely to wear all the paint off of those pearls of hers.

By the time the deed was done, I turned around to see a spectacle of women. There were men too, like Charlie and Joseph, but they were overtaken by all of Dora's girls standing outside in various stages of sleepiness, waiting to see us off. Nancy May had tears in her eyes as she told Hour what a good girl she was and patted her head. Hour's head looked tiny under the large woman's man-sized hand.

Dora, for her part, hugged me against that bosom of hers like she was trying to squeeze and smother me to death with it. She kissed Hour gently on the forehead, knowing she would hate a hug of that magnitude. Joseph shook my hand and slapped my back like a man might another man, and my chest swelled at the meaning of that.

Within a blink of an eye, Lil' Missy was in front of me. No kidding. She wasn't there, then I blinked, and then she was there. For a second I thought she might be a figment or a specter in the smoke, like the fog that leeched from the night before, but when that cinnamon smell wafted over me, I knew it was her. Pretty soon, she was all I could see in the whole world.

"You write me, okay? I mean it, Jimmy Glass. I can read just fine, and Dora's helpin' us all with our letters and such, so you best write me. Promise?"

"I promise. I'll write e'ery day."

Missy giggled, and it sounded like little song birds.

"Easy now. You'll have your studies, so how 'bout once a week?"

"Of course. I'll write you . . . once a week."

There was a thing I needed to say. I knew I might never again have the chance to say it to her in person again because who knew what the future held? The problem wasn't *wanting* to say it. The problem was in the saying it. Words got locked up in my throat and refused to come out. I moved them around in my mouth like marbles, but each one was too hard and thick and stupid to use, so I kept us in silence trying to string the proper words together fit for her.

"Missy, I . . . I wanna say . . . well, what I was hoping to tell you was . . . I love . . ."

Everything shifted because there were lips on my mouth, Missy's lips. She kissed me on the mouth, in front of everyone. Cinnamon swirled around us so all I could hear was the collective gasp of dozens of surprised folks. Somewhere a few girls giggled. Missy released me from the moment, allowing me to float back down to Earth gently. When I looked around, a whole crowd of smiling faces were winking at me.

"Well, kid. I didn't know you had it in you," said Charlie Utter as he nudged me with the point of his elbow.

Scarlet posies blossomed all over my face, and some

of the girls got brave enough to laugh as Missy turned and disappeared among their ranks. I went and stood next to Hour since she was the only one unmoved by Missy's farewell display.

"I s'pose we should get along now if'n we want to make use of the sunlight," said Charlie Utter.

"Not so fast, Charlie Utter, you old windbag of a man, gettin' everything going too damn early. I ain't said my farewells as of yet."

The crowd parted and there stood Calamity Jane, larger than life and smiling. I drunk her in at that moment so I might take her with us to Sturgis in my mind. When she walked up to me, I felt hot tears fall unbidden down my cheeks. I didn't mean for it to happen, and it weren't manly, but there it was.

"Now, don't look so sad, Jimmy Glass. I know I ain't no pretty thing like Lil' Missy yonder, but surely the fear of kissin' a mug as ugly as this one ought not to make a young man cry."

I could no longer hold back the dam. The tears came, and I flung my arms around that woman without abandon. To her credit, she held me just as tight right back. Sobs, the kind that you can't control, racked my body. I was a boy, the one without a mama, once again enveloped in her buckskinned embrace. By the time I pulled away, I had left a wet spot of tears and snot on her shoulder.

"You are a fine man, Jimmy Glass. As fine as any man I've seen. As fine as Bill."

Wiping my eyes, I nodded to her. All my words were used up, and the few I had left were muffled by the sounds of sobbing all around us.

"Thank you, Jane. I reckon we're even now."

"Kid, I reckon the two of us ain't never gonna be even in this here lifetime. That there is a fact that is fine by me."

She shook my hand like a man might, and I shook hers back like a friend.

Jane kneeled down in front of Hour while she stared, unmoved, at the floor. There wouldn't be much of a reaction to good-byes from her. I wasn't even sure Hour knew what the concept meant after her explanation of Pa's death, but Jane wasn't going to let her leave without trying to say her piece to the little girl.

"Hour, honey, you gotta go now with yer brother. There's this great school where yer goin', and it has comfy beds for you and lots of mice for Fred, and yer just gonna love it there. You mind the teachers and yer brother and you'll be just fine."

"Jane?" asked Hour without lifting her gaze from the floor.

It was a little thing, but it made Jane's lower lip begin to quiver. Her own river of tears was beginning to cut trails through the canyons of dirt on her face. She managed to swallow enough of it back to answer.

"No, no baby. I can't come with you. I hafta stay here. They don't teach no schoolin' to the likes of me. Besides, who's gonna argue with Dora if I ain't around?"

Jane tried to smile, but it was strained. Not for the first time, I wished Hour was normal. It wasn't for me this time. It was for Jane. Despite all her gruff exterior, all she wanted was for this little girl to hug her.

Maybe she wanted a semblance of the embrace she had with Hour during the fire. For all Jane had done, she deserved it, but you can't force a child like Hour to be normal, no matter how much you wanted it and who you wanted it for.

"All right, little Hour, the most beautiful girl ever, it's time to say goodbye. I ain't gonna try to make you say . . ."

Hour's face looked up into Jane's then, cutting off her words. It wasn't the mechanical way she tended to do sometimes. The movement was a deliberate one, as though she were thinking it out step by step. I felt my mouth hang open at the sight. My sister was here and present in the moment. She was right there with us and listening like any little girl might. With all the effort in the world of creation, she managed four little words, each in itself a thing to be said clear and loud and proud. Each enough to bring down even the strongest of people.

"I love you, Jane."

24

SOMEWHERE ACROSS THE LAND, eighteen
years later, those same tears fell again across the same
dirty face. Sure, it weren't as youthful, but the same
crystalline eyes blinked those tears away as they did all
those years before. I sniffled for what I was worth and
poked the fire with one of the nearest sticks to distract
from my less-than-manly state of being. It wasn't until
both of our sleeves were damp with brine that we spoke
of real things once again.

"Why don't you go rustle us up some grub, Jimmy
Glass? I haven't eaten in a coon's age, and I reckon I
could eat 'bout anything right 'bout now. Cooky's over
at the chuck wagon yonder. It's the one painted uglier
than Charlie Utter's old box."

The leaves crackled and a twig snapped as I stood from my post and walked away from the woman who changed my life forever. In fact, every step I made was noisy. My last trail boss told me I couldn't sneak up on a deaf drunkard in the boots I bought. He was right, but those boots cost me more than I could have imagined when I was twelve and living in Deadwood. There was a lot of pride in owning something outright you never thought was possible before.

I sauntered up to Cooky's wagon and waited my turn behind a man I recognized as the host of the show. The moonlight gleamed off the waxed tips of his elegantly groomed mustache. He wore a fine suit and checked the time on a chained piece with the nearby torchlight. The man smelled of tobacco and appraised me when I approached.

"You the one been talkin' with Jane?"

"Yes, sir."

"How you know her?"

"We knew each other in Deadwood a long time ago. Just catchin' up."

"I see. Jane is a nice gal, as far as those types go, but watch your wallet, if you take my meaning."

"I'm afraid I don't, sir. You callin' her a thief?"

It got my spine up, but I showed no sign of it to the fellow.

"No, I reckon not a thief the way the dictionary might define it, but that woman'll talk you into buying plenty for her. I can attest to that first hand. I bet she sent you here to buy her dinner?"

I smiled. It couldn't be helped.

"Yes, sir. She did just that."

"If I was you, I'd haul, son, before your pay is gone for good. Just a friendly warnin'. Calamity Jane is a great lady, and a hell of a performer, but aptly named if you catch my meanin'."

A tray of food was provided and the man with the waxed mustache took it in hand. He paid the aproned cook inside the wagon and nodded to him. Cooky scowled, glared at me, and then looked back to the waxed man. I wondered if there was a wad of spit sitting there in the mess of beans on his plate with the look he gave.

"Next," he barked without any fanfare.

"I guess that's me," I said, stepping in front of him to place my order.

"Oh, and don't worry about me getting dinner for Jane. I will owe that woman until the end of my days, I reckon."

Tipping my hat, I bowed a bit to excuse the confused man with his dinner. He said no further words to me but turned around and walked away. When I faced the wagon once again, I found that Cooky was looking upon me in a kinder light. Perhaps, after all, I would not be eating his spittle with my dinner as I assumed the last customer was doomed to do.

The menu read as most chuck wagons did. Everything was brown and hot and named something other than what it really was. My choices consisted of Sonofabitch Stew, Mysteries, and Mexican Strawberries. I ordered two of each, and tipped Cooky a little extra in the hopes my food would truly be spit free.

Sonofabitch Stew I had heard of before. It was pretty much a mug stew with anything and everything handy thrown in—heavy on the potatoes. Mexican Strawberries were easily identified as beans, but the Mysteries were, well, a mystery, until my trays showed up on Cooky's counter. Each order had a link of some sort of sausage. My best guess would put the name having to do with the mystery of what sort of meat was in the casing. I hadn't seen many dogs around and hoped it was due to a high population of coyotes and not the ingredients in Cooky's sausages.

Regardless, I thanked Cooky and headed back to Jane with my trays of hot brown food in hand. She thanked me when I handed her a tray, then offered me a swig of her whiskey. We sat there, eating and drinking in amicable silence for a spell, neither one of us wanting to broach the next subject we both knew was bound to come up. It weren't for fear, and it weren't because we were awkward around each other. Neither of us had a yellow streak in us, and we had spent the last few hours reliving the past together.

The thing of it was, all that time, it left a hole. Jane and I sat a few feet from one another, next to a tall fire in the darkness of the evening, but those few feet might have well been a mile for the distance eighteen years will add to them. Somehow it was easier talking about the past. It was a time in our lives when there was no gulf of years, no hole in the middle. Back then, we were friends, and talking about back then was comfortable. Now, reaching across to her to finish the untold story was like trying to shout it across a canyon.

"I still write Dora," began Jane.

Her edge of the canyon got a little closer.

"Yeah, she still in Deadwood?" I asked.

"More or less. She lives there sort of permanent, but she travels a lot too, to visit her other places in the other cities. She and Joseph are still married. Still together."

"That's good. Seems like ev'rywhere you turn, the story's otherwise. If there was two people supposed to be together, it were them, I reckon."

My edge of the canyon crept closer still, and Jane looked up at me with that crooked stare of hers. I knew that stare, even after eighteen years I knew it. The gulf between us shrunk even further. I could see the question skitter across the plain of her mind before it even left her lips.

"You and Missy ever . . .?"

I smiled and poked the fire with my stick again. The sparks dazzled the night and lit up our section of the dark with little false fireflies.

"We wrote, and we still do. She's runnin' Dora's place in Belle Fourche. I've visited her a few times. Life of a cowboy don't lend itself to sittin' still, so we visit when we can."

Jane smiled.

"I figured that filly might've ruined you on all others. You were so smitten by her back then. Never seen a worse case of it."

"Yeh, I won't lie none. Not to you. I ain't never loved a woman like Missy. Not ever. I tried a few times, but nah. Never quite got over that one."

We laughed a while at the absurdity of love and silly

campaigns our young hearts force on us in its glorious name. By the time the real question came, Jane and I were practically next to one another. The grand opening of time that had yawned before was now only a crack in the Earth. I gazed up into those crystalline eyes of hers, the ones that looked so much like Hour's, and awaited what I knew would come next.

"Your sister, is she . . .?"

"Not dead, if that is your meanin'."

"It is. How is she?"

"Hour is a woman unto herself, thanks to you."

I paused to let Jane release the breath I could feel she was holding in. All these years, and she never knew if her good deed helped that girl. She had never known what became of the troubled child she found in Deadwood. Eighteen years Jane had waited to hear that news. Eighteen years she had been holding that breath.

"The nuns at the boardin' school, they had dealt with such children before. No beatin's like others might have gotten. They gave her a routine and played to things she liked. Animals mainly. She learned to read and write, and a speech teacher worked on her talkin'."

"She's normal now?"

"No, she ain't normal, but she is independent. There's some stuff she ain't never gonna be good at. Folks conversate with her, but she gets confused sometimes when what she says makes 'em mad and the like."

"She talks to people?"

This one came out like a burst of steam, and I was again reminded how long it had been since Jane knew my sister—when four words strung together was a miraculous thing. I had watched her almost every day for a time as she improved measure by measure. Looking back to Hour eighteen years ago and thinking she might someday speak with people and look them in the eyes without trouble would have taken my breath away too.

"Yeh. She's even married, Jane. Has her a young doctor up in Kansas City. He's a kind fella. I sure do like how patient he is with her. They have a piece of land out there where Hour has her work. She's one of them animal doctors. Works on horses mainly."

"Horses. She works on horses?" she asked.

The tears were flowing again in a trickle down the worn grooves around her eyes. Her words were small and breathless, a strange sound coming from the legendary Calamity Jane. Shock chilled me a bit and I wondered for a moment if I should go sit beside her. The idea of needing to comfort Jane was a foreign one, and I wasn't sure how to act on it or if I should act on it at all. How did a mere cowpoke go comfort a person like her? Was it even possible?

Jane wiped her face with her sleeve and continued without my help.

"She purdy? I always figured she would be. I s'pose she must be to get a young doctor and all. Funny how what you want fer a girl can also be the thing you fear fer her too."

"She's gorgeous. A picture," I said.

"A picture. I knew it. I just knew she would be a picture of a thing."

"You always made quite an impression on her you

know."

"How you figure?"

"She kept the name you gave her when she got married."

"She didn't take that feller's name?"

"No, she did, but when she changed her last name she also added a middle one. Her name is Hour Glass Williams."

"Hour Glass Williams, the horse doctor. As I live and breathe. You know, I thought about her so many times. Her and you. I always wondered . . ."

Jane's face drifted off somewhere I couldn't follow. It was somewhere inside that eighteen years where I never went, where I didn't know her. The place was dark and forbidden for the likes of me and Hour. I frowned and looked down at my boots.

"We tried writin', you know. We wrote Dora, but she wrote back sayin' you left Deadwood. She promised to try to foreword on our letters, but your trail went cold fer a spell, and we stopped trying. I didn't think I'd ever see you again, Jane. Where did you go?"

"Oh, I went my way. Here and there. Was in Texas fer a spell. Got married and had me a daughter. A proper one this time."

"What happened?"

"I did, kid. Bein' a mom and a wife, it ain't a life fer the likes of me. I love my girl. I loved her enough to give her to some fine folks who would be good to her. Ain't fittin' to have a mama drunk as a skunk all hours of the day. Still can't sleep in a proper house with a roof. What sorta mama can't sleep inside like a civilized person, I ask you?"

"You're too hard on yerself, Jane."

"Ah, I can stand the gaff. I know what I am. A wanderer, like you, Jimmy Glass."

A gentle silence fell between the two of us like a newly laundered sheet in the wind. Nothing bad loomed inside it, but nothing good did either. It was a purgatory sheet of silence, but neither of us minded much. It wasn't until the question came to me that I thought to end the quiet around us. Once the question was there, there wasn't much I could do to not fixate on it. It was how my mind worked. A wanderer's mind, as Jane might call it.

"Jane, I have a question fer you."

"Shoot from the hip, kid. I ain't holdin' back nothin'."

"Did you even really know Custer?"

The night air was broken by Jane's sudden barking laughter. It came from her in a sudden burst and nearly knocked the wind out of me. Somewhere in the distance, a pack of coyotes howled, and the nearby horses stamped the earth, startled by the sudden outcry. It was an infectious thing, for soon, I was laughing along with her. We didn't stop until the wind had left us and our eyes were blurred from tears. My sides ached from it.

"That was an unexpected goddamned question!"

"Ah, but did you?"

"It don't matter a lick, kid. All them high n' mighty officers were tha same as far as my story goes. Whether it were General George Armstrong Custer, General Crook, or General Terry, they was all a bunch of know-it-alls who didn't listen a lick to their scouts' advice. Just look at the famous fuckin' demise of General Custer."

"Why don't you ever tell the true stories? Me and Hour, all those people you nursed in the pest tent, the stagecoach full of folks? You saved our lives. Why don't you tell people those stories? You're a real hero, Jane."

"I don't know nothin' 'bout that kid, but if there's one thing I have learned in this world of shows and legends, it's that folks don't want real stories. They wanna hear that I knew Custer, and they wanna hear I brought Jack McCall to justice. They wanna hear the stories they heard a thousand times before. The only thing that makes my story worth the dime they payin' is the name attached to it. No, kid, if'n you wanna be a legend, best leave the truth outta it. No one wants to hear the truth, not from a dried up old bit o' leather like me."

"I would," I said to the old bit of leather in front of me.

"Ha. Well, you never were very bright, I must say," said Jane while laughing.

We both chuckled our part without knowing where to steer it. I had asked my questions, and she had learned her piece of the puzzle, but something seemed missing. I didn't want to leave her here, but what else could I do? An offer to come with me to Kansas City came to mind, but she wouldn't accept that. Not in three lifetimes. She had a wanderer's heart, and there was no cure for that sort of thing.

"Farewell, Jane. You may not see it, but you saved us. To me, that's better than any tall tale even you could invent."

I stood and collected my hat. There was more on my tongue, more than just a farewell, but I couldn't form it. The measure of it was there, but the refined edges were not. A feeling lurked in my mind, an ugly one, that I would never have a chance to see this woman again. Surely, if that was so, something more should be said.

"Jimmy, tell Hour . . . Well, just tell her, won't you?"

I tipped my hat and nodded to her. There was more, so much more to be said. All those prophets and poets they taught me about at St. Martin's would have been able to find the words, the right ones. Alas, I was merely a mortal, and a small one at that. I turned on my heel and began my journey away from Calamity Jane, feeling every inch unworthy of my current place in the world.

It was then that the wind struck me, and with it, it carried her words. If I were a betting man, I would have placed a silver dollar on that wind coming from the direction of a little farm outside Kansas City. Maybe it came from an unknown place in Texas or a rowdy spot in Deadwood. Those words, the perfect words, were now mine to use.

"I love you, Jane."

I said them to her without looking back, never seeing their impact.

The wind whipped up beneath them and echoed their song again and again and again. Two sentences that should have been one but for a poor girl's handicap. The breeze picked them up and carried them off over the plains and across time. Words that swirled only moments around a cemetery where Wild Bill and Jane would rest in the future. Friends and neighbors and family added to them. All the people who were touched lent their voices. They rang like a bell in the air all around us now and back then and into the soon-to-be so Jane might never want for hearing them again in her lifetime.

I love you, Jane.

Legends may weep, and if they do, we mortals ought not to witness it, for who are we to judge their tears?

25

AS SOON AS I saw the rider headed my way, the day turned itself a measure hotter than before. My wrists itched suddenly beneath the sleeves, and beads of sweat formed where the bandana touched my neck. I was on the road to Belle Fourche, and the only person in the world who knew that fact was Missy, yet something told me this fellow was here for me. A little notion somewhere in my mind said it. Even though it were nothing more than a whisper, I could still hear the damn thing. A good portion of dread rode along with me suddenly, and the weight of it was nearly too much for my horse to bear. The rider approached, and I could honestly say I never knew the man. That fact didn't lift my burden though.

I slowed my horse's pace to a stop and the fellow

did the same. He looked barely older than a school boy. He was tense and itchy, an urgency haunted that gaze of his, and I aimed to know what it was. I nodded to him in greeting.

"What's the hurry?"

"You wouldn't happen to be a Jimmy Glass, would you?"

The sound of my name coming from the lips of a stranger was disconcerting at best. I tried my hardest to hide that fact. Nothing could be gained by showing your cards too early in any situation. However, it was my reckoning that only men with news of death or illness rode with the names of men they didn't know, and my spine shivered with the possibilities.

"Yessir, that's me."

"Oh thank the good lord. That woman said she'd tan my hide if'n I took too long findin' you. I reckoned she'd do it too. She scared me half to death."

"What woman?"

"The Madame woman. Diddlin' Dora herself. She said to tell you to meet them at the Belle Fourche train station by evenin'. I reckon it's important. She paid me a whole dollar just to tell you that."

"Thank you," I said, flipping a coin in the young man's direction.

I trotted ahead as he fumbled off his saddle to retrieve his coin from the grass. No part of me wanted company on this trail, especially not from messengers who didn't know me but knew my name. The fact of the matter was I had been headed to Belle Fourche, already pert near there at the outskirts of the town, to see Missy. I had written to her a month ago to plan the trip, and now the great Madame Dora DuFran was sending messengers to reroute me. Dora mainly stayed in Deadwood these days, and Missy ran her place in Belle Fourche. It weren't odd that Dora would be paying a visit to Missy's neck of the woods, but something about this smelled sour. My belly wouldn't sit still as I wondered what had happened.

It was just before sundown when I arrived at the train station in Belle Fourche. I thanked the heavens above to see my Missy, just as lovely as I had left her, standing among a pile of luggage on the platform. Reds and purples from the yawning sun lit her from the west. Fading rays sent her shadows streaking across the wooden platform. A gentle breeze moved her hair away from her eyes like a lady in a picture. Angels didn't look that good.

My initial thinking had been along the lines of something sinister happening to Missy, and to see her face smile when I approached relaxed an intensely chewed up part inside my chest. She wore blue and black from heel to head—a vision if I ever saw one. I lifted her in my arms and swung her round. She kissed me as I took in her scent.

"I have missed you," I whispered beneath her hat.

She played at batting me away, smiling all the while.

"You ain't gonna start that marriage talk again, are you? I don't think I have it in me to turn you down a third time. Not with this new scruff."

Missy ran her fingers through my newly trimmed beard. It was short to be sure, but with age, the patchy sparse bits had blossomed into a far more manly spread across my chin. Once, in an intimate morning moment, Missy had told me of her fondness for beards, so I took it in my head to grow one for her.

"I have many things to ask you in private, but for now, I want to know why I got grabbed by a messenger on the trail here? What's goin' on? Where's Dora?"

Missy's face fell, and the enchantment we had been weaving together unraveled around us. As if called from the ether, Madame Dora DuFran, in all her finery, made her presence known with a loud stomp of a boot on the floorboards next to us. Joseph stood next to her, a bit pudgier than I remembered, but smiling widely at me. Dora, for her part, stood with her hands on her hips, a sideways smirk on her face as she appraised me.

"Mr. Jimmy Glass," she said with her grandiose voice.

I was a child again, a silly twelve-year-old boy, and despite myself, I lept into the grand woman's arms. Without abandon, without shame, and without any thought to others around me, I held that woman. God bless her, she hugged me back. I was still her man, just like I had been all those years ago. A tender part of me would always be that man for her.

When we released, she slapped my arm and dabbed at the spots underneath her eyes. I had made her tear a little, and it was apt to ruin her makeup. Joseph leaned over and shook my hand while she fixed herself. I marveled at the fact that I was taller than he was now.

"What's happenin', Dora? A messenger found me and said to come here. We coulda met at the saloon. I was headed there to see Missy."

"We weren't gonna be there, kid. It's Jane. She came up this way a piece ago lookin' real bad. I came up here and gave her a job at the Belle Fourche place cleaning and the like. But the drinkin', it's the same. Her body can't take it anymore. She started slowin' down something fierce."

"I told her she could stay as long as she wanted," interrupted Missy. "I said she didn't hafta clean and the like if she needed to rest. Dora told her the same."

"You can imagine how well that went over," added Joseph with a sad laugh.

"This mornin' we found a note by her bed saying farewells and the like. Well, it was as close as Jane gets to sayin' the farewells. But it said she was going to Deadwood to be with Bill."

"To be with Bill? That means . . ."

"That means she's aimin' to go and die. The damn fool she is. She wants to run away and die in a ditch like a dog or somethin'. Well, we ain't gonna let her. That woman ain't passing this life without a friend next to her. I won't have it."

Dora looked likely to start crying again. Joseph placed a tender hand on her shoulder, and she straightened up.

"The train folks said she boarded the train to Deadwood last night, but the conductor had to stop in Terry just outside Deadwood proper because Jane was drinkin' and vomitin' everywhere. Terry ain't nothin' but a mining camp, but they procured her a room at the Calloway Inn. She's there and she's alone. Not for long though."

"I'm comin' too."

"Damn right you are, Jimmy Glass. Joseph already purchased your ticket."

The train ride was one of magic. Nothing spectacular inhabited the train so to speak, and the conductor did his duty with no more vigor than any other, but being among these people sparked a homesickness in me I hadn't known lived. My ever-present wanderlust took a back seat in the train, letting me have a little bit of home.

Jane was dying somewhere, yet it didn't seem possible. Calamity Jane was a hero, and heroes, they didn't die. Did they? Was it possible? For me, she was invincible. Jane was a marvel, but she was dying somewhere alone. A piece of me refused to believe it.

Here I found myself, arm in arm with the most beautiful woman I had ever known and speaking to two people to whom I owed my life. We laughed and talked of times far gone. Dora and Joseph told story after story of the great calamity that was Jane. I relived my first encounter with her, and my embarrassment at thinking she was a man.

It was impossible, wasn't it? Amidst all that cheer and love, surely it couldn't be that somewhere a woman as powerful a force as Jane was withering away. Even now, she was a specter haunting our section of the train, letting us not forget the parts we might have missed in her story. She seemed to float near Dora especially, trying to make her refrain from leaving out the fights where she had bested the great Madam. I just couldn't reconcile it all. Legends don't die.

"What about her daughter?" I asked when the conversation had lulled. "Back in Abilene, Jane said she'd had a daughter. Shouldn't we write her or somethin'?"

Everyone looked to Dora for answers. After all, she would be the person to know such things. She sighed and stared at nothing in particular with the vacant look of regret.

"Maude, yes. Jane gave her to a woman named Sadie Beck ta raise. Sadie was a sister-in-law or somethin' of the sorts I think. The story was never the same when I asked. As I recall, Jane tried to visit Maude a few times when she got older, but she was . . . well . . . drunk. We all know how she gets. After a spell of visits, Maude told her to leave and not come back."

We all nodded silently, and I tried not to judge a girl I didn't know. A mother who gave you up is hard enough, but a drunk mother who gave you up would be a might bit harder to take for long. Jane was a mighty potent force. And that could wear down even the most patient person over time.

"I still have her address, but I didn't think she'd want to be here. Jane didn't say much about it, but her face was a shade different when I saw her after their last fight."

Uncertainty didn't sit right on Dora's face. It screwed the edges of her mouth downward in an uncomfortable fashion. Missy reached across the void to take Dora's hand. They shared a brief look of feminine sympathy, a kindness Joseph and I could only guess at.

"Perhaps she'll change her mind. Best to write her

when we get to Terry. Don't you reckon? I can help you find the words," said Missy, squeezing her hand.

"Thank you."

When we reached Terry, the moon was high and the town quiet. In Deadwood or Belle Fourche, this hour would have witnessed plenty of raucous talk and drinking, but here it seemed that the world was already in mourning. Briefly, I wondered if we were too late.

The conductor pointed across a small thoroughfare to an even smaller hotel before tipping his hat to us and bidding us good night. We crossed the silent road and entered the hotel where a tall man greeted us from behind a counter.

"We are lookin' for a woman," said Dora. "She came in last night, sick. The conductor helped her get a room here. Goes by the name Jane."

"Yeah, I know the one. I hope you folks have some money to pay her way. Sent a doctor up to her an' every-thin'. Said she weren't long fer this world with the state of her innards."

Dora leveled a glare at the man, and he softened under the pressure of it.

"I mean, of course we gave her every consideration."

"You better had," I chimed in. "That's Calamity Jane you have up in yer room. *The* Calamity Jane. You best thank yer lucky stars you have the good fortune to house her. This'll put yer little hotel on the map."

His face fell and the man started wringing his hands. A cold sweat draped itself over his face like a veil of water beads.

"Oh my. That's who she is? Well, obviously then,

the . . . uh . . . the room is free of charge. And the doc. I wouldn't dream of . . ."

"We will also require two rooms," said Missy, her nose sufficiently in the air. "One for my husband and I, and one for our friends."

"Yes, yes of course. Friends of Calamity Jane stay free of charge as well."

He fumbled with room keys and told us where Jane was staying.

"There's a grand restaurant just right . . ."

"Thank you," interrupted Dora, shutting the man down with the raise of one finger.

We ascended a very rickety staircase without further discussion with the hotel's manager, Missy's arm in mine. I leaned in close to whisper to her.

"My husband and I? Tryin' somethin' on, are you?"

"Maybe. Or maybe hotel people ain't partial to renting rooms to unwed couples. Trust me, I know from experience they normally ain't."

Dora was the first in Jane's room. She didn't even try to go to her own room until she had seen Jane with her own eyes and dubbed her living. We three, for our part, stood outside the door with a pile of bags while an argument commenced inside the hotel room. Jane might be dying, but she pitched a tolerable fit. The sound of her relieved my nerves and lifted my spirit. She wouldn't die, she couldn't die. Not Jane.

When Dora emerged from the fray, her mask was slipping. Bags hung beneath her eyes, and even though there was a fair amount of rose in her cheeks from shouting, it was superficial on her graying skin. My hopes vanished at the sight of her.

"She ain't good," Dora said with a breath long held.

"Is she . . . goin' to die?"

It was Missy who posed the question, but all of us asked it.

"I think so. It ain't good."

"When?"

"I don't rightly know, but here's how I see it. The damn fool wants to die alone, but we ain't gonna let her. It ain't right. So, I will take a shift tonight. I'll stay with her so she won't go alone. Then, Joseph can take her in tha mornin'. Jimmy can have the afternoon, and so on. If'n one of us thinks it's time and can get tha others, do so. Okay?"

We all agreed, and Dora readied herself for the fight that was coming. She entered the room and ducked just before a glass shattered on the wall where her head had been only a second ago. I made to go in and help her, but she waved me away.

"Get your fat carcass outta here, Dora DuFran! I ain't wantin' nobody seein' me this'a way. I told you, god dammit!"

Joseph made a motion to go in with her, but Dora's hand stopped him as well. Her face hardened, and she shook her head.

"You got the shift in the mornin'. Go get some sleep, Joseph. Both of you, I got this."

Dora shut the door just as another barrage of cursing hit our ears. Not knowing what else to do, I helped the man to his room with all of Dora's luggage and bid him a good night. Missy and I went to our room where sleep became an illusive enemy. We spent some tender time together as we were wont to do. That part was nice, but the usual relaxed feeling it gave me after never came. I fidgeted under the quilt and Missy smacked my knee.

"You keep that up, and I'll send you off to sleep with Joseph," she teased.

"Na, he ain't as fine at this part as you. He does snore less though."

Missy slapped my knee again, and we laughed as I held her closer. Silence fell again over the two of us. It was an old blanket, that silence. Warm and tender and full of things unsaid. The peculiar thing about an old friend like that was it often encouraged the type of talking that was not fit for the hard light of day. Anything, I supposed, was better than being left alone with those unsaid things.

"You worried about Jane?"

"Yes'm. I hate feelin' helpless. I want to do somethin', but I don't know what."

"Me too."

"I ain't worth my salt, am I?"

"What do you mean, Jimmy?"

"Hour don't need me anymore, I can't help Jane, and you ain't gonna marry me."

"Who says I ain't gonna marry you?"

I sat up and looked into her eyes. Her hair was splayed so pretty on the pillow, like curvy sun rays on snow. A little smile pulled at one side of her mouth, but I wasn't reading the tale behind it. This was a game somehow, I just knew it, but the rules were hidden from me.

"You did . . . twice."

"You weren't listenin'. I said 'no.'"

"Yeah, what am I missin' exactly?"

"No ain't never."

I laid my head back down on the pillow, and she fit herself into the crook of my arm. It was her place, this spot. She knew it were hers too. Missy always found a home there, her head on my shoulder with one arm wrapped around my chest. This place was made for her.

Truth was what it was. Hard facts were difficult to ignore. Many years had passed since I knew the blonde slip of a girl at Dora's place in Deadwood. Many more had passed since she knew the gangly protective brother of a broken little girl. I was older now than Jane was when I met her. Funny, that idea. Funny and strange and sad all at once.

We were different, older for sure. Without a little girl to protect, the years had made a wanderer out of me, but they had been kinder to Missy. Sure, she had little sagging pockets around her belly, and those cheekbones didn't hold her skin the way they used to. A spring chicken she was not, but to me, she would always smell of cinnamon. In my truth, she was and would always be perfect, and that was the only truth that mattered to me.

"I don't bed anyone else. Not anymore. I haven't in a while."

"So, what does that mean?"

"It means no ain't never."

Sometimes, life tells you to stop. It won't get better

than that, it says. Best not to push her. I felt that then. Even though I wanted to press the issue, I refrained. Pulling the quilt up over us, she moved closer to me. Cinnamon swirled around us, and finally, sleep came to me.

With the morning came breakfast downstairs in the hotel's adjoining restaurant. Dora made a brief appearance, long enough to grab some bacon, coffee, and bread. She looked frazzled and drained, as though she had done battle the evening before. I was eager to see Jane, but after seeing Dora, I worried after how our reunion might go. She spoke little about Jane's condition, but none of what she said was promising.

Around three in the afternoon, Joseph came knocking on our hotel room door. I answered it to find him looking beaten down with a cascade of coffee splashed on the front of his shirt. He stank of bile and vomit, and my heart sank further.

"It's your turn, Jimmy," he said sullenly.

I nodded to the man, and he lumbered away back to his room.

Jane's room was quiet when I walked inside it. The thudding of my heart was all I could hear inside my own head. Looking around, I took inventory of the damage. Several broken glasses littered the floor. There was a white wash basin broken in two next to the only chair in the room. A tray that once might have contained breakfast laid smashed in the corner. It appeared as if someone had attempted to clean up some of the wreckage but given up. When I laid eyes on the actual woman, the sight was all too familiar.

The buckskins she normally wore were in a pile in the corner, and she wore a man's long underwear beneath the quilts of the bed. Her hair was black in appearance but not in natural color, soaked with sweat and wildly stuck to her pillow. Jane twisted and writhed with feverish agitation. The smell was that of heat, an unnatural heat, along with bile and sweat. She lay there grappling with an unknown foe, her skin looking hollow and drained of blood, as if she were being replaced with wax.

It was eerie, the similarities, and for a moment, I was transported back in time to another place with a different dying woman. Even the damn quilt had a star pattern on it. My breath caught in my throat. I hadn't even known I made a noise until Jane opened her eyes to look at me.

"Jimmy? Jimmy Glass?" she asked weakly.

I grabbed the chair and pulled it up to the side of the bed as she stared at me through graying eyes. They were red-rimmed and cloudier than when I last saw her. She searched my face for a long time, and I tried to smile at her.

"Is that you under that awful beard?"

"It's me, Jane."

I reached under the blankets and found her hand. It was clammy and hot to the touch with fever, but I held it in between mine anyway. Jane was in a sort of awe, staring at me. This wasn't at all what I had expected. There seemed to be no more fight left in her. A terrible note of sadness accompanied that thought.

"I'm cold," she said.

There was a spare quilt folded at the end of the bed. I stood, and draped it over her.

"Is that better?"

Jane didn't answer. She merely gazed into my face, apparently enamored with something. Not knowing what else to do, I took her hand again. When she blinked, it was a slow, deliberate blink. Every time she did it, it looked to all the world like she was closing her eyes to sleep, but then she'd struggle to open them again and stare in wonderment at my face.

"Did Hour send you?"

"What? No, Jane. She's with her husband. She don't know I'm here. But I'll tell her. I'm gonna send fer her. There's a telegraph office . . ."

"No. No. Ain't time. I got a letter fer her over yonder. Give it to her, would you, Jimmy?"

I looked in the direction of her gesture, and there sat a small stack of letters. Apparently, it was one of the only things she had that was hers in the room. I wondered briefly if Jane owned anything anywhere anymore.

"Give it to her."

"I will, Jane. I'll make sure of it."

"The others go to my daughter . . . my other one . . . my blood one. Dora knows where she is. They need to get to her. It ain't much or even . . . enough . . . but it's important."

"We'll make sure, Jane. She'll get them."

She smiled then. It was a weak little thing. A smile I normally only saw on her when the liquor had taken her over and she was near sleep. But this wasn't sleep, this was something else, and Jane hadn't had any liquor. She shook her head slowly, struggling to focus on my face.

"Jane? Jane, you okay?"

"I still can't believe it's you, Jimmy Glass. Outta all the fuckin' people in this world, you're the one that is here to send me on. I coulda sworn it'd be Hour. That Injun gal, she said . . ."

Her tongue sort of lolled and ended her sentence there. Those once crystalline eyes of hers were gray as they rolled up in her head. Her body was still now, no longer struggling against its unknown foe. Life drained from her face right in front of me. She lacked the will to move. I hadn't thought it possible, but her stillness was more terrifying than her fits. I tried desperately to hide it, but my voice shook under the weight of fear.

"Jane? Jane, how are you feeling? Are you still cold?"

"I ain't feeling nothin', Jimmy Glass."

The words came out lethargic and slurred. Something inside me, something that knew more than me, told me that this was the end. This was it. I ran to the door and hollered out into the empty hallway.

"Missy, Dora, Joseph, come now!"

I slammed the door behind me, satisfied with the sound of shuffling in the hallway. There wasn't time to check who it was. I didn't dare leave Jane alone the way she was. Nothing to do but hope the proper people heard me.

When I got back to Jane, she looked almost gone, but her eyes found me again in the murky world she now found herself in. I held her hand, but she didn't hold mine back. That part of her was already dead.

"Bill. I want to be near Bill."

"Don't worry, Jane, you will be. I promise."

There was a commotion behind me as an unknown number of people entered the room. I didn't look, I didn't dare look at them and turn away from her. Every breath of hers was a struggle, and I held on tight to her hand as she slipped away between my fingers. The part of her that was Jane pulled gently away from me like an ebbing tide. I held on tighter to her hand, but there was no use in it. You couldn't pull back the waves. They left when they so pleased.

In an instant, Dora was there on the opposite side of the bed. The look on her face, the longing of it, made me want to turn away. Tears came silently at first, but the racking sobs followed close behind. It weren't right, seeing a woman like Dora in that way. Letting go of Jane's hand, I stood and turned to be face to face with Missy. Her eyes were screwed up with sadness and tears. Her lower lip quivered.

"Jane?"

"She's gone," I said.

That was all there was to say. Words were not meant to be spoken in a time like this for they would do nothing but come up terribly short. Joseph went to Dora and held her. Missy collapsed in my arms and sobbed there for a long while. We four, the friends of Calamity Jane, were there for her passing on August 1, 1903.

I found very few words in the coming three days. There were matters to attend to and a funeral to arrange. Terry was blessedly close to Deadwood, and we transported Jane's body by train to the place she wished to be buried. Missy and I went on ahead to make arrangements for the funeral and to make sure there were rooms available at Diddlin' Dora's for the two of us. I didn't recognize any of the girls there, and Dora had even hired a new cook. Nancy May had gone off to California. It still felt like the old place to me though, alive and breathing with the number of people in it, and I was glad to be staying there.

Upon our arrival, we were approached by the Society of Black Hills Pioneers. They had heard of Jane's passing and wished to help us in her burial. Arrangements were made at the Mount Moriah cemetery and at the First Methodist Church. Deadwood hadn't been big enough to host a proper church the last I'd seen of her, but that had been some time ago.

On the fourth day of August, we set to the task of laying Jane to rest. Dressed in our Sunday best, the four of us joined a barrage of people spilling into the First Methodist Church of Deadwood. Some wept like fools in front of the closed casket containing what remained of our friend. Others tittered and gossiped among each other like hens, looking this way and that. I wondered how many here actually knew Jane, and how many were here because of the spectacle. Being present at the burial of a legend would be a tale to tell the grandchildren. Still, I scowled when I caught the hens in the act.

Dora and Missy had indeed sent word to Jane's daughter along with the letters Jane had written and charged us with passing along. There had been no reply. Whether the silence had been purposeful or just out of not receiving the notice in time, we didn't know for sure. I wondered if perhaps her daughter would try to attend the funeral, but there was no way to know her in the crowd, having never seen her face. Most of those paying their respects were a sea of strangers to me.

In Deadwood I enlisted a messenger to take Jane's letter and my own to Hour. Whether she would want to have been present or not was a hard thing to tell. Death didn't seem to hit her the way it hit others. When people passed, they were simply gone to her. Flown away. Regardless, it turned out she couldn't come. The doctors wouldn't allow it, not in her condition. News of my sister's pregnancy didn't reach me until Terry. I didn't bother trying to telegraph her about Jane's funeral. Hour might try to run herself ragged to make it out to Deadwood if she knew, and that would be bad for the baby. She would get the letters. I was joy-filled for Hour, and at the same time, my gut sat melancholy, knowing there would be no way she could be there with me.

The thought occurred to me to look for Charlie Utter or perhaps his brother. Might they come to bid their farewells? I hadn't seen Charlie in ages, and he had been kind to us. I said as much to Dora, but she said something about his moving to Panama so that was the end of my inquiry.

Everyone said the service was a lovely one. I took their word for it, being that my judgment on such subjects was limited. The service was blessedly brief; that's what I knew. Religion was never a thing I could ever grab ahold of for long. Probably because I was fashioned after my pa that way, I reckoned. I sure tried, but religion was like a slippery fish to me. I never had it in me to hold on too long or too tightly, but I bowed my head at the proper parts.

After the services, everyone followed the casket to the cemetery. Mount Moriah was higher up on the hill than the original Ingleside Cemetery where my pa was buried. That cemetery had filled quickly in the early days of Deadwood's youth, and Wild Bill's friends had paid to have him moved to the new Mount Moriah Cemetery. The procession of mourners still passed the old cemetery though, and I found myself looking for my father's grave.

There were so many more now, and I had to admit that all these years had erased its exact location from my mind. Still, I looked, crooking my neck as subtly as I could. We could only afford a wooden marker back then. Would it even still be there? Had time and weather washed it away already? A hard blow hit my chest, and I felt the urge to cry.

Missy, ever present at my side, took my hand and squeezed it, as if knowing my thoughts without words. I breathed in her scent and swallowed my pain down. It stuck for a bit in my throat, but I managed to work the lump away. I was here for Jane today, not Pa. I had wept my tears for him years ago.

We climbed the hill to the cemetery where a grave had been dug in the dark earth next to Wild Bill Hickok himself. The preacher said a few words over the coffin as four men lowered her down with ropes. Dora threw something on top of the grave as it sank. With a closer look, I saw it to be a bundle of wild flowers tied with a lace ribbon. Tears streamed down her face, and I knew in an instant she had picked them herself even though the madame surely had the money for store-bought. Words came to me from ages ago. I muttered them to myself.

"It does make it look nicer."

"What?" Missy whispered.

I shook my head as if to say it were nothing. She wouldn't understand.

Others threw tokens in with Jane's coffin. Tokens, flowers, one person poured a little whiskey on the lid of the coffin. An act that received a scowl from the preacher, but I figured it were an appropriate thing.

It was my turn to leave something here for Jane. Some token of how I felt.

From my belt I retrieved a small knife I carried everywhere with me. It weren't much of a blade, but it was true and sharp. It slipped from its buckskin sheath easily. The sheath weren't the same leather as it had once been because I had replaced it to keep the knife in good condition. It was the knife bit of it that meant the most to me, and that was still the same as the day she gave it to me.

I stepped forward and ran the blade down the length of the heel of my right hand. Sorrow must have numbed me for I barely felt the knife as it opened my skin. A tiny line of red opened into a steady dripping of blood. It all was a terribly familiar feeling.

I held my hand over the grave and squeezed my hand into a fist, allowing a few drops to splatter on the wooden coffin below. When I stepped back, Missy was waiting with a blue handkerchief in hand. She wrapped it around my hand tightly and laced her fingers with mine to keep the bandage on. Her face looked so distraught.

"What'd you go and do that for?"

"I didn't much feel like cryin'."

ABOUT THE AUTHOR

Michelle Rene is a creative advocate and the author of a number of published works of science fiction, historical fiction, humor, and everything in between. You may have also seen her work under the pen names Olivia Rivard and Abigail Henry. She has won several indie awards under her Michelle Rene name for her historical fiction novel, *I Once Knew Vincent*.

Michelle's favorite places in the world are museums, galleries, and libraries. Everyone who creates tells a story of some kind or another. Whether she's painting, writing, or making a video game, Michelle is dedicated to her obsession with story telling.

When not writing, she is a professional artist and all around odd person. She lives as the only female, writing in her little closet, with her husband, son, and ungrateful cat in Dallas, Texas.